THE RIDDLES INSIDE THE ENIGMA

Two members of the station staff lay on the floor, dead, in their survival suits. Evan bent over the nearer figure, saw a small tear in the suit, just below the ribs.

A small laser enlarged the tiny tear in the tough fabric, and he rolled it back.

Where the corpse's stomach should have been, was a round cavity filled with dark green liquid. Resting in the center of the placid pool were three disks. Tentacles radiated from them in all directions. But as he was staring at the things, one of the small tentacles trembled.

It lifted.

It squirted something at him.

Evan wrenched back violently, smashing his head

The fluid struck the visor directly in front of his right eye...

SENTENCED TO PRISM

Alan Dean Foster

A Del Rey Book

BALLANTINE BOOKS • NEW YORK

A Del Rey Book
Published by Ballantine Books
Copyright © 1985 by Alan Dean Foster

Library of Congress Catalog Card Number: 85-90718

ISBN 0-345-31980-X

Manufactured in the United States of America

First Edition: September 1985

Cover Art by Barclay Shaw

Here's one for Don and Dana Carroll to peruse
while they're fixing Italy...

1

A FINE DAY IT WAS; CLEAR AND CLOUDLESS, bright (oh, how bright!) and cheerful, a day on which all things seemed possible. Even dying. Dying had not been on Evan Orgell's schedule for the day, but that was the result he was on the verge of achieving. And there wasn't a damn thing he could do to prevent it.

Because his suit was broken.

All around him the extraordinary, phantasmagorical world called Prism teemed with life. His visit to Prism was supposed to set him up for life. Now it appeared likely it was going to set him up for something else.

The air centimeters from his face was rich with oxygen he couldn't breathe. Nearby burbled a stream of fresh, cool water he couldn't drink. It flowed through a forest full of plants and animals he couldn't eat.

Prism's sun warmed his face. It was intensely bright but no hotter than the star which circled Evan's own world, Samstead. At midday the temperature was positively benign. He could breathe the air of Prism, drink its water, eat his own rations, and yet he was going to die. He was going to die because his suit was broken.

It shouldn't be. It was a very special suit, even by the unique standards of Samstead. It had been built especially for this visit. The engineers and designers had constructed it to protect him from every imaginable danger, every conceivable threat a world like Prism could pose. What the suit's builders did not foresee, could not have foreseen, was the utter alienness of Prism's inhabitants, not to mention their insidious cleverness.

It wasn't entirely their fault, he had to admit. The engineers were used to building survival suits for work on worlds whose lifeforms were nothing more than variations on a familiar theme, that theme being the carbon atom. Prism was different. There evolution had proceeded from a different beginning to wildly different conclusions.

It was that evolution which had broken his suit.

The bright sun continued to beat down on his unshaded form. While the temperature outside his artificial epidermis remained pleasant, it was starting its inexorable upward climb within. Evan desperately wanted a drink of water. He tried to roll over. The permanently sealed servos refused to respond and he stayed as he'd fallen, flat on his back.

His left arm wouldn't move at all. The right groaned as he stretched for the water. It was a radical break with procedure, but he thought he might cup some water in his one operable hand instead of trying to draw fluid from the helmet tap.

Assuming he could do this, though, how could he deliver the water to his mouth through the suit's impenetrable visor? His right arm went limp and he gave it up, exhausted by the attempt, just as he'd been exhausted by Prism ever since he'd touched down on its glittering, disorienting surface.

It had all seemed so simple and straightforward back on Samstead. An unparalleled opportunity for advancement within the company. There was no way he could fail to carry out the assignment. He'd never failed before, had he? Not Evan Orgell.

Methodical, brilliant, incisive, overpowering. Also impatient, overbearing, and arrogant. All those descriptions had been applied to him from the beginning of his career by those who admired him as well as those who hated or simply envied him. All were to varying degrees accurate. Failure was not a term which applied to Evan Orgell.

Until now. Because his suit was broken and survival suits just didn't break. Until now. It was something that did not happen.

As Prism shouldn't have happened.

He lay there on his back, trying to gather his remaining strength and regulate his breathing while he considered what to try next. The first thing was to get out of the direct glare of the sun. Using his right arm as a lever, he slipped it beneath him and pushed. The servos whined, his body lifted, and he managed to roll a couple of meters to his right, beneath the torus of a cascalarian. A tiny triumph, a very minor achievement, but it made him feel a little better.

The cascalarian occupied the same ecological niche on Prism as a shade tree on Earth or Samstead, but it was not properly a tree. It possessed neither leaves nor chlorophyll. The tripartite central trunk was three meters high. From there stiff spines grew parallel to the ground. These supported a transparent glassy torus which was filled with a great variety of life, some of it motile, all of it part of the parent growth. It reminded Evan of an imploded Christmas tree.

Everything grew toward the central trunk and the center of the torus. There was no outward expansion. Competition for living space within the torus was fierce and constant, yet all of it was part of the cascalarian's own closed system. The various shapes were competing for food. Which was to say, for sunlight. Like the majority of lifeforms on Prism, the cascalarian was a photovore.

The thin outer shell of the torus magnified the sunlight falling on it. Within the protective magnifying shell the internal lifeforms were colored lapis blue and aquamarine. Here and there a few patches of royal blue—something twisted and throve. There were also unhealthy-looking patches of pink sponge, but they were rare.

The cascalarian was an organosilicate structure, as were most of the dominant lifeforms on Prism, for it was a world based as much on silicon as carbon. A world of glass, beauty, and confusion.

No matter. Shade was shade, he mused.

By turning his head he could look down at the stream. The cool, pure, fast-running stream that could save his life, if he could get to it. The stream was alive with snowflakes. Twenty of them would fit easily in the palm of his hand.

Snowflakes had tiny transparent legs which ended in broad flat pads. Attached to their backs was a single curved sail about the size of a thumbnail. They congregated where the water was still, partying on the surface tension. As the sun rose or fell they adjusted their stance to receive as much of its light as possible, crowding and shoving each other for the best place. Each photoreceptive sail was a different metallic color: carmine red, cobalt blue, deep purple, emerald green. A pair of tiny crystalline eyes marked the location of each head, and the eyes were colored the same intense hue as their owner's sail.

Powered by Prism's sun, the creatures dashed silently back and forth across the water, using tiny vacuuming mouths to suck up the mineral-rich silicoflagellata washed down from above. Thoughts of predation began to worry

Evan. He was in no danger from the cascalarian or the brightly colored snowflakes, but he knew that Prism was home also to creatures which would gladly take him apart. Not for meat, but for the valuable store of minerals his body contained. The human body was a mine of highly prized trace elements. So was his suit. A big scavenger would draw no distinction between man and clothing and would devour both with equal pleasure.

His body was particularly rich in iron, potassium, and calcium. A mine. My mine is mine, he thought, too tired to laugh. The sun continued to raise the suit's internal temperature, despite the cascalarian's shade. He blinked against his own sweat. He had to do something soon.

No. He had to do something sooner than that, because something was coming toward him. He was sure his vision wasn't that far gone. Whatever was approaching wasn't very big, but then, it wouldn't have to be to do some real damage, given his helpless semicomatose state.

He couldn't see it clearly because the special discriminatory visor of his suit helmet wasn't functioning properly. The visor was necessary because many of Prism's lifeforms were organized according to fractal instead of normal geometry. They tended to blur if you stared at them for very long, as the human eye sought patterns and organization where none existed. Fractals existed somewhere between the first and second dimension or the second and the third. No one, not even the mathematicians, was quite sure.

It didn't matter so long as you looked through the Hausdorf lenses. They were built into the visor of his suit helmet. Which was broken. As a result, fractally organized figures didn't look quite right when viewed through unadjusted transparencies. Like the whatever it was that was slowly coming toward him.

It was more than merely disconcerting. You could go crazy. Fortunately he was too tired to care. So very tired.

He could feel himself drifting, falling asleep or fainting, he wasn't sure which. Not that it mattered.

He only hoped that the alien entity stalking his motionless form would start by eating the damn suit instead of its helpless occupant.

2

THE STORM RAGED AS EVAN STRODE BRISKLY down Korbyski Avenue. He was enjoying it. Powerful thunderstorms were a frequent visitor to this part of Samstead. The wind, heavy rain, and lightning were exhilarating. Naturally, the weather didn't affect him at all because, like everyone else on Samstead, he was wearing a suit.

He happened to be clad in a developmental engineer's duty suit, status semiformal. Its internal stabilizers allowed him to stride without strain into a seventy-kph gale. Evaporators and dispersers kept his face visor clear. The thermosensitive weave kept him warm and dry. The light, flexible material was dyed dark green. Black stripes ran diagonally across his chest, left shoulder, and left leg. Two bands of lighter green crossed his right shoulder. Evan was partial to subdued attire.

The street was crowded with citizens rushing about their daily errands. Each wore a uniquely decorated suit and none paid any attention to the near hurricane battering the city.

Suits were comforting not only to those who wore them but also to everyone else, since a suit reflected not only its wearer's personal taste, but also his or her profession, wealth, or private interests. Evan passed one woman who was having trouble controlling her offspring, who were fiddling with their stabilizers in order to float freely in the wind a meter above the pavement. He could hear her shouts clearly over the omnidirectional universal communicator. She was late for some kind of business lunch and didn't have time to indulge naughty children. Besides which if they didn't settle down, behave, and walk properly, they were going to miss ballet class.

That threat convinced the youngsters to reset their stabilizers. They dropped gently to the street and toddled along silently in their mother's wake—though every so often the boy would rise a couple of centimeters off the ground until a sharp backward glance from his mother would force him to return quickly to the pavement.

Evan smiled at the byplay between mother and son, turned another corner, and found himself confronting a towering structure with a concave facade. He started through the central courtyard toward the imposing entrance. Over the doorway was the legend THE AURORA GROUP, rendered in blue crystal. In the center of the open courtyard and dominating it was a three-story-tall fountain in the shape of the company logo, three worlds forming a pyramid. The fountain played smoothly despite the constant wind. The water was contained by carefully programmed hydrostatic charges.

The door recognized him and let him through. As he entered the foyer his suit automatically adjusted to the warmer temperature inside. At the touch of a button on his right wrist, his visor and hood folded back into the neck of his suit, forming a neat high collar of the style favored by British admirals of the seventeenth century.

By the time the elevator deposited him on the fortieth floor the suit had dried itself and removed its own wrinkles.

Nothing in his appearance suggested that he'd spent the previous half hour strolling through a whirlwind. Samstead's weather was the reason for the invention of the Samstead duty suit. What had evolved from necessity had been metamorphosed by custom and fashion into something considerably more elaborate. Scientific invention had unintentionally paved the way for the establishment of a social convention that was unique to Samstead.

Seram Machoka was waiting for him. Since no desk was visible in the president's office, it was apparent that the meeting was going to be conducted on an informal basis. That suited Evan just fine. He was at his best when the diplomatic niceties did not have to be observed.

He walked right in, unchallenged by human or mechanical intervention. It all looked very casual, but his progress was being monitored by company security. There was no reason to stop him. He was a known company man, in a known company suit.

Machoka smiled and waved Evan to a couch without rising from the lounger on which he reclined. Then he turned away as if suddenly disinterested to look through the transparent outside wall at the storm still engulfing the city.

He was wearing a supervisorial communicator's suit modified to resemble leather. A series of concentric circles and alternating bands of yellow and white decorated the upper half of the suit, rising from his waistband to his right shoulder. The left side of the suit bulged slightly. It was stuffed with tactile controls and contact points. A desk was nothing more than a quaint formality. Machoka's suit could put him in contact with every division of the company.

Evan waited patiently, supremely confident as always but hard pressed to restrain his curiosity. He'd never met

Machoka before. There had been no reason for the two men to meet. Evan was an employee of the company and Machoka its president. They moved on different levels. Now there was reason for those levels to interact, and he was intrigued.

His colleagues at work had teased him about the summons though Evan wasn't easy to tease. That was part of his personality, the part that sometimes angered those who didn't know him and put off those who did. He couldn't understand why he could gain everyone's respect but not their affection. He was friendly and outgoing, always willing to help anyone with a problem. Could he help it if he was smarter than them? His tall frame didn't help in cozying up to acquaintances. Tall people intimidated, short people ingratiated. We're still primitives at heart, he always reminded himself.

A few close friends understood him well enough to take his daily Olympian pronouncements with a grain of salt and to joke with him about the drawbacks of his personality. They were there to congratulate him on his summons. It might involve a big step up the corporate ladder.

At least Evan's size wouldn't put Machoka on the defensive. The company president was as tall as Evan, though much darker of skin and scarcer of hair. He wore spiral tattoos on his forehead and neck, and big round metal earrings. A titanium arrowhead was glued to his shaved forehead. His personal adornment was confined to the skull. He wore no rings or bracelets and nothing on his suit. The suit was all business.

Eventually Machoka turned away from the storm to regard his visitor. "Do sit down, Orgell."

Despite the office owner's admirable efforts to convey a feeling of ease and relaxation, Evan sensed the tenseness in the president's voice.

He folded himself into the couch. It was close to the

transparent wall. A couple of meters from his left side the gale smashed raindrops against the plexalloy.

Something in Machoka's suit beeped softly. Irritated, he threw Evan an apologetic half smile while his fingers danced over the rightside controls. He whispered toward his chest and Evan heard him say quietly, "No more calls for the next hour, please." There was no way of telling whether he was commanding a machine or a person.

Several telltales on the right side of his suit immediately went dark. Only one remained active. It glowed a steady red.

"It's a pleasure to meet you, sir," Orgell said politely. He had not expected to be more relaxed than the company president, but it was becoming clear such was the case. It only left him feeling that much more confident. He had not the slightest doubt he would be able to carry out whatever assignment the company had in mind for him. He always had.

There is a small group of people who are convinced that they can do anything, absolutely anything asked of them. Evan Orgell was one of them. Of course, he wasn't omnipotent. He couldn't do everything. But he was *convinced* that he could. That kind of conviction carries a power all its own.

Machoka tugged at his left sleeve until he'd revealed a slim bracelet. So Evan had been wrong about the absence of body jewelry.

"What do you think of this?"

Evan leaned forward to study the bracelet. It was bright yellow and faceted all the way around. "I'm not a gemologist. I couldn't tell you if it was a natural stone or artificial, much less if it's worth anything."

"It's natural." Machoka seemed to be trying to hide his amusement and it occurred to Evan there might be more to the adornment than first met the eye. The president rose, walked over to stand close to Evan, and stuck out his arm, palm up. "Here. Take a closer look."

Evan did so, wondering what he was supposed to be looking for. Many facets cut by a steady hand, he decided. A dark wire appeared to run through the center of the crystal with smaller wires branching out from it. Inclusions of some sort, or an integrated support matrix added by the jeweler to strengthen the stone. He said as much to Machoka.

The older man couldn't conceal his pleasure any further. "No, you're not even close."

Evan was a little miffed. He had serious work of his own to do, and if the president of the company wanted someone to play guessing games with, he could damn well find another candidate.

Machoka sensed his discomfort, adopted a more serious mien. "Touch it." He gestured with his wrist. "It has a most interesting feel."

Frowning, Evan reached out with his right hand. He received the impression of something slick and waxy before a sharp sting made him jerk his hand back. The bracelet twisted slightly before resetting itself on Machoka's wrist. As it twisted, it separated for an instant. Evan could just make out two small yellow imperfections at the point of separation: eyes. Then the head slipped neatly back into a groove in the tail and the bracelet relaxed once more.

Machoka raised his hand and admired the ornament. "Not much of a charge, but I imagine it's enough to scare off the majority of predators."

"If it was supposed to be funny, it wasn't." Evan nursed his tingling hand.

Machoka looked down at him. "I was told that you had a terrific sense of humor—except when the joke was directed at you." This time Evan wisely said nothing. "We're calling it a Spanset. It's an organosilicate lifeform."

Evan's curiosity quickly overcame his upset. "Like a diatom?"

"Far more advanced than that."

The Spanset clung to Machoka's wrist without moving, looking exactly like a chunk of cut citrine. "So it's alive. What do you feed it? I can see right through it and I don't see anything like a stomach or normal internal organs."

Machoka turned to the transparent wall and held up his arm. The light passed cleanly through the Spanset's body. "They can be trained to recognize individuals. It identifies me through my body's electric field. That's what the biologists tell me, anyway. Feed it? It's a photovore."

"A what? I mean, I know what that should mean, but I've never heard the term used before."

Machoka turned back to him and shrugged. "It's the best thing we've been able to come up with. It's a light-eater. It lives on sunlight." He ran an affectionate finger over the crystalline surface, which did not stir. "It possesses its own little photovoltaic system. Instead of converting sunlight into chemical energy, as plants do, it converts light directly into electricity. That's fine for a machine, but not for a living creature, and the principles are driving our research people crazy. Mathematically it's all possible, but applying the math to a living thing is something else again."

"Where did it come from? What's the world like?"

"Easy. One miracle at a time, Orgell." Machoka resumed his seat. "As to what its home world is like, we don't know yet. But we do know where it is. Prism."

Evan's expression twisted. "Are we talking physics, philosophy, or the beautiful eyes of the new Records Department Comptroller?"

"It's a world. A new world."

"Sure is. First I've heard of it, and I don't miss much."

"It was intended that you and everyone else miss this. One of the company's hunters stumbled across it. Very few people within the organization know about it, and we've worked hard to keep the discovery out of the media. Now one more person knows about it."

Conscious of the small honor just received, Evan proceeded cautiously. "I can see why you're trying to keep it a secret." He nodded toward Machoka's wrist. "If that's an example of the commercial possibilities—imagine jewelry that defends itself against thieves."

Again the president gestured with his wrist. "This is nothing, nothing. A bauble, a toy. According to what little we've learned about this place thus far, the possibilities there are..." He swallowed, started again. "We can't even begin to imagine the possibilities. I certainly can't. Scientifically I'm little more than a layman. I'm an administrator, not a chemist, not a products analyst." He rose abruptly and began pacing back and forth in front of his visitor.

"Orgell, we don't know what we've got here except that it's big. Bigger than anything anybody's dreamed of. Bigger than any single project the company's ever tackled before. This world is not just new; it's radical. It's so strange my people are still arguing over whether biologists or geologists should be in charge of exploration and initial development. This business of organosilicate lifeforms is not unique. Some exist here on Samstead, some on Earth. But not on this scale. And the whole class of photovores is brand-new."

Evan eyed the Spanset again. "It exists solely on sunlight?"

"No. It does ingest modest doses of certain minerals and salts. Call it a kind of food." He hesitated. "You'll get a full briefing before you go."

"Before I go where, sir?" Evan asked quietly, even though he'd already pretty well divined the answer.

"Prism, of course."

"I'm neither a biologist nor a chemist, sir."

Machoka turned to his right and touched a panel on his chest. A leather-backed video screen about ten centimeters square emerged from the arm of the lounge-chair. The president rested his chin in one hand while he studied the display thus presented, spoke without looking up from the screen.

"No, you're not. You're an interdisciplinarian, a jack-of-all-trades. You take a little from this field and a little from that and come up with solutions to problems." He looked up from the display. "We already have specialists working on Prism. Evidently they are not getting the job done. It seems they are in some difficulty."

"What kind of difficulty?"

"We don't know. That's part of our problem. We don't know because we haven't been able to make contact with the station there in quite a while. If it was something easily repaired or coped with the station staff would have handled it by now. They haven't. It may be nothing more than a simple breakdown in communications requiring a part they don't happen to have in stock."

"Then why bring me into it? Send in a communications crew."

"You were one of those responsible for the development of the Avilla Off-World Exploration software, weren't you?"

"Not exactly. I was *the* one responsible for its development."

"So even though your in vivo off-world experience is limited, you have via computer and the software you designed actually been on and coped with literally hundreds of difficult and complex new world crises?"

Evan nodded. "That's right."

"So in that regard you're probably better prepared to deal with whatever problem has arisen on Prism than most of our field people."

"Perhaps. That still doesn't explain why you don't send in a crew. If you want to send a generalist, then I'm your man, but I don't see why you don't surround me with a few specialists."

Machoka was drumming the fingers of his right hand on the arm of the couch. Suddenly he gave the top of the video screen a hard slap, driving it back down into its cubicle.

"You asked why you haven't heard about Prism's discovery. You deserve an answer."

"I think I've already inferred one."

"Then you deserve confirmation. You haven't heard about it because the Aurora Group's presence there at this time is, well, let's call it semilegal."

Evan tried not to smile. "Does that mean someone else might refer to it as semi-illegal?"

"Only if he were less than tactful," said Machoka quietly. "We've managed to set up a small research station on the surface. That's all, so far. That's where what little information we've acquired to date has come from."

"Along with your pet."

Machoka admired his wrist. "Yes. Communications at best were infrequent and subject to heavy coding. Despite such precautions I fear they are being monitored. It's not easy keeping the discovery of an entire world hidden from the rest of the Commonwealth.

"If we announce our discovery, then by Commonwealth law Prism is thrown open to development by any company or individual that wants to go to Terra or Hivehom and file a Research and Exploration Claim. Soon you have government types from the Standards Bureau running all over the place making sure that you're not abusing your permits, infringing on the claims of others, and generally making it difficult for your own people to do business."

"I understand."

Machoka nodded slowly. "I was certain that you would. The point of all this is that if the project *is* being monitored, we have to keep our activity to a minimum. That precludes sending out a fully equipped evaluation team. That's just the kind of activity those bastards at Reliance, or Coway-Thranx, or the Helvetia Consortium, or any of our other less principled competitors would be likely to take notice of. And if we hire a free-lance team from outside the Group, we risk our secrecy further.

"But it's most unlikely that the presence in the area of a single Aurora executive would spark any undue interest. Since we don't know the nature of the trouble on Prism, we have to send in a generalist to find out what's going on before we can decide how best to rectify it."

"Meaning me."

"Meaning you, yes. The very fact that you are not known to our competitors as an off-world specialist works in our favor. They cannot be aware of your work on the Avilla software." Machoka considered the section of lounge which had swallowed the video screen, decided against resurrecting it.

"I don't have to tell you that this is not to be discussed with anyone else. If any of your coworkers ask where you're off to, tell them you're being sent to Inter-Kansastan to attend and report on the semiannual conference on genetic manipulation of cereal grains. You'll be going in that direction in any event and so your passage shouldn't arouse any suspicions. The crew of the ship you'll be traveling on has instructions to make a single fast pass by Prism to drop you off. You'll be picked up when you request it and not before."

"Just a minute. How can I request pickup if the problem is with the station's communications system?"

Machoka smiled broadly. "Wait until you see the suit you'll be working with. Unless their deepspace beam has been snapped by an earthquake or something, you'll be able to tie right into the base generation system with your suit electronics. There's a lot more to this suit than your Avilla software. Our engineers are rightly proud of it." He paused, steepling his fingers.

"There are some on the Board who say I'm being too cautious in this matter. I think not. There's too much at stake here. This is too important to the company, to me, to all of us. There are fortunes and futures aplenty to be made from this discovery and its subsequent exploitation—*if* we can keep it quiet for a year or two. That means keeping greedy s.o.b.'s like the people from Reliance and Helvetia in the dark. It also means keeping everything secret from the Commonwealth Council. Not to mention the United Church. I don't want that bunch of pious moralists poking around Prism until we're thoroughly established there.

"If we can keep it quiet for a year or so we'll be set. After that it won't matter if the whole Commonwealth knows about Prism. We'll have such a lead in research and exploration that any other company that wants to go into Prism will have to pay for the use of our knowledge, if only because it'll be cheaper than starting from scratch themselves. That goes for the government and the Church as well."

"And if we're found out?"

Machoka shrugged. "If by a competitor, we lose a great deal of money. If by the government or the Church, we may lose our freedom. Looked at from any angle, Prism is a great risk."

"Risks hold fascination. Prism sounds fascinating to me, not risky."

"Your confidence again. May it stand you in good stead. Then you accept?"

"Of course I accept. Did you think I might refuse? I've never turned down a company assignment yet."

"They told me this was how you'd react. I know about your attitude."

"There's nothing wrong with my attitude," Evan replied defensively.

"No? I was told that you're arrogant as hell."

"I am not arrogant. Just confident of my abilities."

"Well, that's what's needed here."

"I've already handled more than a thousand theoretical off-world problems during the development of the Avilla software. I doubt that there's anything on Prism that I haven't already dealt with in theory if not in practice. I'm sure I'll be able to isolate the problem and compose a solution for it."

"I hope so too, Orgell. I hope that this world doesn't present you with that thousand-and-first problem, the one you haven't had to deal with yet."

Evan found he was growing impatient. If Machoka was trying to scare him he was failing. "Don't we know anything about this world except that it's 'different'?"

"Certainly. The usual predevelopment basic information. I am told that the climate is agreeable, the air palatable, and that there are no native diseases that can affect us. Not germ-based, anyway. Of course, research is still in its infancy, but from everything that's come through so far the place sounds like an exotic paradise. This may turn out to be a holiday for you."

Sure, Evan thought. Except that the holiday-goers who'd preceded him to Prism weren't communicating with anyone anymore. He rubbed absently where the Spanset had stung him. The unexpectedness of the jolt had shocked him more than anything else, but still—what if that was just a sample of the defensive mechanisms employed by the local lifeforms?

"I wish I could tell you more, but you'll be given all the information you'll need to carry out your mission. After all, you're not going to be thrashing around the planet's surface. That's what the specialists at the station are there for. You're really going to be a glorified courier though I'm hoping you'll be able to solve the problem by yourself and save the company some time and money."

"I'll certainly do my best, sir."

"Yes, that's what the reports all say. Don't let it give you a swelled head."

"Not unless the atmosphere there is lighter than you're telling me."

"So you do have a sense of humor. Good. You'll have help right up until drop-off time. Don't hesitate to ask for anything you need. We'll give you proper cover. You're traveling first-class to an important interworld conference on genetics. Better bone up on your Mendelian mantras in case you have to sound professional. If you need anything from the company library..."

"My own is well equipped, sir, but thanks for the offer."

"Another one of those voracious readers who devour information on a plethora of subjects, eh? I wish I had that kind of luxury time. Unfortunately someone has to run this company, and I'm him. All I have time to read are columns of figures and personnel analyses. Dry, dead stuff." He held up his arm to admire the Spanset one more time. "Nothing exciting like this. I envy you your visit. I want to see this world more than I can say, but I can't trust the day-to-day operation of the company to anyone else. Even if I could, it'd be impossible to keep my comings and goings a secret from our competitors. So—you'll have to be my eyes and ears on this trip, Evan." It was the first time he'd used his visitor's first name. A ploy, Evan knew.

"Any particular suits I should pack, sir?"

"Standard private traveler's comfort suits. The company will provide you with some new ones, if you like. You may as well be comfortable during the civilized portion of this trip. It's a long way."

"How will my nonappearance at the genetics conference be explained?"

"I see that you're taking this in the proper spirit. Don't worry. A suitable explanation will be provided, in case anyone bothers to track your movements that far. I don't think anyone will, but we'll play it safe just in case. Don't start worrying yourself with details. They'll be taken care of. Just get to Prism, find out what's going on, compose a report that even I'll be able to understand, and tell us what those people need so they can get back to work.

"I said that we'd like to have Prism to ourselves for a year or two. We'll be very lucky to keep it secret for a year. We may not have half that, no matter how careful we are. That means that every hour, every day, is one more hour and day to widen our advantage over our competitors."

"I can leave tomorrow, if necessary."

"Good." Machoka rose from the lounge. Evan sensed that the meeting was at an end. He stood, and the two men shook hands.

"I'll be interested in a firsthand report when you get back," Machoka said as they walked to the elevator. "Maybe you can make some of what I've been shown comprehensible. I've run back the chips from Prism at slow freeze and I'm damned if I can understand half of what I'm seeing."

"I'll be looking forward to that meeting, sir."

Evan was provided that same information to peruse on his home reader, and he could sympathize with Machoka's confusion. Despite his remarkable store of personal knowledge he found himself having to halt the playback and refer constantly to his reference texts.

The straight science was bad enough, all this business of a world inhabited by photovores and organosilicates, but there was also the matter of the creatures' appearance. The lifeforms depicted in the preliminary report could not exist. Surely they'd been invented by a coterie of drunken artists trying to pass off their ravings as reality.

Part of the problem was that so many of the recorded images were indistinct. The report apologized for this, saying something about photographing fractal geometries without the aid of Hausdorf lenses. Fractal geometries? Hausdorf lenses? Back to the reference books.

His mind was spinning when he reported the following day to a branch of the company he hadn't even known existed. It was housed in a small factory complex on the outskirts of the city. From the outside the building looked quite ordinary. Inside it was anything but.

That's where they showed him the MHW.

3

He'd heard about them but he'd never seen one except on the occasional news report dealing with the exploration of a new world. Certainly he'd never expected to be fitted for one. Yet the MHW standing before him was to be his.

The Mobile Hostile World suit, of which his was the latest and by far the most advanced model (or so the engineers who were showing it to him boasted), was designed to provide an explorer on a dangerous world with complete lifesupport and protection. It was solid and stiff instead of flexible like the day work suit he was wearing.

They put him in the MHW, let him get comfortable, and then ran him through a complete checkout of suit systems. Even that little instruction and preparation was unnecessary, since the suit could instruct its wearer on how best to utilize it. He had no trouble with the instrumentation, and the majority of controls were operated verbally. The suit was a true marvel of modern engineering, an extension of his own body. Its operator would be well protected on the surface of Prism or any other world. His last concerns about the forthcoming journey vanished.

Another storm was battering the city as he returned home, but he couldn't see it. He could see only his future expanding before him. A vice-chairmanship perhaps. First company consultant. He might be perceived by some as arrogant (honestly, he would never understand where people acquired such notions!), but that wouldn't slow his climb up the ladder of success. Achievement was what mattered to men like Machoka, and Evan Orgell would deliver. His twenty-five years with the company were coming to a head. All he had to do was locate a problem, propose a solution, and file a simple report.

What Machoka didn't know was that Evan would have paid *him* just for the chance to visit a place that promised to be as fascinating as Prism.

He made his way home as rapidly as possible, ignoring the rain. The streets were crowded as usual. Several city employees were working nearby to clear a clogged drain. One wore a suit full of plugs through which he delivered power to two coworkers, whose suits were equipped with repairing and reaming arms.

He passed a doctor and nurse. They looked like candy canes in their familiar red-and-white-striped medical suits. The red stripes were softly aglow, indicating both were off-duty. Their suits contained sufficient medical equipment between the two of them to enable them to perform anything up to medium-difficulty surgery on the spot. A more serious operation would require the addition of specialized suited technicians.

Evan had once read about something called a "hospital" in an old history text. Apparently the ancients had actually hauled even the severely injured all the way to factorylike buildings for the purpose of treating them, instead of doing the necessary work on the spot. Imagine, subjecting an accident victim to the trauma of movement!

A civil policeman in his armored pale blue suit stood chatting with a media vendor. The latter's suit boasted several flashing tridee screens, each equipped with a hardcopy printout for those who wanted to purchase. While staring at one screen Evan almost bumped into a woman advertising a forthcoming tridee. The flexible screen she wore from neck to knees wriggled with scenes from the forthcoming play. To ensure that preoccupied passersby looked at the ad, the video playback would disappear at unpredictable intervals and the screen would become completely transparent—but only for a second—before the advertisement resumed.

Three kids had halted outside a confectionery shop. He noticed them only because they were bawling and crying loud enough to drown out everything else coming over his communicator. The adults hurrying by ignored their cries, for the children were already being attended to—by their suits, which wouldn't tolerate unprogrammed or unnecessary digressions. Only a parent or school administrator could alter that programming, and so the children would have to learn to be satisfied with the fruit juice and milk their clothing would readily provide.

Such musings reminded Evan that he was hungry himself. He nudged one of the controls set into the left arm of his suit. The small dispenser mounted on the right shoulder slid forward until it was properly positioned. A few cassava chips were followed by a dose of hot Samsteadyon tea, heavily sugared. The snack was more than enough to put spring in his step for the rest of the walk home.

Naturally he didn't unsuit until he was safe and secure within his apartment. No use courting arrest for outraging public morals.

The spacious rooms were cluttered and disorganized,

in sharp contrast to their occupant's mind. Tapes and chip files were piled in corners, on furniture, even in the kitchen. And the books, of course. Evan's few visitors never failed to remark on the presence of the books. Real books, printed on tree shavings.

A storage chip might hold a hundred, a thousand times as much information, but there was no pleasure to be gained from holding one in the palm of your hand. A real book provided tactile and visual enjoyment as well as information.

One of these days he'd have to get the place cleaned up. He'd been telling himself that for ten years. His lady friends tried to do it for him, without success. Possibly his ferocious response that he wouldn't be able to find anything discouraged them from pursuing the long-range excavation necessary to complete the work. Or maybe it was because none of them hung around for more than a few months. Eventually they all drifted off into the company of less brilliant but more amenable men.

Except Marla. Marla kept coming back. She was a structural designer, and a good one. She was smart enough to understand Evan's profession and hold up her end of a conversation with him. What differentiated her from the others was that she also could see deep enough into his psyche to realize that for all his intelligence he was basically as insecure as everyone else. Their relationship grew slowly and steadily. Each preferred to dance at arm's length from the other, both afraid of commitment while desperately desiring it but wary of making a serious mistake this late in their lives.

Another year, maybe less, and he'd propose. If nothing else, they were too practical to continue paying for two homes when they spent so much of their free time in each other's company.

The depth of their maturing relationship was defined by Evan's kitchen.

He'd allowed her more leeway than he ever had any

of her predecessors in cleaning it up. As a result, it was now possible to use the cooking facilities to prepare a halfway hygienic meal. The bathroom was next on her agenda. When she reached the front door they would get married.

She deserved to know how the meeting had gone, now that he was comfortably ensconced in his apartment. He used the wall relay to call her. She was quietly pleased for him, recognizing how important the assignment could be to his career and their future. She was also as cautious as ever, identifying potential problems and pitfalls he'd overlooked in his first rush of excitement. There was no yelling and shouting; only quiet discussion and thoughtful analysis. That was something else that set Marla apart from the many women who'd visited Evan's apartment. There's much to be said for youthful passion, but when one reaches his forties it's time to consider more than physical abilities. Living with someone is, after all, very different from loving someone, and requires a good deal more patience and understanding.

She promised to look after his collection of tropical fish and other personal matters, wished him success and a speedy return without any display of tearful emotion. She told him how very much she would miss him. He felt very warm and secure inside when the monitor in the wall finally winked off. A couple of touches on the controls filled the room with reassuring Mozart and changing pastel patterns on the screen.

Then he went through the ritual of unsuiting, placing the empty metallic cloth skin in its holding slot in his copious closet and setting the storage unit for a standard clean and check. There were the usual few seconds of discomfort at being unsuited, though of course he was still tightly sealed within the larger inflexible suit that was the apartment. One could buy a bulky life suit, essentially a mobile apartment, but locally they were banned due to the population density of the city. Strictly a novelty for nomads and country folk.

A check of his console revealed a long list of company-coded information awaiting his attention. Pulling up a chair, he started running them through the decoder.

He'd only been offworld on two previous occasions. Once to Earth for an important company conference and once to New Riviera for an expensive company-provided vacation. While coordinates for Prism weren't given, time of travel was. It shouldn't have surprised him, not given the dimensions of the Commonwealth, but he was still a bit stunned. It was farther from Samstead than he'd ever expected to travel. He was going to be a long way from home.

With nothing to worry about, he told himself. Not with that advanced MHW surrounding him.

As he stared at the monitor he considered going over to Marla's before he left. He wasn't sure she'd be pleased. Neither of them cared much for unexpected surprises. Both of them were planners. It was another reason they got along so well together.

No, they'd said their good-byes. The next time he spoke to her he would be home, ready to regale her with tales of grand successes on alien worlds. He would attack Prism as he had every other complex problem the company had handed him, solve the research station's troubles, relax until his pickup ship came for him, and work on the presentation speech he would doubtless be asked to make for Machoka and the board of directors.

He was already planning how he and Marla would spend his bonus.

The KK-drive ship which picked him up from the orbital station ran irregular routes. Its passage close to the sun of an unexplored system would cause no comment. His section was heavily populated by company employees being sent hither and yon, to be planted like seeds on this world or that in the hope profit would blossom in their wake.

He was relaxing in the first-class lounge, watching the antics of the otters and fish in the central tank, when she interrupted his viewing. She was blond, what they called straw blond. Her skin was almost transparent, and her eyes just kissed with blue. As if to belie the delicacy of her coloring she was strappingly built. Feminine for all that, though.

She wore a mauve dress that covered her from ankles to just below her chin. Garnets sparkled around the hem and neckline, worked into the material in a few simple designs. What made the outfit especially interesting was the intermittently variable opacity of the material. It would change from a solid mauve to a kind of red smokiness that concealed while revealing. Evan was reminded of the advertising girl he'd encountered not long ago. He wondered if the degree of opacity could be varied or if it was a fixed attitude of the material itself.

She noticed his attention, smiled, and walked straight toward him.

"Hi." Her voice was surprisingly deep. "First trip out?"

"No. Third. That's a lovely outfit you almost haven't got on."

She giggled. That was unexpected and forced him to revise his initial estimate of her age downward. She'd been walking by herself since she'd entered the lounge. Unmarried, no boyfriend traveling with her. Parents?

Either she read his mind or else his expression was more predatory than he thought. "Don't worry. I'm by myself and I'm of age. You want to see my ident?"

"Why would I want to?" There. That was sufficiently ambiguous so that she could take it any one of several ways.

Her reply was equally duplicitous. She sat down next to him and they chatted like old friends. She seemed content merely to flirt and tease. That suited him well enough.

The verbal play was welcome, particularly since the rest of the passengers seemed an unusually dull lot. Interesting conversation can be hard to come by when you're a lot smarter than everyone else. Especially if you tend, as Evan did, to spend most of the time talking about yourself and your own achievements.

The girl, however, seemed more than willing to sit and listen to him for as long as he chose to spin stories of his admirable accomplishments. Her name was Mylith.

"So you're going all the way to Repler?"

He laughed. "Nobody goes that far."

"This ship does."

"Just some of the cargo."

"Oh. I hadn't thought of that." In one hand she held half a dozen glass straws. They were fused together. Each was a different color and each contained a different liqueur. She would sip from one straw and then move on to another as he talked.

The dress never became more than milkily translucent. Never transparent. The guessing game it forced on his eyes was still intriguing.

"Where are you getting off?" she asked.

"Inter-Kansastan. Genetics conference."

She made a face. "Sounds dull."

"It probably will be. Ours not to reason why, though. Just to do what the company tells us to."

"I suppose. I'm not quite so enthusiastic." She put a hand on his knee. "Where else have you been? You said this was your third trip out."

He told her about the conference on Earth and the vacation on New Riviera, and she didn't ask him about his destination again, but for some reason he still felt uncomfortable. No reason to. He was just nervous. Asking a fellow traveler his destination was perfectly normal shipboard conversation.

Eventually they returned to the subject of her unique attire. With a sophistication that belied her age and which he found slightly offputting, she allowed as how since he found it so interesting, he might like to see the rest of her wardrobe. He thought about the invitation long and hard before explaining that he was really very tired and had a lot of reading to catch up on before retiring. If she was disappointed she didn't show it, but she didn't approach him again. From time to time over the next few days he saw her talking to other passengers and occasionally a crew member. He wondered if she'd made any successful assignations since he'd turned her down.

By the time she departed on an intersystem shuttle he was mad at himself for having passed on what might have been a memorable opportunity. He'd always been over-cautious. His mind assured him he'd done the right thing. It was not the time for extracurricular involvements. Secrecy and a low profile at all costs. But the rest of his body was pretty upset at the decision.

The great ship drove on through space-plus, following a course through a region of abstruse mathematics only advanced computers could understand, passengers and crew confident that they would emerge in the right place relative to the rest of the universe when they dropped below light speed and back into normal space. Two more such jumps relieved the ship of all its passengers save one.

A last jump put them in orbit around an unnamed world.

The company officer who came for Evan as he was using his window scanner to examine the cloud-shrouded world below looked like a gnome misplaced in time. A tall gnome. Save for a few lingering brown patches, his hair was pure white. He wore a neatly pointed beard and walked with a slight stoop, further enhancing his fairy-tale appearance. That is an impolite analogy, Evan told himself. There is nothing fairy-talish about a spinal defect modern medicine couldn't fix.

He looked to be in his late seventies and his voice was

strong and sure. A man accustomed to giving orders. He was polite to Evan but not deferential.

"So you are the one they selected."

"Yes, I'm the one they selected. Time to go?"

The older man nodded. "You've seen the MHW? Fine. Let's get you suited up. I'm not supposed to linger in this vicinity any longer than necessary."

Evan indicated the light green comfort suit he was wearing. "What about this one and the rest of my personal belongings?"

"That looks suitable for an interior lining. Light and smooth. We'll see to the rest of your stuff. You won't need what you've got on now inside the MHW, but you'll want to have something more comfortable to wear around the station."

"Then what I've got on will do. You're sure I won't need anything else down below?"

The older man grinned. Evan couldn't tell the prosthetic teeth from the real ones. "The suit will take care of all your needs, including those you haven't thought of yet. I've been well briefed on this mission. That's quite a toy you're going to have to play with. I'm Garrett, by the way."

"First name or last?"

"Middle."

Evan smiled back at him. If the company wanted to play coy with a semilegal visit to a semilegal project, that was okay by him. He could understand the need.

Garrett led him back through the ship, past the now deserted passenger lounge with its glowing otter tank, through the communal dining parlor, back into a world of conduits and throbbing machinery.

They passed through a security door into a small holding area. Two women were swarming over the MHW, passing instruments over and through the hollow shell. Final checkout, Evan mused.

It was good to see the suit again, an old friend from

home. Nearly three meters tall and broad in proportion, it towered above the humans working around it. The flat gray duralloy exterior was unmarred, as was the transparent plexalloy bubble that would allow him a three-hundred-and-sixty-degree range of vision. The entry door in the belly stood open.

"Something special, isn't she?" The note of pride in Garrett's voice took Evan by surprise.

"Are you one of the designers?" The two technicians ignored them, intent on their work.

"Who, me?" Garrett laughed. "No, I'm just a field rep. I had a chance to do some work with the prototypes for this beauty. It's nice to be in on the first use of the first fully operational model."

Evan admired the smooth exterior lines. "You have to admit it doesn't look like much."

"Not from the outside, no," Garrett agreed. "I think the appearance is intentionally deceptive. This suit will take care of you and comfort you, provide for you, and even entertain you in everything from near absolute zero to a few thousand degrees above. I won't list her tolerances for you because you're probably familiar with them already and it would take too long to read them off."

"They didn't tell me anything on Samstead about maintenance."

"No need to. The suit can take care of itself for a full year, and you'll be down below a lot less than that."

"I hope so. Surely it doesn't stock enough food and water for that long?"

"Power yes, food no. It's packed with concentrates and it can synthesize plenty more. Flavor the stuff, too, I'm told. As for your defense systems, the suit will explain everything to you."

"So I was told. There wasn't time for much in the way of hands-on instruction."

"Not needed. A six-year-old could run this suit. Once you get inside and key it, it'll fill you in on anything you need to know. Once keyed it will respond only to your voice and your body's signature. It's damn discerning. Wait till you have a chance to use the chameleonics. Not true invisibility, but the closest we've come."

Evan nodded absently, took a last look at the interior of the ship. He was anxious to be on his way. Triumph and glory awaited. Well, a commendation and promotion, anyway. The company didn't go in for the flashy stuff.

"Might as well get on with it."

Garrett nodded and spoke briefly to the pair of technicians. They lingered over a last check, reluctantly moved aside. Evan stepped up to the ladder which protruded from the belly of the suit.

"Key activation MHW eight oh six."

"Activation key," the suit replied in a pleasantly modulated voice. "Welcome, wearer."

Garrett nudged Evan in the ribs, grinned proudly.

"My name is Evan Orgell. I will be inhabiting you during the visit to and exploration of the planet below. What further identification do you require?"

"None, Mr. Orgell. Recognition and key complete." With a *whirr*, the suit knelt, rendering the ladder superfluous. One of the technicians removed it. "Come aboard."

"Thank you." Ignoring the two female techs, Evan removed his leisure suit and stowed it in the appropriate compartment inside the right leg of the MHW. Clad only in his underwear, he bent and entered.

There was enough room inside for him to stand up and turn if he wished to, but he was content to settle himself into the snug, thickly padded operator's chair high up in the chest. His arms and legs slid neatly into the waldo sockets provided for them.

The suit was now tuned to his own muscular system. Experimentally he tried his limbs. The far more powerful limbs of the suit responded accordingly. If he desired he could tear the starship apart piece by piece.

A voice reached him from outside, picked up by the

suit's aural receptors. "Everything look okay, Orgell?"

"Outstanding. I take it you're going to put me down close to the station?"

"As close as we can. The drop coordinates are programmed into the suit and it will handle any necessary adjustments of the parasail."

"Something I've been curious about from the beginning. Why don't we use the ship's shuttle?"

"You ought to be able to guess the answer to that one," Garrett said somberly. "We've taken every precaution, but there's still no way of telling for certain if we're being shadowed or not. If we are, long-range scanners could pick up the movement of a shuttle. No way can your suit's drop be detected. Too small and no power output to show up. It's a passive drop. Don't worry. She'll get you down."

"I wasn't worried. Just curious." Evan wondered how much he believed his own disclaimer.

One of the technicians finally spoke up. "We're positioned. Lock's over there." She pointed, as if Evan could miss seeing the gaping opening in the side of the hold.

He nodded, was delighted when the suit nodded with him. He walked toward the big cargo lock and the suit moved obediently in tandem with his legs. Once inside, he turned to look back as the door closed behind him. He could watch the gauge set in the door go from green to red as the air inside was exhausted.

"Nervous, sir?"

"What?" It took him a second to realize it was the suit itself which had addressed him. "No, not at all."

"Your pulse is racing."

"Excitement and anticipation, that's all."

The suit accepted this explanation without rejoinder. Evan glanced down at his immense metal frame. This is how Goliath must have felt, he told himself. Invulnerable. Omnipotent.

The lock lights went out. Garrett wished him good luck.

Then the outer door was sliding past, revealing the black void beyond. Knowing it was unnecessary but feeling the need anyway, Evan took a deep breath.

Then he stepped out into nothingness.

He felt a slight jolt as the ship's tractor beam took hold of him. He was turned, properly oriented, and shoved planetward. At first it didn't even feel as if he was moving, though he knew better. The suit told him as much, providing facts and figures, relative velocities, and all manner of physical confirmation.

Soon instrumental proof was unnecessary; the curvature of the world below swallowed space until all he could see was Prism. Then the huge parasail deployed, its engines reversing thrust and slowing his descent. He began to glow, descending feet-first. The visor automatically darkened to protect his eyes from the light. Moments later he began to bounce, like a stone skipping across the surface of a pond, as Prism's atmosphere thickened around him. Throughout the drop, the suit kept him cool and comfortable.

Gradually he began to make out shapes, land masses, below and ahead. Then he was dropping over water, a lot of water, and he had a few anxious moments while he wondered just how accurate the suit's programming had been. But he underestimated his rate of descent as well as the angle, and he was soon back over land again. That was better. The suit would keep him alive in any environment, but he didn't relish the thought of walking to his destination through several hundred kilometers of deep ocean.

Soon he was close to ground and slowing rapidly as the parasail worked hard against gravity. His visor lightened, but not completely. He wondered aloud what the problem was. The problem, as the suit told him, was Prism itself. It demonstrated by returning visor shading and polarization to normal. The surface below was so bright, so full of blinding lights and colors, that he couldn't look at it. He acknowledged the success of the demonstration and permitted the suit to darken the visor again.

Something huge and yellow darted toward him suddenly, hurtling from a thick cloud. A burst from the suit's needler sent it hurrying away before he had a chance to get a good look at it. One quick comparison showed how alien was the world beneath him: the attacker had looked more like the parasail than a bird.

More interesting still was the ground below. It was covered in forest, but a forest like none he'd ever seen. It was green, yes. Also purple and vermilion, royal blue and a deep emerald green, and a hundred shades in between. Some shapes were broad and expansive, others tall and thin as fairy towers.

"Organosilicate growths," the suit explained, drawing upon its programming. "Some contain symbiotic or parasitic chlorophyllic forms. Others do not and rely on other means of sustaining life."

"Like the photovores," Evan murmured.

"Yes, like the photovores." A small corner of the suit visor became a miniature tridee screen and Evan was given a quick refresher course in what was known of the unique world of Prismatic botany.

"There are true carbon-based lifeforms on Prism," the unknown narrator declaimed drily, "as well as purely silicon varieties. There are also the organosilicate hybrids. These seem to be among the most successful types, drawing as they do on the strengths of both molecular structures for greater flexibility. In particular, the organosilicate plant types appear to dominate their respective ecological niches, the organic carbon structures being capable of photosynthesis which is enhanced by silicate forms which serve to protect the more vulnerable woody growths while concentrating sunlight upon them."

Evan continued to listen to the lecture, but with only half his attention. The rest was devoted to the white sausage-shape buildings which had suddenly appeared beneath him. They occupied a clearing in the forest. Several smaller secondary structures had been erected nearby. A long straight, cleared area could only be a shuttle runway.

He stared hard as the parasail carried him over the station, but even with the visor's magnifiers on he saw no sign of anyone moving between the buildings.

"Company frequencies. Let them know we're dropping in."

"That was attempted from the ship, sir, without success."

"I know, but just because their long-range communications are out doesn't mean that nothing's working on the local bands."

"As you wish, sir." Several minutes passed as they cleared the station perimeter. "Nothing, sir. No response at all."

Not encouraging, Evan thought. Something pretty bad must have happened here to obviate even suit-to-suit communications. He was reminded that he wasn't on Prism simply to say hello and shake hands. He was also beginning to believe that Prism station had experienced more than a mere breakdown of communications.

Surely if any of their equipment was functioning they would have detected his presence by now and come out to wave at him. But the station grounds remained deserted. Nor had anyone appeared by the time he touched down a couple of hundred meters outside the station perimeter. The cautious approach had been preprogrammed into the suit, an apologetic voice explained when he asked why they hadn't set down inside the station itself. If some unknown catastrophe had overwhelmed the station's staff, it would better to come up on it gradually instead of dropping down in the middle of it. Evan had to concur, mildly mortified that his clothing was acting more sensibly than he.

The suit disconnected itself from the now useless parasail. Evan took a few experimental steps, jumped five meters into the air, and assured himself all suit systems were functioning properly. Then he turned a slow circle to study the remarkable forest surrounding the station.

He was a well-read man with a voracious interest in natural science, but nothing he'd encountered in the literature of the real or the imaginary had prepared him for the environment in which he now found himself. The first thing he noticed was that despite the extraordinary clarity and intensity of the sunlight, it was difficult to isolate individual growths. Not only because the Prismatic flora grew in nonsymmetrical fractal shapes, but also because so many of them were highly reflective. While much of the reflectivity was a natural consequence of the silicate composition of the growths, some of it was intentional. Reflectivity can become an efficient defense against predators. It's hard to attack something when all you see is what it reflects. The research complex had been constructed in the middle of a forest of warped mirrors.

In place of trees there were the gigantic cascalarians, whose solid transparent toruses of silicon dioxide were alive with miniature ecologies of their own. Tall thin towers of copper- and iron-colored silicates grew twenty meters high. Each was no bigger around than a soda straw, but the whole grove was given support by a subterranean network of glass fibers that spread through the sandy soil. Evan was particularly taken with a bright yellow aluminosilicate bush that resembled four interlocking helixes. The bright colors were due to the presence in each growth of trace minerals extracted from a soil that was more akin to the sand of a deserted beach than a healthy black loam. Instead of rotting, decomposing organics, the earth of Prism was rich in silicates.

Set amid the taller "trees" were open glades of intensely hued smaller growths. One such field was filled from side to side with small silvery rotors mounted on stems. Breezes set the whole field to spinning, like a floor lined with children's toys.

Evan bent to study them. The suit took all the strain off his back and would hold him in that position permanently, if he so commanded. His visor was centimeters from the tiny spinning flowers. Not all were silver. A few showed touches of tangerine-orange and pink. In the entire steadily spinning meadow there was not a suggestion of green.

Pure photovores then, every one of them. He wondered if the rotors served a function. Perhaps the winds on Prism blew out of the sun and the miniature propellers kept each growth oriented toward the light. Something new caught his eye: places where the rotor blades had been eaten away.

A short search turned up several of the grazers; tiny black-and-white-spotted beetle shapes equipped with mouthparts like a belt sander. Simultaneous with their discovery was the explanation for the rotors themselves. His guess about sun orientation had been way off. Each stiff breeze caused the rotors to turn, which threw the grazing bugs to the ground. They would have to climb the stems to resume eating. So the rotor design was intended to keep the grazing to a tolerable level.

"Why are they eating?" he wondered aloud. "If these growths are pure photovores, there's no organic matter in them."

"The grazers are also photovores," the suit informed him. "They are after the mineral salts which are concentrated within the small growths. Such salts are necessary for proper body development and functioning. I do not have details on the chemistry yet. They were not included in my programming."

Doubtless because the research team hadn't gone into such details yet, Evan mused. He began to wonder how the "bugs" reproduced. Did they lay eggs, or glass beads, or what? The possibilities were endless and unnerving. He was thankful he wasn't a biologist assigned to this world.

He straightened and started toward the camp.

A wall of rainbows blocked his path, a curving lattice-work of pale green crystals too beautiful to trample; he took care to edge around them. As he drew near, the bladelike shapes quivered visibly. He checked an internal readout. There was no wind. But the blades were definitely in motion. His helmet was also picking up a high-pitched whine.

"What are they doing?" he inquired warily.

"You are a motile form which has entered their growth space. As such, you represent a threat. The plant is responding. Look down to your right. Another motile is also within the prohibited area."

Evan hunted through the lesser growths around the base of the rainbow cluster until he located something that looked like a slug enveloped in an amethyst shell. It was very close to the pink and rainbow blades. Abruptly it halted and began to quiver. As Evan stared in fascination the purple outer shell shattered. The carbon-based slug tried to retreat to cover but was immediately set upon by half a dozen long wormlike forms that erupted from below the sandy surface and began to tear at its unprotected flesh, quivering amid the fragments of purple silica that lay glittering on the ground.

Evan took a couple of steps backward. Instantly the whining faded away. The rainbow hedge ceased moving.

"Ultrasound," the suit said. "A useful defensive mechanism on a world of silicates."

Giving the hedge a wide berth, Evan continued toward the station perimeter, his mechanical legs eating up the ground in huge strides.

It was impossible to take a step without destroying something. Transparent bubbles no more than three centimeters in diameter, which held in their centers individual blobs of chlorophyllic material, covered the ground. The bubbles served to intensify the sunlight falling on the energy-producing organic matter within.

With each step Evan smashed dozens of them under-foot, but there was nothing he could do to prevent it. Fortunately, the ground cover was exceptionally resilient. Looking back, he could see the bubbles began to re-form soon after they'd been broken. Even so, despite the reassurance of this rapid regeneration, the constant crunching noise in his ears was disconcerting.

He was beginning to think that nothing bigger than the unfortunate slug moved about freely on the planet's surface when something that wasn't a member of the station staff interposed itself between him and the nearest building.

4

DESPITE THE CONFIDENCE HE HAD IN THE MHW, Evan was still intimidated. The creature was twice the size of the suit. Its body oozed around a single rotating globe lubricated with what looked like glycerine. The globe fitted neatly into a huge socket in the creature's underside. Using the globe like a ball bearing, the Prismite could pivot and turn with astounding agility. The globe was translucent, and Evan could clearly make out the dendritic inclusions within.

Four dark red eyes like enormous rubies were glaring at him. They surrounded a twisting, powerful silicate trunk. The tip of the thick protuberance was lined with sawlike blades.

"Local carnivore or the food-chain equivalent," Evan observed with forced calm. "I presume it can't hurt us?"

"Naturally not. It apparently intends to try, however. The action should be instructive."

The suit was correct in its assumption. The globe spun, kicking up sand and bits of ground cover as the rotund killer charged. At the same time the flexible trunk snapped out straight as a lance and all the saw blades at the tip lined up. It also demonstrated another neat trick which took Evan completely by surprise.

Half a dozen glassy cables emerged from the body and shot out to lasso the MHW.

"Your vital signs are racing," the suit admonished. "There is no need for concern as long as you are secured inside me."

"I know that." Evan was upset that the suit should think it necessary to reassure him, equally angry at himself for responding like a child. He tried to calm himself. His pulse slowed.

Despite the pull of the cables the suit did not budge. Weight and stabilizers kept it upright and in place. There was a splintering sound as the trunk-lance struck the suit's chest. Vicious silicate sawteeth began to grind against the duralloy. They would have made a bloody mess of anything as fragile as human flesh and bone, but the outer surface of the MHW wasn't so much as scratched.

Evan watched with interest as the futile attack continued. When he felt the suit had had enough time to record everything of interest, he spoke. "End it. We've spent enough time here."

"Yes sir."

The carnivore persisted even though its teeth had been ground almost flat against the duralloy. It would have to be discouraged. A small tube emerged from beneath Evan's left arm. There was a crackle and a bright flash of light. The six cables dropped away and the monster retreated, wobbling crazily on the single globe. It fell over, the globe spinning and tossing sand into the air as it struggled to regain an upright stance. When it finally did so, the thing pivoted and sped off into the forest, weaving drunkenly as it smashed through crystalline growths or bounced off those too large to roll over.

"What did you use?"

"A powerful electric charge, sir. I was programmed to be highly selective in my choice of weapons. Standard defensive measures would not be very useful here. A laser, for example, might be reflected back at us. But a strong electrical discharge disrupts the internal systems of silicate photovores. The results are satisfactory with the added benefit of not killing a local lifeform needlessly. Sometimes it is better to sow confusion than death."

"I'm sure the conservationists who designed you would agree," Evan murmured. He surveyed the ground ahead. "Anything else likely to threaten us?"

"No sir."

"Then let's not waste any more time."

"Excuse me, sir, but I should prefer to avoid the growths directly ahead."

Evan frowned inside the suit. Nothing but low ground cover lay between them and the station perimeter. "What growths?"

"Allow me to adjust your Hausdorf lenses, sir." Evan's visor flickered, darkened slightly, and suddenly half a dozen humped growths appeared not more than three meters in front of him.

"Where the hell did those come from?" They looked like tumbleweeds sculpted out of crystallized maple syrup. Their edges blurred even as he stared at them.

"They have been there all along, sir. My programming identifies them as Fransus clumpings. It is not yet determined whether they are plant or animal."

"Right now I'm not interested in their classification. Why didn't I see them before?"

"Human eyes cannot see into fractal dimensions, sir. Fransus clumpings exist entirely within pure fractal space, between the second and third dimensions. Apparently not all local lifeforms can see into fractal space either. A wonderful camouflage."

"By all means, let's go around them." If something could exist entirely in fractal space, it was conceivable it

had defensive weaponry which could function in fractal
space. Evan had no desire to test the effectiveness of
something he couldn't see.

It was clear that the station's defensive perimeter had
collapsed. The grounds were alive with organosilicate
forms. More than communications had failed there.

As he strode between the buildings he saw that Prism
was taking the installation apart. Huge vitreous vines were
draped over one structure after another, while smaller
growths followed in the wake of the larger, hunting for
cracks or broken windows. The walls of plastic and metal
were being methodically reduced to their basic chemical
constituents and then consumed. The extent of the
destruction hadn't been nearly as obvious from above.
Now that he was in the midst of it he began to wonder if
anyone had survived.

Where was the station staff?

"Try suit-to-suit frequencies," he commanded the
MHW.

Again there was no response. He resorted to shouting
through the helmet's voice membrane, his voice rising
above the squeaks and whines that resounded around him,
also to no avail.

He called up a map of the station on his visor. A few
more strides found him standing outside the communications center. It was thickly overgrown. Long thin ropes
of green glass enveloped the curved roof and walls. Thin
tendrils protruded from bunches of bright red spikes and
penetrated the disintegrating walls.

The door was shut, sealed from the inside. He could
have forced it easily with the MHW, but since he'd resolved
to disturb as little as possible, he sought another entrance
instead. There were several which hadn't been installed
by the station's builders.

On the sunny side of the building, where the overgrowth was thickest, he found that the red spikes had

combined with a massive green cable to rip a hole in the wall large enough to admit him, suit and all. He crawled through.

As he did so he noticed how the red spikes were pushing steadily deeper into the plastic while the flexible tendrils sought cracks to penetrate. They looked like vanadanite crystals gone berserk. One whole section of wall had been reduced by some kind of solvent to a mass of plastic foam. He put his sheathed hand right through it. When he pulled it back, the resultant hole was alive with frantic, squirming black shapes that were eating the plastic.

Inside he commenced a detailed examination of what was left of the communications center of the station. Everything, from floor to furniture, was under attack by Prismatic lifeforms.

"I thought HW buildings were designed to be completely animal- and insect-resistant," he murmured.

"Normally they are," the suit replied. "However, this is not a normal world. The lifeforms have no precedents in the lexicon of Commonwealth discoveries. It is a unique environment that calls for unique countermeasures."

"Which the staff here wasn't prepared to take. That's clear enough."

He turned abruptly, went back for another look at the hole in the wall. "I wonder how it's done."

From beneath his right arm a sampling hose reached into the plastic muck, inhaled briefly, and withdrew. Several minutes passed while the analytical laboratory built into the suit did its work. The answers appeared on his visor screen soon after, in the form of long complex molecules that were breaking apart even as he stared.

"Polycyanoacrylates are tough, but very vulnerable to distortion. Most of the potassium is missing. When the small creatures remove that, the rest of the wall resin is reduced to garbage."

"Why potassium?"

"Who knows?" the suit said. "Perhaps they ingest it to increase their internal electrical conductivity."

"Maybe." He looked back into the room. "I'd still like to know what happened to the staff."

He found three of them a few minutes later in the next room, where the transmission and receiving instrumentation was located.

Like the exterior door, the one leading to the inner chamber had also been sealed from inside. Unlike the other, it had been penetrated somehow, the seal broken. One figure was lying against the deepspace transmitter console. Perhaps he'd been trying to send a last, desperate message. Evan could only guess, because the man was as dead as his companions.

The figure was barely identifiable as male. The flesh was intact, but all the bones had been eaten away from inside. A hunger for potassium again, and calcium too, Evan surmised. The fleshy envelope that remained was not in very good condition. He was glad of the suit which filtered the air he breathed. Silicate forms or no, obviously enough common bacteria were present to initiate the process of decomposition.

The man's life beacon was intact. The light that pulsed from the tiny sensor embedded in his right wrist, however, was a pale, weak red, indicating that the beacon had been active for some time.

The theory behind the beacons was simple and straightforward. Any threat, danger, or trauma that sufficiently and adversely affected the beacon's owner would automatically activate the device, radiating strong signals to bring help. Everyone traveling to or working on a new world was required to have one installed. Despite the protection afforded by his MHW, Evan had one in his own wrist.

But there'd been no one left on Prism to respond.

The second occupant of the chamber also showed the

flashing light. The third did not. His battery had given out prematurely.

"I guess they never got their message off."

"No sir," said the suit quietly. A laser pointer came to life, drew Evan's attention to the back of the console.

Two barely visible transparent filaments ran from a tiny pinecone-shaped growth that clung to the back of the console. They crawled up the console and vanished through a minuscule hole in the metal. Evan touched them and they quivered slightly.

Disdaining tools, he used a hand to rip away the back panel, involuntarily jerked his hand back as a huge ball of downy tendrils spilled out onto the floor. They twisted slowly and deliberately, curling in and over themselves as each sought a new purchase.

What he could see of the complex interior of the communications console had been reduced to mush. Chips and circuits ended in bubbles of moist fiber. "Sample."

Out went the suction tube a second time. Tendrils were stolen for analysis and then spit out again.

"Yttrium," the suit eventually announced. "A minor but important component in much communications equipment. This growth is after the yttrium in the components."

"So it eats the whole inside out of the console just to get at a tiny amount of one rare earth. A real gourmet." Evan traced the path of the two invading tendrils to the pinecone growth. "Surely they ran regular checks on their equipment. I can't believe somebody missed seeing this."

"Excuse me, sir, but you are operating under a misconception. The tendrils did not arise from this small growth on the floor and then penetrate the console. The tendrils are growing from the inside out."

That explains it, Evan thought. A spore or something had slipped through the building's filters and lodged inside the console. Maybe it had come in on somebody's suit and somehow been shielded from the disinfecting unit mounted in the floor by the front door. Possible sources of infection were many. The staff had probably had no idea of the extent of the damage until it was too late.

Leaving the console, he walked over to the second figure. The woman had been in her late forties. She was lying comfortably on a couch. Perhaps she'd been asleep when the final blow had fallen. She was almost intact.

Blue, olive green, and yellow tendrils emerged from the couch to penetrate every part of her body. Except for the presence of the tendrils she might have been resting comfortably.

Evan reached out to run a hand along one leg. Through the suit's tactile sensors the limb felt normal. He used both hands to tear the tough duty suit from ankle to thigh. The skin was undamaged, though wrinkled and dried. He ran a hand along the bare leg.

As he did so the skin peeled up like parchment. Beneath, where muscle and bone should have been, was a lump of solid green glass. Tiny shapes, like oversized corpuscles with legs, were moving about just beneath the transparent surface. They scattered, fleeing from the unexpected light.

Evan drew back, feeling the gorge rise in his throat. For an instant he was tempted to burn the abomination. Logic held him back. The woman was already dead. More than dead. Cremation would entail a useless waste of energy.

Nothing so obscenely deceptive marked the demise of the third occupant of the building. The young man had been neatly dismembered, like a child's doll awaiting repair. Arms and legs lay less than a dozen centimeters from their joints. The head had been removed to an equal distance from the shoulders. A man in six pieces, waiting for somebody to put him back together again. It was neat enough to be disturbing.

Evan found he was glancing occasionally over his shoulder. Stupid, he told himself. The MHW would warn him of any approaching danger and deal with it before he was so much as aware of its presence. He forced his attention back to the corpse. Other than having been separated into six pieces, it appeared to be undamaged. Nothing was missing—no, that wasn't quite true.

"There's no blood."

"It would have evaporated by now," the suit suggested.

"Maybe, but there aren't even any stains. There ought to be stains." He knelt to examine the floor. Standard universal matting; rubberized, flexible, and supportive. But it should show stains. Therefore the blood had been removed before it had a chance to reach the floor.

"Iron, sir," the suit hypothesized. "Iron, and potassium again. Apparently different lifeforms here go after different minerals. It is clear that they make no distinction between the station itself and its inhabitants. Both are nothing more than sources of valuable minerals."

Evan couldn't keep the edginess out of his voice. "Not me. I'm nobody's mine."

He returned to the communications console and tried a number of the apparently undamaged controls. None of the telltales on the panel lit up. A weak glow from one readout indicated that the nullspace generator buried deep beneath the station was still intact, but that was understandable. It was sited in solid ferrocrete thirty meters below the surface. That was SOP. So the beam *could* be powered if it could be purged of hungry, invading lifeforms. He clung to that thought gratefully. It was hard to maintain a positive attitude amid so much devastation.

"I don't see any reason for optimism," he muttered aloud, "but we're obligated to check out the rest of the station."

"Yes sir."

It took the rest of the long local day to prowl through the remaining structures. Some were empty save for their complement of opportunistic colonizers. Others contained surprises more gruesome than anything he'd seen in the communications building.

In the last warehouse he surprised three motile carnivores working a corpse. The fragments of the victim's suit identified him as a member of the life sciences support team, but that was about all Evan could tell about him.

Each of the carnivores (a term more descriptive than accurate, Evan knew, since they couldn't properly be termed *meat*-eaters) was the size of a large dog. They were tripedal, with each foot ending in a supportive pad. Organic bodies were wrapped in protective silicate exo-skeletons boasting sharp black spines. They ignored Evan's entrance completely, so intent were they on ingesting the remainder of the unfortunate staff member. Droplets of solvent oozed from their mouths.

Logic be damned, Evan thought angrily. "Burn 'em!"

"Perhaps one should be preserved for future study." As the suit made its suggestion the three scavengers turned and attacked. Their powerful jaws had no effect whatsoever on the MHW's exterior, nor did the solvent they secreted.

"I said burn them," Evan snapped loudly. This time the suit didn't respond verbally. Instead, it extended a laser and methodically melted each of the attackers into a puddle of slag and carbonized flesh.

They died silently, fighting to the last, their persistence as horrible as their appearance.

"Let's get out of here." Evan turned. "We still haven't checked the dormitories." He pushed impatiently through the pink tendrils that had already begun to seal off the entryway. A brief electronic squeal accompanied each destructive swing of his metal-encased arm.

The first dorm building was empty, but the second contained a surprise—two bodies untouched by dissolving parasites. They lay in their beds on the second floor. Each man had a neat hole in his head just above each ear. The second man held a needler tightly in his right hand. The other lay sprawled across his bed at an unnatural angle.

"This one shot that one, then lay down and committed suicide."

"Why?" the suit asked. Intelligent as it was, deductive reasoning wasn't one of its strengths.

"Impossible to know for certain, since neither of them can tell us. Despair, perhaps. I imagine everything went to hell pretty quickly near the end."

What particularly interested him, though, were not the two additional bodies but the neat row of survival suits, twenty in all, hanging on their holders on the back wall of the room. None looked damaged. He pulled one off the rack and inspected it carefully. Intact and ready to receive its owner. Each suit would have been fashioned for a specific staff member; it was important that they fit perfectly. None was as massive as the MHW encasing him, but they seemed tough enough to resist the assaults of black-spined scavengers and predatory plant-life.

Yet none of them had been donned by their owners. The staff of the station had been slain, every one of them, before they could get into their suits.

Again he looked at the pair of dead men, lying unprotected on their beds only seconds away from the potential protection of their suits. What kind of attack could strike that quickly? Or was everyone at the station the victim of something more subtle, like overconfidence? Once more he found himself looking over his shoulder, nervously eying dark corners. These were highly trained people, the best, the most resourceful. Nothing, not even a world as alien as Prism, should have been able to surprise them so quickly. And they were, every one of them, dead, slain before they could don their suits.

Suddenly he didn't care. Suddenly all he wanted was to repair the deepspace communicator and get the hell out of there. For the first time in his life, Evan Orgell was frightened. It was a brand-new sensation and not a pleasant one.

"Easy, sir. Relax. There is no danger. I am not a

standard-issue survival suit. I am the MHW, and everything is under control."

Evan slowed his breathing, took a sip of iced fruit juice from the helmet dispenser. "Sorry. I'm not easily unsettled." He swallowed more juice, took a last look around the room. "Let's get over to Administration and Records. We've got a job to do."

He spent the rest of the day and most of the next running through those records which had survived the attentions of the local life without coming any closer to an explanation of how two dozen highly trained people had been overwhelmed and killed without so much as having a chance to don the survival suits that might have saved them. They hadn't been torn to shreds by some unimaginably huge carnivore, nor had they all been destroyed internally by the same kind of parasite or disease. Except for the pair who'd been needle-shot, cause of death remained a matter of some uncertainty.

He did not work in silence. The forest surrounding the station, and, for that matter, the station itself, was filled with the cries and hums and squeaks of creatures largely unseen. Occasionally a deeper roar reverberated through the silicates, but nothing materialized to attack him. Still, he took no chances and slept within the security of the MHW.

The records contained information that would be invaluable to the company. All of it fit comfortably in the MHW's copious storage chips, where it would await transfer to company facilities. The irony was that the information couldn't be utilized until he also produced an explanation for the disaster which had devastated the station.

Nowhere within the lengthy discourses and dissertations that had been filed by the station's staff was there anything to hint at the catastrophe that was going to befall them. Yet something capable of such rapid and utter destruction must exist. He was surrounded by proof of its existence.

There was one final mystery.

The dormitory where he'd found the two dead men held twenty-four racks but only twenty survival suits. Personnel records indicated twenty-four expedition members. He had buried the remains of twenty scientists and technicians. The time had come to locate the other four. Of course, he could have gone to work on the beam first, but even as anxious to be away as he was, he would rather die than leave a job incomplete.

"They have to be around here somewhere," he told the MHW. "Trouble is, we've found several bodies with dead beacons."

"I will run a sensitive." Evan waited while the suit performed the high-intensity scan. Within a modest range it would pick up even the slightest emanation from beyond the station perimeter.

"Observation tower."

It was the one place Evan hadn't personally inspected because it seemed an unlikely place to find survivors. The tower elevator was broken, the controls having been chewed up by tiny plant and animal forms, but the four metal struts that supported the three-story structure were still in place, though one had white bubbles forming on its flanks. A precursor to consumption, Evan knew.

He chose the next strut to the left and started climbing, the suit negotiating the almost vertical ascent without straining. As soon as he'd gained the top he punched in a window and climbed through.

Two of the missing four members of the station staff lay on the floor inside, dead, and in their survival suits. The instrumentation surrounding them had hardly been touched, the destructive lifeforms not having reached so high yet.

What of these newest corpses? Had they had time to don their suits before disaster struck or had they already been wearing them when the rest of the camp was devastated? He bent over the nearer figure. Behind the protective visor was the face of an older man. Gray hair and mustache, strong features. Even in death he looked competent. His eyes were closed, his expression serene. He might have been sleeping.

Then Evan saw the small tear in the fabric of the suit, just below the ribs. It was almost unnoticeable. He reached toward it.

"Don't touch that," the suit said warningly.

Evan jerked back his metal-clad hand as though he'd put his bare flesh into a flame.

"What is it? Another local lifeform?"

"Several. Death here is confirmed. There is no need to touch the body."

Evan frowned, discovered that he was sweating slightly despite the reaction of the suit's coolers. "What's the matter? Surely there's nothing here that can damage you."

"Preliminary investigation suggests caution is more sensible than bravado. Survival suits are woven of acryvar. They can be melted, but they are not easily torn. I will enlarge the opening further to provide a better view." Again the small laser put in an appearance, its beam set for cutting this time instead of killing.

In a second the slit was half a meter long. "Now open it, but carefully, and keep control of yourself."

"I'm always in control of myself," Evan replied irritably. Despite his self-assurances, he found that his stomach was turning. He was convinced he'd already seen everything the planetary lifeforms could do to a human body.

He was wrong.

Where the man's stomach should have been was a round cavity filled with dark green liquid. Resting in the center of this placid pool were three disk-shaped objects. Tentacles radiated from them in all directions. They looked like a cross between starfish and fried eggs. As he was staring open-mouthed one of the small tentacles trembled, lifted, and squirted something at him.

It struck the visor of his suit directly in front of his right eye. He wrenched back violently, smashing his head into the roof of the chamber. The MHW's internal compensators protected him from concussion, but he was still rattled.

A second squirt struck him over the other eye. The fluid had no effect on the suit. Following this second assault the remaining two starfish disks reached up and over with their own tentacles, grabbed the flaps of the suit Evan had pulled aside, and covered themselves up again.

Evan discovered that he was shaking. "What the hell was that?"

"Defensive reaction utilizing gastric juices."

"Well, if the idea is to shock or surprise a potential intruder, it succeeded."

"The intent is considerably more lethal than that. Look to your feet."

Evan leaned forward, looked down. Several drops of the liquid which had been sprayed on his visor had dripped onto the floor. Smoke was rising from half a dozen places where the fluid was eating through the metal.

"That's gastric juice?" Evan had to work hard to keep his voice even.

"Very few substances can harm a strongly bonded silicate form. That's nitric acid. So is the pool occupying the stomach area of that unfortunate gentleman. I suspect his companion here has suffered similar treatment."

"If that's nitric acid in his gut, then there shouldn't be anything left of his belly, much less the rest of his body."

"I suspect that the creatures which secrete it have somehow lined the stomach cavity with a material impervious to their own juices. Thus secure from outside interference, they can dissolve bones and flesh at their leisure."

"Hell," Evan muttered. "I only hope the poor bastards

were dead before those things infested them. You're sure about the other one?" He nodded in the direction of the second body.

"I detect the presence of identical acidic compounds."

"All right, how did their suits get ripped? Survival suits aren't supposed to tear."

"Evidently these did. I should think the acryvar capable of withstanding the effects of nitric acid, but perhaps the suits were weakened by something else before the bodies here were invaded. Again we have many questions, sir, and no answers.

"Of course, once the integrity of a suit has been violated, many varieties of native life could subsequently gain entrance. Then it would not take much to induce death. A dilute injection of nitric acid into the bloodstream, for example."

"Spare me the details." Evan made a last search of the observation deck, checking drawers and consoles. The several large storage cabinets were all secured. Using the suit's strength he broke the locks. The cabinets contained assorted instruments, computer storage chips, and personal effects. There was no sign of the two survival suits that were still missing. Having no one else to discuss the matter with, he sat down and talked to the MHW. "This is the last refuge. We've been all over the station. So where are the others?"

"I think it reasonable to assume that the suits are with their owners, though in what condition I cannot imagine. They certainly did not save these two unfortunates. We must at least begin to consider the possibility that the missing suits and their owners have been completely destroyed."

"Even if that's the case," Evan argued, "their beacons would survive."

"Nothing can be taken as assured on this world. Granted that what you suggest is so, if they have been ingested in large pieces, then the beacons in question may have been carried in the gut of some scavenger a considerable distance from the station."

Evan sighed. "I wish you wouldn't keep bringing up facts that contradict my hypotheses. In any case, we have to account one way or another for both the missing suits and personnel. Who's still unaccounted for?"

The screen on the inside of his visor lit up. "A security and supplies technician, Aram Humula; and a xenobiologist, Martine Ophemert."

Evans considered. "There's an outside chance they might still be alive, you know. If they were outside the station perimeter when the disaster struck, engaged in field work or something, they might have survived."

"Why then have they not returned?"

"Several possible reasons. Fear, confusion. They may have been injured and are holed up somewhere awaiting help. Or," he added uneasily, "they might be worried that whatever destroyed the station is still in the vicinity." He ran his fingers over one pristine console. "Most of the instrumentation up here is in good shape. No power, of course. As fond as the local lifeforms are of rare metals and mineral salts, I can imagine what they've done to the station's power grid by now. Maybe that's what happened to the defensive perimeter. Maybe it never had the chance to stop whatever it was that got in here because the power had been cut off. Backup included."

"That is possible," agreed the MHW. "A beacon locator was built into me specifically for this mission, but its range is—"

"I know. I'm familiar with your specs." He let his gaze wander out across the crystalline, spectral forest, wondering how much of it he was seeing and how much more lay beyond the range of his vision, Hausdorf lenses notwithstanding. "We won't find a better place to signal-seek than from up here. You might as well make a three-sixty scan. Take your time and work as far out as you can."

"Excessive scanning is inadvisable."

"You'll have plenty of time to recharge. The days here are long and you couldn't ask for more intense sunlight. Besides, you have plenty of reserve power."

"I know, but I am programmed to be cautious when it comes to high power expenditures."

"Well, we should only have to do this once."

Movement caught Evan's eye. Several dozen tiny flying creatures had attached themselves to his left leg. They were bright yellow, with tiny green eyes and spiral wings. The length of their piercing mouthparts was twice that of their bodies. They were frustrating themselves on the duralloy skin of the MHW.

Evan brushed them off, caught the last one, and held it up to the light. It struggled to get airborne again while emitting a short, sharp whine. He crushed it between his fingers. It didn't collapse in on itself so much as it splintered. The whine went away.

Meanwhile the MHW had extended a single gleaming metal rod from its backpack. The rod unfolded to form a rectangular antenna.

"Scanning," the suit informed him unnecessarily.

Evan waited quietly while the machinery did its job. Starfish that made their homes in pools of nitric acid in your belly. Glass fibers that dissolved away your bones. Suddenly the opportunities afforded by his visit to Prism paled beside the comforts of home. He wanted off this world, and soon.

He'd planned to regale his friends and colleagues with elaborate stories of his adventures on a strange alien world without precisely identifying it. Now even that pleasure was to be denied him. By choice, because he hadn't seen much on Prism so far that would enliven a party by the telling of it.

"I have one beacon fairly close in," the suit said, interrupting his reverie.

Evan nodded, wondering if the suit would correctly interpret the movement. He moved to the smashed-in window, took a last look at the bodies, and began to climb down the support strut.

Huge strides quickly carried him beyond the station boundaries. In a small field of blue rotors he found suit number twenty-three—and its occupant.

The MHW ran an ident light over the bands that criss-crossed the chest, analyzing the frequency of the feebly pulsing beacon.

"Aram Humula."

Evan nodded as he bent to examine the body. It was a good thing the emergency beacon had been implanted in the wrist, because the rest of the body had been crushed almost flat.

5

So much for possible survivors, he thought. One more blank on his report filled in, one left to go. A few small digging things scurried for cover as the shadow of Evan's helmet covered them. They had four-centimeter-long legs and spiral bodies of brown glass.

"Nothing subtle about this one," he murmured to the suit. "Looks like he was run over by a ten-ton transport." With a finger he nudged aside shards of Humula's fragmented helmet. "Plexalloy visor. Should be as strong as the rest of a standard survival suit. Something made garbage out of it."

"Yes sir. Excuse the interruption, but I think you should know that something is crawling up your right leg."

Evan idly glanced down. The climbing creature was smooth-backed and curved. Instead of legs, it laid down a track of glue just ahead of itself. Four long, graceful antennae patted the path ahead, relaying information to the patient crawler. Evan could not see any eyes. The composition of the light blue glue intrigued him. It occurred to him then that the gunk might be acidic. "Suit integrity check," he said, his voice a little higher than usual.

"I would warn you immediately, sir, if there were any problem with—"

"Run the check."

It took less than ten seconds. "Suit integrity is intact, sir."

Was Evan imagining it or did the suit sound slightly miffed? "Thank you," he replied sarcastically. The creature had stopped moving. "What's it doing now?"

"Trying to penetrate, sir. Still another voracious local lifeform. I should guess that its red coloring is due to the presence of large amounts of alumina in its silicate exoskeleton. It is not a photovore."

"I can see all that. Get rid of it." He started to reach down with an arm. The limb froze halfway.

"That would not be advisable, sir. There is no point in putting excessive strain on my fabric."

Within the suit, Evan frowned. "What are you talking about? It can't tear the duralloy."

"No sir, but I can. I can damage myself. You see, the adhesive slime the creature is secreting is extremely powerful. You could rip the creature to shreds but the glue would remain on my exterior. Wouldn't a complete removal of all foreign substances be preferable?"

"Of course."

"Then relinquish control of your left arm, please."

Evan did so, watched with interest as the small laser came back to life. The creature died instantly when the beam pierced it but it took nearly five minutes to boil away the rest of the extraordinary glue it had secreted. By the time the messy task had been completed, Evan could see several more of the glue producers making their way toward him through the ground cover. A couple of casual giant strides carried him well beyond their reach.

"Another integrity check," he muttered. The suit complied without comment.

He refused to admit that he was concerned. Admittedly, the survival suits that had been provided for the station staff were not in a class with his MHW, but it was still unsettling to see how poorly they'd fared in protecting their wearers. It took only seconds to run a check and he wasn't in the mood to take chances.

Twenty-three of the station's twenty-four inhabitants were now accounted for. Find the twenty-fourth and he could prepare for the return home. In the time it would take for a company ship to reach Prism to pick him up, perhaps he could find out what had happened. He was less and less sure he wanted to. "What about the remaining beacon?"

"I have been solidifying a fix on it, sir. It is extremely weak, though that may not be due entirely to loss of battery strength."

Evan's interest perked up and he forgot about the corpse that now lay half a dozen meters behind him. "What are you getting at?"

The MHW turned toward the northwest. "The nature of the fluctuation is not constant."

"You mean, it's moving?"

"Within a small area, yes. That is the most reasonable explanation."

"A survivor!" A survivor might be able to tell him in detail what had happened to the station and its staff, saving him days of drudgery and securing his triumph.

Of course, there could be other reasons for the beacon's restricted range of movement. The beacon and the wrist it was embedded in might be resting in the belly of some carnivore. Or the moldering corpse of Martine Ophemert might be drifting back and forth in the eddy of a river.

He forced himself to put a leash on his excitement even as he directed the suit to start tracking. It was unlikely anyone could have survived for so long without the support facilities of the station. There was plenty of water, but food was hard to find and possessed unique methods of defending itself. Still, if this Ophemert was sufficiently resourceful and if her survival suit was still intact, she might still be alive.

If that slim possibility panned out, he would have a chance to play the hero. He'd always wanted to be a hero. It would suit him. Hard to become a hero in the civilized, regulated confines of a major city.

So there were several reasons for wanting to find Martine Ophemert alive.

The suit did all the work, choosing a course through the vegetation and operating the long metal legs. It was easy to be bored.

"Let's see the plot." He slowed to a halt.

Instantly the visor video came to life. Bright green lines formed a small grid. In the center of the grid and off to the left pulsed a bright red dot.

"Abstracts don't tell me anything," he grumbled.

"Depending on topography we should reach the place in four or five days, sir."

"Not bad." It would give him the opportunity to observe and record a better cross section of local lifeforms for the company archives. "Resume tracking." He readied himself for the resumption of motion.

The suit did not move.

"What's the matter?" He was suddenly fearful the beacon had chosen that moment to die.

It did not involve the distant, tantalizing signal, however.

"Look down at your feet."

Evan complied. A vitreous yellow-green gel was crawling up both legs. It appeared to bubble straight out of the ground and was already up to his knees.

"What the hell is it?"

"Cyanoacrylate structure. Quite unique, sir."

"Everything here's quite unique. It doesn't look like

much. Come on, let's get moving." He pressed his right thigh against the appropriate sensors. Servos whined in protest but the leg wouldn't budge. The gel continued its rapid climb up his lower limbs.

"All right, I'm convinced. It's unique. Now break free."

"I cannot, sir."

"What do you mean, you 'cannot'? It's just a different kind of glue, like the stuff that other thing was secreting."

"Your pardon, sir, but it is not merely a different kind of glue. It is not being secreted by a single small animal but is oozing directly out of the ground. It is a far denser compound with a considerably more versatile molecular structure."

Evan refused to panic. "Then burn it off, like you did the other."

"Yes sir." Once more the laser was brought into play. Evan found he was beginning to sweat as the minutes passed without any reduction in the volume of gel.

"It's not working."

"I could have told you that, sir. The gel is capable of dispersing the heat of the beam throughout its substance. It cannot penetrate my exterior, of course."

"At the moment that's not very reassuring. You *have* to break free."

"I am considering the problem, sir."

Evan fell quiet to let the suit's computer devote all its efforts to finding a solution to the current predicament. He tried his legs again, was unable to move them at all. The gel was working its way rapidly up his thighs. It was thick and syrupy.

He wondered where it was coming from.

What would happen when it reached his neck and began to cover his helmet? What would happen when he was completely encased? They'd already encountered one species which utilized nitric acid as gastric juice. What else besides adhesive gel could the abomination buried beneath him produce? The process reminded him of the way in which a spider immobilizes its prey in a silken cocoon before it begins to dine. Something huge had to be down below, concealed by the sandy soil. It was wrapping him up, slowly and methodically. To produce so much gel so quickly it had to be of considerable size. Would it come up beneath him or would it pull him down under the surface? Down into the darkness, where he wouldn't be able to see, where he'd only be able to feel it probing and picking at the suit, hunting for a way in.

But it couldn't break into the MHW. He was sure of that, though not quite as positive as he'd been a day earlier. And if it couldn't, what then? If it let him go, all well and good. If not—if not, it might choose to keep him for a while. A day, perhaps, down beneath the surface. Or a couple of days. Or more. Until his air began to run out because it couldn't recycle.

He would be buried alive, entombed within the suit. The impregnable MHW would become an impregnable coffin.

He had to get out of that inexorable, crawling grip. Reaching down, he used both massive metal hands to dig into the material. There was resistance from the gummy substance and when he tried to pull it away from his hips he found he could not. Worse, his hands were now glued to his sides. The gel continued its uninterrupted progress up his body, flowing outward now to encase his hands and lower arms as well.

"You know," the suit informed him thoughtfully, "if I were able to synthesize a powerful acid like certain local lifeforms it might be that it would damage this gel. Unfortunately, I was designed to synthesize only foodstuffs."

Evan ignored the MHW's lament. He wasn't interested in what it couldn't do.

Think, he shouted at himself. He'd been put down here to find answers and provide solutions to problems. He needed one now. The suit could only do his bidding. Beyond a certain point it could not initiate action, could only respond to his requests. He fought to remember everything he'd learned about Prism since the cursed moment when he'd touched down on its surface.

At the same time he couldn't help but stare in fascination as the malevolent goo came crawling up his arm, surmounting the elbow and hurrying toward his shoulder. When it reached that point it would start for his neck.

Something moved, ever so slightly, under the ground.

Acid might be effective, but the suit couldn't synthesize acid. What else could it do? What else might prove effective against an inanimate assault? What else did the inhabitants of Prism utilize to . . . ?

"You can generate frequencies on every wavelength, can't you?"

"Yes sir. As part of my internal communications system I am able to—"

"Try ultrasound. Remember the spiked plants we encountered outside the station? Try that; put all the power into the broadcast that you can! Even if it's potentially harmful to me."

"Excellent suggestion, sir."

A slight hum filled the suit. Evan knew he wasn't hearing the sound the MHW was generating but rather the suit's instrumentation operating at far more than communications strength.

Several minutes passed. Then the gel stopped its advance, centimeters from his visor. It began to solidify, to harden around him.

"I believe we may have found a possible solution."

"Don't stop! Pour it on."

He stood there, listening to the humming from within. If the suit overdid it and burned out a component or two . . . But the MHW continued to fill the air with sound waves far above his range of hearing.

Not Prism's, though. The forest around him was suddenly alive with frantic, outrageous lifeforms fleeing in all directions, a blur of fractal shapes and silhouettes.

His helmet audio pickup conveyed a new sound to him. It sounded as if someone had dropped a basket of eggs on his head. It was repeated, with increasing frequency.

All over his body the hardened gel was starting to shatter. Something heaved underfoot and he nearly fell. It was the last time he sensed motion from below. The cracks continued to multiply and widen. Then the solidified gel was flaking off, in tiny chips at first, then in big, waxy chunks, tumbling off his arms and torso. Experimentally, he tried to lift his left leg. It took three tries before he broke free of the weakened casing. Now he was able to use his hands to rip away huge pieces of the encumbering substance.

When he'd cleaned the last fragments from the exterior of the suit and had climbed to the safety of a large, sloping chunk of schist, he looked back at the place where he'd almost been entombed like a fly in amber. There was nothing to suggest a trap, nothing to hint that something vast and lethal had lain in wait in that spot just under the ground.

As blowers dried the sweat from his face he relaxed by lambasting the suit for its failure to detect the danger.

"I am sorry, sir. I was not designed to cope with so subtle an attack. One looks for fang and claw, not ooze. It began so slowly that I was taken by surprise. Sometimes it is difficult to tell the difference between a perfectly natural occurrence and a hostile act. There are those worlds on which rain is lethal to the native lifeforms. I had believed the first secretions to be nothing more than a manifestation of some local climatic or plutonic condition, which I am more than prepared to deal with."

"Next time jump, then analyze," Evan growled, refusing to be appeased by logic. "Or ask. Maybe I don't have your capability for instantaneous retrieval of information, but my brain is a damn sight better at rapid analysis."

"Of course, sir." The MHW was appropriately contrite.

"I do not wish to burden you with unnecessary queries involving moment-to-moment operation."

"That's all right. Go ahead and burden me." He surveyed the terrain ahead, trying to see into the depths of the glittering, adamantine silicate forest. The sky overhead was blindingly bright. Crystal shells crunched underfoot as he stepped off the rock and their bright green growths hastened to regenerate the protective transparent bubbles.

"Let's find that damn beacon."

"Yes sir."

Covering meters with each of the suit's long, tireless strides he resumed the search, the sensors clinging tenaciously to the weak electronic spoor that marked the location of the twenty-fourth and last member of the research station staff—or of her body.

In the days that followed he had numerous encounters with the lifeforms that swarmed over Prism's surface in fractal profusion. None of them threatened his progress. All were appropriately imaged, digitalized, and locked away in the MHW's memory for future study. Some were more outlandish than believable and a few so outrageous in shape and form Evan wasn't sure he'd be able to convince his colleagues back home that they actually existed.

He was particularly taken with the needlepuffs.

They filled an entire arroyo, almost hiding the small stream that ran through its center. Each was a different color. They varied in size from tiny globular structures no bigger than his fist to giants four meters in circumference. They were pure silicate forms and they filled the little canyon with frozen fireworks.

From each hidden nucleus a thousand spines radiated outward in every direction. Each spine was lined with additional thousands of smaller spines, and these in turn boasted thousands more, the duplication repeating itself down to the submicroscopic level.

Only his Hausdorf lenses brought order out of this

prickly chaos. Blue and carnelian, onyx and amber yellow and metallic green, the needlepuffs displayed a false fragility that didn't fool him for a minute. Safe within his suit he could stride through them with indifference, leaving a carpet of glittering color in his wake, but anything not similarly defended would have been cut by a billion tiny knives.

Instead of turning constantly to keep themselves facing always toward the sun, the needlepuffs remained immobile. Hundreds of light-sensitive surfaces would always be in position to gulp a few billion photons no matter where the sun hung in the sky.

As for the valuable salts and minerals their hidden bodies contained, that remained safe from any predator. The smallest needlepuff made the most intimidating terrestrial cactus appear defenseless by comparison.

On the fourth day he was stopped by the hedge.

Actually, "hedge" was something of an understatement, wholly inadequate to describe the barrier which confronted him. He found himself facing a solid silicate wall which varied in height from four to ten meters and stretched from horizon to horizon. Each of the growths comprising the hedge was more than a meter thick at its base. They clustered so tightly together that nothing larger than a glass mouse could slip between them.

Two thirds of the way up its trunk, each "tree" was pierced by three or four thick, girderlike branches. The outer surfaces of these projections were highly polished and rotated about a common axis to reflect as much light as possible onto the light-gathering upper portion of the trunk. The rest of the organism had the color and sheen of pink chrome.

The hedge had crowded out all vegetation from its immediate vicinity. The suit estimated the wall to be some five meters thick. They were less than a day's run from the location of the beacon.

"No telling where it stops," Evan muttered, glancing first to his left and then right. "Can we cut through?"

"I can try, sir."

Evan approached the nearest tree and studied the smooth, unbroken surface appraisingly. Then he made a fist and hammered down. A big chunk of pink silicate—(lithium aluminate, no doubt, he mused)—broke free, fell to the ground. For an instant he thought the parent growth might have shuddered slightly, but that had to be an illusion. Surely a plant analog like this one was incapable of generating so visual a reaction to minor destruction. He struck again. The fragment that crumbled under his armored hand this time was smaller than the first.

"Take too long and it's energy-wasteful," he muttered. "Burn through."

"I am not sure that will be any more efficient, sir. A laser is not as effective on highly reflective forms, and from what I can see of their internal structure they are highly dispersive as well."

"Try it anyway. I'm not interested in spending hours punching my way through like a demented boxer."

His arm rose and the laser began to cut. The silicate surface in front of him reacted by bubbling and melting away. The suit's concern seemed unfounded.

Evan waited impatiently while the suit cut a gap wide enough to pass through in the first row of growths and went to work on the second. Work there proceeded a little more slowly, but soon the second row too had been breached. The suit began on the third. Evan could see daylight beyond.

A single tree more than a meter thick was cut clean through and he had to step aside as it fell backward toward him. It shattered when it struck the ground, sending splinters flying. Casually he straddled it as the laser went to work on the last pair of trunks blocking their path.

In the center of the cut-through stump was a darker material the color of morion, an almost black quartz. It bore an uncanny resemblance to the heartwood of a normal tree.

Perhaps the darker material served as the conduit for raw silica drawn from the soil which the tree utilized for growth. Fertile ground for speculation outside his own field.

Then he was through the last barrier. At the same time, a small nova went off in front of his eyes.

Fortunately his vision darkened quickly enough to save him from permanent blindness, but the flare still hurt. Tears streamed from his eyes, trickled down his cheeks despite the efforts of the suit's humidity control to soak them up. The visor was black and he couldn't see what was happening. Occasionally the blackness was marred by a brief silvery cloud, evidence of new flashes.

The suit reminded him of his position. "We must move forward, sir."

He nodded absently, staggered through the gap the laser had cut. The silvery mists grew fainter as he moved away from the hedge. Soon the visor began to lighten. After a while he could see again. Forest ahead, sky above. He turned and looked back toward the barrier recently breached.

Flashes continued to fill the gap, but they were greatly lessened in intensity and frequency. The energy required to generate the bursts must be considerable.

"Interesting." He turned to continue on. Neither leg responded.

"I fear I have sustained some damage, sir."

"Damage?" That word wasn't supposed to be in the MHW's vocabulary. "From what? A little light? What kind of damage?"

"The growths which form the line behind us are slow to react to attack, sir. Perhaps because they rarely are attacked. As a result they have evolved a unique method of defending themselves. Unique and yet obvious. It is quite remarkable."

"I'm sure it is. This world is one remarkable discovery after another. You can detail it for me later." He tried to walk again, with the same ineffectual result.

"I am very much afraid, sir, that my lower motor drive has been burnt out."

Evan sensed the short hairs on the back of his neck beginning to stiffen. "What do you mean, 'burnt out'?"

"If you care to look down, sir."

Evan did so. It took an effort because the suit servos were not responding smoothly. Behind him, the hedge was now putting forth only intermittent, feeble flashes that were somehow familiar.

Black scars ran the length of the MHW. In a few places the supposedly invulnerable duralloy exterior had been melted completely away, revealing smoking components and circuitry. The area around the suit's right knee was gone entirely. Thin wires and connectors hung from the hole. Wisps of gas drifted out, showing where the super-cooling insulators had been violated. He was leaking liquid nitrogen from several joints. No wonder he couldn't move.

Anxiously, he looked back at the hedge. Another burst of light, a long pause, and then a last. At the same time it struck him. What he was seeing in action was an ultra-violet laser.

But that was insane. People used lasers against hostile primitive lifeforms. Primitive lifeforms didn't use lasers against people.

The suit confirmed the impossible. "Remarkable, sir, most remarkable. There are no previous records from anywhere in the Commonwealth of a living form lasing naturally. Perhaps such an evolutionary development here should have been anticipated."

"It's not possible—no," he hastily corrected himself, "obviously it is possible."

"It is fortunate that we are no longer perceived as a danger. I reacted as quickly as possible, sir. I was barely able to recognize the threat in time to protect you from serious harm."

"I still don't see how one or two plants could generate enough energy to cut through duralloy."

"One or two could not. However, we were not attacked just by those growths we were cutting through. Apparently a danger to one is perceived as danger to all. It took a while for the hedge to mount a collective response to our penetration. On Earth, trees under attack warn one another by chemical means. Here the method must be different, but it is no less efficient, and the response considerably more so.

"These growths are photovores, like many we have seen. Unlike those encountered previously, however, these apparently have developed the ability to concentrate enormous amounts of energy within themselves and then to release it all at once, in powerful bursts. As each growth adds its own quota of energy to the pulse, the effect is magnified repeatedly. We were attacked by a single entity ten meters in depth and five in height and at least several kilometers in length, that constitutes a laser of considerable potential. Strong enough even to penetrate duralloy.

"I am sorry, sir. I was designed to cope with assaults from unexpected nonsentient alien lifeforms, but as nothing like this has ever been encountered before it could not possibly have been foreseen. Prior experience on new worlds suggests an explorer needs to be ready to fend off tooth and claw, venom, or sheer muscle. I am capable of dealing efficiently with infinite variations of same, including such unlikely forms of attack as ultrasound and acid, which we have already encountered. I was designed to defend against hostiles which can bite, cut, bludgeon, spit, secrete, or vibrate. I was not designed to cope with a lifeform which can lase."

Evan considered this while he watched the hedge begin to repair itself. He wasn't overly concerned. The suit had suffered some damage, that was all.

"How long will it take you to fix the trouble?"

"It is true that I am self-repairing, but only to a degree. Even I have limits." A pause. "It appears on introspection that the damage extends to internal functions more complex than motor drives. I am attempting to isolate the fire—"

"Fire?" Evan's eyes widened slightly.

"—and prevent its spread to more sensitive components. It is not easy. Integration precludes much isolation without compounding—"

How long will it take you to fix it?" He was growing warmer.

"You do not understand the extent of the damage, sir. It is not as if something broke. I carry ample spares for replacement where required. But entire integrated blocks have been vaporized, along with their connections. The cooling unit has also been affected and this compounds the problem."

So I'm not the only one who's sweating, Evan thought anxiously.

"I am sorry that I have not been able to live up to my designers' expectations, but they could not have anticipated, a n t i c i p a t e d, a n t i c i . . ."

As he sat in his seat the voice of the MHW, the strong, reassuring voice that had comforted him from the moment he'd stepped out of the ship high in orbit above Prism, the voice of knowledge and infinite resourcefulness, the voice of Commonwealth technology, died.

"We have to find a place where you can shut down nonessential functions while you repair yourself. That means we have to move." The faint siren call of the beacon was forgotten now. Everything else was forgotten. He tried to take a step. This time not even a complaining whine greeted his efforts. He jammed his leg viciously against the sensors. He might as well have been kicking granite.

"Come on, suit," he whispered nervously, "respond."

He nudged switches on a panel near his belly. "Manual emergency override. Basic systems functions, respond. Come on, damn you, respond!"

Only the echoing silence of dead metal, loud in his ears.

The audio membranes filled the suit with the unshielded sounds of Prism: electronic whispers and buzzes, harsh whistles and ratcheting growls. Unsettling sounds, alien sounds, suddenly much closer than they'd been before. Behind him the trees rose immobile, drained and drinking in the sunlight, a tall pink wall separating him from the ruins of the station. They took no interest in the tall, immobilized metal shape standing not far away. They weren't interested in him anymore. He was no longer perceived as a threat. And rightly so.

Then he was falling, unable to slow the descent or stop it. He'd halted on a slight slope and the suit's internal stabilizers had finally succumbed to the pervasive damage. He couldn't do anything to regulate the fall, of course. His own muscles were nowhere near strong enough to hold the heavy metal and plastic MHW upright against the pull of Prism's gravity.

There were no compensators to cushion the shock when he struck. His face bounced off the inside of the visor and blood started from his nose. At least he'd landed on his back. Whether that was sheer luck or a parting gesture by the suit's systems he had no way of knowing. He put his head back and waited for the bleeding to stop. Nor was he in danger of being blinded by the glare outside, since the material of the visor was largely self-adjusting. As he lay there in the bright light of day it compensated for the increased glare. That rapid chemical response to light was all that had saved him from being permanently blinded by the first burst of the hedge laser.

It was still comfortable within the suit, though several degrees warmer than optimum. That would soon begin to change. He knew that the cooling system was ruined and that if he lay in the sun very long he'd cook as efficiently as if in an oven.

Nothing lay unattended for very long on the surface of Prism, however. It wasn't long before he had company.

It was crawling onto the visor and he flinched even though he knew it couldn't get at him. Short red legs propelled a squat, triangular body. At the fore point were two bright green crystalline eyes mounted on weaving eyestalks. They swiveled to stare down at him.

What did they see? What was the mind like behind that shiny, slick-backed body? Could it feel, or was it no more than a mobile machine? The glassy stare was not enlightening.

The lower foresection of the body between the eyes dropped open. Out came something small, thin, and spiral-shaped. It started to drill into the visor, directly over Evan's right eye, at high speed. He could hear it whine through the audio pickups. He sweated a little heavier for a few seconds until it became clear his visitor was incapable of penetrating the plexalloy.

The creature kept it up for more than a minute before finally giving the transparent material up as a bad job and moving away. It hadn't so much as scratched the visor. Even so, Evan found his stomach was churning.

It returned a couple of minutes later and decided to try the place where the visor was sealed to the body of the suit. Each of its legs operated independently of the others. Again the disconcerting whine, again the suit's integrity remained intact. Of course, if it found one of the places lower down where the hedge had sliced open the duralloy—but maybe it wasn't even interested in him. Maybe it was after the minerals in the suit itself. Still, Evan knew from personal observation at the station that there were plenty of scavengers who would find his body more than palatable. He was full of magnesium, potassium, calcium, zinc, iron, and all sorts of tasty spices. If he lay there long, sooner or later something would come along that would be ready and able to take him apart.

A second driller joined its cousin. Evan lay quietly, trying to ignore the intensified whine as he considered possible courses of action. He'd always been good at planning and organizing with a minimum of resources, but the latter usually included more than a dead survival suit. Now it was broken, and he was going to die. He could not think of a way out.

The drillers went away before nightfall, leaving him to ponder his fate in the darkness. He was only four days out from the station. Four days suit time, that is. Considerably longer for a human traveling on foot without the assistance of mechanical muscles.

Less than a day to the location of the feeble beacon. The beacon that moved around within a confined space. Even if Ophemert was dead, her suit might still be functional. If that was the case and he could salvage it, his chances of making it back to the station alive would be improved immeasureably.

Or maybe she was still alive. Perhaps she'd been out on a field trip, had been informed of the disaster in time to save herself, and was even now awaiting word that it was safe to return. He could convey that information to her and they could return together.

Except that he knew there was no way he could survive on Prism's surface without a suit. A suit was vital to his continued survival. It moderated the temperature, supplied food and water, protected its wearer from the elements, provided communications, advice, and even entertainment. All he had now was his light day-suit, the one he'd brought along to wear within the civilized confines of the station. How could he trade the armored safety of the MHW for a suit of thin, nonfunctional artificial fabric?

If he didn't, his only alternative was to remain within the corpse of the MHW and hope that the company would come looking for its wayward explorer. One day they would. Trouble was, one day might be months in the future. By then he wouldn't care when they found him.

Dawning of a new day found him rummaging around inside the suit, having slept well despite his fears. He found that he was able to extricate most of the concentrates from their storage compartments by hand, as well as the majority of vitamins. If he wore only his underwear, he might be able to rig a pack from his day-suit pants. He would then have food for a while and a means to transport it.

Evan Orgell was not passive. However assured the demise fate appeared to hold out to him, he refused to accept it as inevitable. Some might call such an attitude arrogance. Evan would have defined it as persistence in the face of adversity.

Maybe his suit *was* broken, but his legs still worked. He'd done a lot of walking on Samstead and thought he was in pretty good physical condition. He could still run and dodge. Human beings had been running and dodging for millions of years, just as they had survived without suits. Surely he, a modern man, could do as well as his ignorant ancestors?

No, he could manage physically without a suit. Mentally was something else again. He'd been outside without a specialized suit only twice in his life, both times to go swimming with friends at the beach. On a dare, they'd gone in without surf suits to propel them through the waves and protect them from the sun and salt. It had been a nerve-wracking ordeal, but he'd survived it.

He discovered that he was shaking as he contemplated what he was about to do. That was interesting. A new experience. Welcome to Prism. He forced himself to wait until he'd regained control of his muscles before starting in on the latches that sealed him inside. Each opened easily at his touch. The emergency manual release was a bit more complicated, but eventually it, too, yielded to his ministrations.

The latch was freed. All he had to do was twist the handle a hundred eighty degrees and shove. He did so, and as terrified as he was by the thought of it opening and exposing him suitless to the world outside, he was even more frightened that it wouldn't.

He pushed. The only advantage he had over a newborn chick emerging from its egg was that he knew what kind of world he was being born into.

If that counted as an advantage. At the moment, he might have found a little ignorance comforting.

6

TWO THINGS STRUCK HIM FORCEFULLY AS HE emerged: the overpowering brilliance of the daylight reflected from a million silicate forms and a peculiar smell that caused him to inhale sharply. Peculiar, but not bad, the smell was that of fresh air. The first fresh air his lungs had embraced since he'd left Samstead. It was strikingly different from suit air, as sharp and piercing in its own way as the light.

The air gave him no trouble, which allowed him to concentrate on the problem of seeing. In order to see at all he had to squint, and still the tears poured from his outraged eyes. He would need some kind of protection if he expected to go more than a hundred meters from the suit.

Ducking back inside, he worked his way up toward the visor and searched for a release. There was none. The visor was heat-sealed in place and couldn't be removed without the facilities of a fully equipped machine shop. So he would have to improvise.

The food concentrates came in heavy plastic packets. He'd pulled one apart and was studying the material when it occurred to him that he didn't have a single tool; not even a pocketknife. Everything was built into the MHW and secured as tightly as the photochromic visor.

Another foray outside and another search of his immediate surroundings assured him he was in no danger of imminent attack by crystalline carnivores. Crying like a baby, he hunted around the fringe of the suit until he found what he wanted: a section of bubble grass that had been shattered by the suit's fall. One curved edge seemed sharp enough.

The plastic cut more easily than he'd hoped. When he finished he was the owner of a strip five centimeters wide and thirty long. He wrapped it around his head and knotted it in back. He hoped he wouldn't have to do any running.

The next time he stuck his head back out into the light and tentatively opened his eyes he found that he could see without pain, though not very clearly. His first attempt at scavenging had proved more successful than not. He squirmed back into the suit to see what else might be salvageable. It wasn't encouraging.

His leisure duty suit, which he'd expected to wear on the journey home, became a crude pack with the legs knotted and then tied together and the belt secured at the waist. It wouldn't hold much, but so far he'd been unable to find much to carry. He was more concerned about his footgear than anything else. Sunburn he would suffer when his underwear gave out, but his light shoes would have to last or else his feet would be cut to ribbons. Once more he was grateful for all the walking he'd done at home. At least the soles of his feet were tougher than those of the average desk-minder.

He spent a futile half day trying to get at the rest of the food, which was secured within the MHW's dispensers. Without the proper tools he was doomed to failure, but that didn't stop him from cursing the suit's designers fiercely.

One more thing needed to be done before he abandoned the suit permanently; he wrapped one piece of legging over nose and mouth. The air might smell refreshing, but it was full of minute particles of silicon. Silicosis was one disease he intended to avoid at all cost.

Thus garbed and muffled he took a deep breath, thankful that the surface temperature was mild, and stepped clear of the suit. He was standing virtually naked and alone on the surface of a hostile alien world.

He checked his wrist beacon. It came to life immediately, light strong, battery fresh. The light would grow brighter if he came close to another beacon, a feature designed to enable survivors of a disaster to find one another. He was going to use it to find Martine Ophemert's beacon. Its range was short, but he should be close enough for it to be useful.

Eventually it would also guide his rescuers to him. Until that blessed day he had to survive, probably for several weeks or more. It would take that long for the company to get worried enough to send a shuttle after him.

He remembered the line the MHW had been taking prior to its demise: northwest. Orienting himself by the sun, he started off in what he thought was the right direction. If his beacon light did not grow noticeably brighter by the evening, he would backtrack and choose a different tack.

The suit was utterly useless to him now. Still, he abandoned it with reluctance. It was his last real link with Samstead and safety.

The forest closed in around him. Every growth, however innocuous-looking, presented a hostile appearance to Evan. Every one seemed to follow his steps, waiting for just the right moment to explode, or spit acid, or envelop him in some horrible alien web. It took him several hours to realize that not every living thing on Prism was intent on his destruction. So long as he did not threaten them, they were quite indifferent to his presence.

As to which were actually dangerous he couldn't have said. Slick growths which appeared unyielding proved to be soft and flexible when he accidentally brushed up against them, while those which looked cuddly turned out to be full of barbed hooks. He spent half an hour pulling the curved objects of that lesson out of his left leg and resolved to avoid contact with everything, even if it meant deviating from his chosen path and going the long way around.

On the plus side, his shoes were holding up well. The soles were thin but tough, a quality common to the majority of modern footwear. Also, most of the silicate growths that filled the ecological niche for ground cover were softer than their spiky, larger cousins. On some, like the bubble-encased chlorophyllic growths, the danger was not cutting himself so much as it was slipping on the slick glassy curves and breaking his neck. He found he had to skate as much as walk across them.

Water was no problem. If anything, there was too much of it. Late afternoon found him taking shelter beneath a condarite. The big growth reminded him of several dozen glass umbrellas growing one inside the other. Each shell was a different color, but all were tinted green by symbiotic bacteria. Small six-legged creatures with triple light-absorbing backplates lived between the umbrella shells. They crawled out to peep curiously down at him, vanished instantly if they caught him looking at them.

He wondered if growths like the condarite made any use of the water. It seemed likely they would need it to transport salts and minerals for growth and health throughout their structure, but they were devoid of the woody pulp which formed the body of normal trees. Perhaps they made use of some kind of porous silicate membrane. Another question best left to the botanists—or the geologists.

It rained all the rest of that day and through the night. He was up before dawn and on his way again. It would take his system a while to get used to the longer days and nights. Still, he felt refreshed and almost confident as he approached a small pool for a drink the following morning.

He hesitated only because something—it looked like a glass centipede—had chosen the best place for drinking. The thing had just shuffled to the pool's edge and dipped its mouthparts into the water.

As Evan stared, crouched among a soft clump of what looked like steel-wool cactus, the worm began to sizzle. Startled, he jumped backward. The reaction did not spread, however, and he slowly resumed his vantage point.

The water parted and something like a giant amoeba emerged. Slowly and patiently, a gel enveloped the dead worm and sucked it down into the pond. Evan moved forward cautiously and stared downward, risked a peek beneath his plastic eye-shield. Except that the bubble grass grew only to within two meters of the water's edge and then halted abruptly, there was nothing to indicate that the "pond" was actually filled by something powerful, dangerous, and perfectly transparent.

Nearby grew a variety of thin photovore that flourished in thick stands like pale yellow bamboo. An intricate internal structure of struts and braces enabled some of the canes to climb to forty meters or more despite their narrow diameters and apparent fragility. Feeling a little shaky, Evan snapped off a three-meter length and tucked it under one arm. As a weapon it was next to useless, but it would make a serviceable probe.

He used it on the next waterhole, but only after something bright purple and beige rolled out of the undergrowth on four ball bearings to sip at the water's edge. It extended a coiled yellow snout, inhaled its fill, and rolled noiselessly off into the forest. Evan assumed its place by the pool, jabbed repeatedly at the water with his newly acquired staff, and prepared to jump or run as circumstances dictated. He was required to do neither. Nothing grabbed the pole; nothing dissolved it. There was nothing in the pool but water. Then and only then did he bend to drink.

The ball-bearing drinker had been an organosilicate, a protein lifeform shielded by a silicate shell. He found himself wondering how it would taste if cooked over a slow fire. No, not yet. He hadn't been out of the MHW that long. He made a meal of concentrates, added appropriate vitamins, and continued on.

His close escape at the hands of the pool-dweller was forgotten when he noticed a perceptible strengthening of his beacon's light. He was still on course, then, and would not have to waste valuable time by returning to the suit and seeking a different direction. As the long evening set in, the brilliance of his surroundings was minimized. When he was able to see without his crude sunshades, he stowed them carefully in his pack, then reviewed his limited stock of food. He had enough to get him back to the station, but no guarantee that he would find untouched stores of food once he returned. He'd seen how easily the local lifeforms could break into and devour the materials used to manufacture electronic components, witnessed their taste for the basic elements that comprised the human body. He might return in high spirits only to find an empty larder.

If he was going to have to dine on the wildlife, now was as good a time to try it as any, while he still had some regular food to tide him over the inevitable stomach upsets. He would have to hunt carefully among the organosilicates for something palatable.

Might as well take a stab at hunting and gathering now, during the one time of day when he could see without his encumbering plastic eyewrap. He would improvise. Mankind had progressed somewhat beyond the skills necessary for hunting and gathering, and the citizens of Samstead had progressed rather farther than most. Which was another way of saying Evan was acutely aware of his ignorance.

Still another in the chain of ponds lay ahead, sheltered beneath a grove of what looked like glass poles topped by abandoned birds' nests. The nests were actually clumps of delicate fibers that strained to catch the rays of the slowly setting sun. Evan could see them moving, following the shrinking light, drinking in the photons. In the center of each pole was a greenish vein as thick as his leg. It was impossible to tell where silicate life ended and carbon-based began.

Piles of shattered trunks and broken fibers provided good cover, but try as he might, he couldn't locate anything small and edible. Everything was encased in a silicate shell or was composed entirely of inedible silicate materials.

Disgusted, he gave up before nightfall and lay down to watch the fibers atop the pole-trees slump against their trunks. Once more the decreasing light brought forth a multitude of night sounds prodigious in their inventiveness. Constrained screams, shrill whistles, buzzes, and peeps were familiar to him by now. In addition he knew that the air waves were alive with an alien cacophony pitched well above his hearing range.

Of more concern was the awakening of nocturnal carnivores, though so far he hadn't been disturbed after dark. That was fortunate, since the only weapons he possessed were a fragile silicate staff and a fragment of broken bubble grass. He strove to lie as still as possible.

Like the day, the night was comfortably warm, a real blessing considering his meager attire. Hadn't his ancestors made do with nothing at all? But they had been covered with fur.

Well, he wasn't dead yet, and with each hour of continued survival his confidence increased, if not his realistic prospects. Hadn't he survived most of a whole day outside on an alien world without a suit? It was a talent the citizens of Samstead had forgone long ago, resurrected by one Evan Orgell out of necessity. He had traversed a respectable number of kilometers by the power of his own muscles, avoided several dangerous lifeforms, and made an attempt, albeit an unsuccessful one, to obtain local food. He had much, he was convinced, to be proud of.

In fact, it seemed that he had been pretty much left alone by Prism's inhabitants, an observation which led him to consider a radical possibility. If the staff of the research station had not tried to defend their post but instead had abandoned it to the catastrophe which had in the end overwhelmed it, would they too have been left alone? On a world as unpredictable and unexplored as Prism, was passivity better than an active defense in the face of alien attack?

It took his mind off the night sounds as he sat there, scrunched in between two glassy trees as the stars replaced the sun with their wholly inadequate light. When the rush of adrenaline through his system lessened, exhaustion began to creep in and he became aware of how tired he really was.

He didn't know when he fell asleep, but he did not expect to awaken until morning. As worn out as he was, it took something spectacular to wake him in the middle of the night.

What happened was that a star tried to get into his eye.

It was bright blue and it tickled. He twisted and jerked his head violently. Aware that something had settled on his face, he sat up fast and brushed sharply at the star with his right hand. It flew away as he opened his eyes.

Until then he'd slept within the womb of the MHW, the visor darkened to shut out any external sights which might have disturbed his rest. No visor stood between him and the night sights of Prism now. One of them had landed on his cheek and tickled him awake.

The night was alive with dancing jewels. His first thoughts were of the fireflies of Earth or the pinmotes of

Hivehom, but it quickly became apparent that the phe-
nomenon he was observing was no kin to those familiar
luciferase-producing lifeforms. They were something different, strikingly different.

They were much brighter than their purely carbon-
based analogs and they exhibited every imaginable color
of the rainbow as they swarmed in the thousands above
the pond. As he stared, two more darted close to his face
and hovered there. They were bright red, crimson. A third
and fourth joined them, one green, the other an extraordinary lavender color, all hanging in the night air in front
of him like hummingbirds. Their tiny, delicate silicate wings
generated a gentle whirring noise instead of a harsh insec-
toid buzz. They did not blink but glowed steadily, their
lights, like their colors, intense and unvarying.

He waved at them and they retreated a few centimeters. The swarm produced more than enough light for him
to see by. He tried to imagine what kind of system could
produce such a creature, theorized that they must spend
every daylight hour soaking up the sun's energy in order
to be able to fly and glow at night.

Surrounded now, he waved both hands to shoo them
away and watched as they scattered, like gemstones tossed
from a rajah's hand. Rising, he saw that they rested in
the trees and bushes, conserving their stored energy for
the production of light. The silicate forest, which had been
so intimidating by day, was now transformed into a dazzling display of living light.

All was not innocent beauty, however. Something
moved in the dim, multicolored light, and Evan ducked
back between his protective boles. It sounded like a small
machine. In a way, it was.

It was composed entirely of black borosilicates, tough
and unyielding, save for a trio of bright pink eyes. With
an inflexible, gaping mouth it inhaled the flying jewels,
darting and swooping among the dancing clouds on stiff,
curved wings. Fingerlike scoops on the end of each wing

curled and twisted, blowing still more unfortunate prey into the open maw while driving the predator through the air. Evan had not delved sufficiently into ancient history to recognize such devices as propellers but he admired their efficiency nonetheless. The single predator had little impact on the thousands of dancing jewels, which, oblivious to the havoc it was wreaking among them, continued with their nocturnal ballet.

He watched until his stomach began to complain. He was tempted to dip into his store of concentrates, forced himself not to. Better to continue to ration himself. However, his stomach demanded something, so he left his resting place and strolled to the edge of the pond, confident that the black flier would ignore him.

He tested the water with the tip of his staff. While the silica was neither dissolved by acids nor attacked by some unsuspected subsurface carnivore, it did attract some attention in the form of a knot of round little water striders. They were not sharp and slim like the snowflakes who lived on the water tension during the day. They were much plumper, but most of that consisted of a silicate honeycomb that was more air than solid. Like the jewels, they also proclaimed their presence to the night by generating light. They were either blue or blue-gray, however, disdaining the intense displays of their aerial relations. The presence of the staff in the water seemed to confuse them. They kept bumping into it and swirling away dazedly.

Picking one out for closer observation was a simple matter. Evan dropped to his knees and scooped one up in his palm. The honeycombed body boasted a long, screwlike tail, a kind of corkscrew flagellum. Beneath the lightly glowing blue shell was a small knot of pink protoplasm. The tail pushed weakly at his palm, unable to propel its owner out of Evan's hand.

After a moment's hesitation, he set it down on the sandy shore, where it twisted and humped about helplessly. Utilizing a fist-size rock, he smashed the shell.

There was no audible response to this destruction, but the pale blue glow vanished instantly and the creature ceased its thrashing. He was able to pick off the remainder of the honeycomb shell with his fingers. This left him with a lump of pink flesh that lay motionless in his palm. The light of the jewel dancers revealed nothing resembling organs; no mouth, eyes, heart, or anything familiar. Just firm meat and a purely silicate tail.

Holding his breath and closing his eyes, Evan held it over his lips and bit it off clean at the tail joint.

The flesh was firm but not tough, with a rubbery consistency and practically no flavor at all. There was no blood, only a thin transparent fluid that was salty to the taste. He washed it down with some fresh water, inserted his staff into the pond, and fished out a second honeycomb strider, killed it instantly in the same fashion as the first. After several minutes passed, during which time he had not thrown up, he downed the next course of what was to become a filling late-night snack.

He found that the pale-blue striders went down easiest, while the blue-grays made him slightly queasy. Therefore he stuck with the pure blues, throwing the grays back, fishing for the diatomous forms with mounting enthusiasm.

By the time he finished, sated, he had accumulated a small mountain of cracked shells and discarded tails and a minor bellyache due more to overeating than the inedibility of his chosen prey. Wishing for a soft cushion but settling for a pile of shed pole-tree fibers, he leaned back and rested his crossed hands over his full belly. As he did so several brownish shapes descended from above and began to pick noisily at the pile of scraps he'd left behind. If they had eyes he couldn't see them. They seemed to be all teeth and claws.

It didn't take the creatures long to clean up the after-thoughts of his meal and return to the sky on parafoil wings. They left only pure silicate structures in their wake.

Carbon-consumers, like the scavengers feeding on the bodies of the unlucky station staff. Contented or not, he would do well to find a safer place in which to sleep off his repast.

He rose and began searching, grateful for the clouds of dancing jewels and for their light, which was beginning to fade as their stored solar energy started to run down. He needed a refuge fast, before total darkness reclaimed Prism's surface. A tree would be good, if he could find something climbable that would support his weight.

As it turned out he found something much more accessible: a place where flood waters from the stream which fed the chain of ponds had gouged out a cave in a soft bank. Crawling in, he found that the cave floor was smooth and dry. Blocking the entrance as best as he was able with rocks, he piled cool sand beneath his head and instantly went to sleep...

Sunlight streaming through the opening finally forced him awake. He twisted onto his side, reluctant to part with the last lingering shreds of reassuring sleep. He was stiff and slightly damp but not cold. The sun was insistent.

He rolled over. As he did so his right hand contacted something hard and slick. It moved, the reaction bringing him to full wakefulness much faster than the intruding sunlight. He had company in the cave! Whatever it was lay between him and the entrance, so he scuttled frantically back against the rear wall of his refuge, clutching his pitiful shard of bubble grass in one hand and waiting for what seemed like the inevitable attack.

The other occupant of the cave watched this activity blandly out of olive green eyes. There were only two of them, but that was all that was reassuring about the alien. It was less than a meter in length and resembled a loaf of french bread baked in dark blue glass. This body was supported by ten canary yellow legs. Body and legs were opaque, so Evan couldn't tell by looking at it if it was an organosilicate or purely silicate lifeform.

As he eyed it warily it did something no other creature he'd previously encountered had done: it blinked, both green eyes being temporarily covered and then exposed again by a pair of black silicate shades that closed over them from the sides. His gaze moved to the forest of cilia that covered the creature's back. At first he'd thought the yellow growths were some kind of fur. Now he could make out the miniature dish-shape that tipped each strand. All of them were straining toward the sunlight flooding the outer part of the cave, the tiny silicate cups drinking in the brightness. Another photovore, he decided.

His suppositions were confirmed when it retreated a few steps in order to place its receptors fully in the light. It kept its gaze on him all the time and the thought occurred to him it might be as fearful of him as he was of it. He relaxed somewhat.

The cilia receptors fluttered as they were placed in direct sunlight. Not only was the alien charging its system; it was enjoying the early morning heat as well, since the conductivity of silicon increased with the temperature. It leaned forward to nibble at the sand with half a dozen small pincers arranged around its mouth.

As he watched it eat, his initial panic dissipated. Evan grew aware of a soft, steady humming noise. It emanated from somewhere inside his visitor and sounded much like a small motor set on idle. At first he thought the sound unvarying, but the longer he listened the more he became aware of subtle modulations. It was a disarming sound, soothing, relaxing, almost a mechanical purr.

He forced himself to concentrate on those crunching mouthparts. How long before the alien came to the conclusion that the cave contained a more accessible concentration of useful minerals than raw sand?

Keeping as much distance between himself and the creature as possible, Evan started crawling around the inner rim of the cave, making for the entrance. As he moved, the alien continued with its breakfast. It also moved its head to watch him. The cilia on its back rose to track the rising sun.

He was very near the cave opening when the steady hum from the alien suddenly rose in volume. Evan fairly jumped for the outside, scrambling on hands and knees, and promptly bashed his head against something unseen. Dazed, he sat back, gingerly felt his forehead, and waited for his vision to clear. Could he have misjudged his sprint for safety so badly?

He had not. During the night, a transparent window had been placed over the cave entrance.

He ran his fingers along the smooth barrier, glanced sharply back at his unexpected roommate. Some kind of protective secretion, he decided. There was no other explanation for the construction. The alien had wandered into the cave sometime during the night, had ignored or not noticed its other occupant, and had put the shield in place to keep out undesirables while it slept.

Unfortunately, in sealing intruders out, it had also sealed Evan in. The humming lessened in intensity. Keeping his attention fixed on the creature, which was eying his own movements with equal alacrity, Evan made a fist and slammed it against the transparency. It didn't look especially thick, and it was riddled with tiny holes, but as with so much he'd already encountered on this world, appearances proved deceiving. Despite his efforts, it did not respond to the attentions of mere human muscles.

He turned away and began looking for a good-sized rock. As he turned, the alien moved toward him. Scrambling backward on hands and knees, he backed into a small alcove, determined to defend himself for as long as he was able.

Except there was nothing to defend against. Ignoring him, the alien approached the barrier. It glanced back once to assure itself of his position, then turned its head to face the glassy wall. A tiny hypodermiclike tube emerged from beneath its mouth, jetted a stream of odorless liquid onto the barrier. Evan stiffened, remembering previously observed secreters of dangerous acids, but this one didn't act like a corrosive. There was no hissing and steaming and the barrier didn't melt into a puddle of silicate slag.

The stream ceased. The alien settled back and waited. While it did so Evan found himself a rock with some heft. It wasn't much of a weapon, but it made him feel better. The creature continued to ignore him.

There was a loud cracking sound. As Evan stared, a jagged line appeared in the barrier. It was followed by another crack, then a third. The cracks began to run together and the transparency started to fall apart, crumbling like spun sugar. In a couple of minutes the wall he'd been unable to dent was a pile of powder on the cave floor. Enzymes or acids, the only difference was one of perspective, he thought.

But the alien still stood between him and the exit. While he watched, it consumed the silicate powder, much like a spider consuming the fragments of its own web, and then nudged a couple of rocks out of its way. The cilia on its back pointed toward the sun regardless of the position of the body.

Apparently satisfied with the exit it had created, it crawled over the few remaining stones and out onto the sandy beach outside. Then it turned to face him. Frowning and keeping his eyes on it, Evan crawled out after it. As he emerged, it backed away from him.

Its gait was more of a waddle than a walk and he almost smiled. Sharp mouthparts or not, it was hard to take anything with so comical a method of locomotion too seriously. Besides, if it harbored any malign intentions toward him, surely they would have manifested themselves by now.

He stood and stretched, trying to unbind his cramped muscles. He still held tight to the rock he'd picked up, in case the creature exhibited an abrupt shift in temperament. But he felt fairly confident now that he was outside.

The alien had been far more threatening when Evan was reduced to moving on hands and knees. Outside the cave, he towered over it. He could step over it without straining.

He felt confident enough, in fact, to return to the cave long enough to gather up his few belongings. Back outside, he removed his broken bubble-grass cup and used it to scoop water from the pond. As he drank, he tried to pretend he was swallowing the cold fruit juice his suit used to provide on demand.

When he'd sipped his fill he splashed the cool water on his face, wiped off with a sleeve of his underwear. A series of erratic beeps made him turn.

He'd half expected the alien to be gone by now, to have waddled off into the underbrush in search of a better place to sun itself. Instead, it had moved a little closer. It stopped when he turned to look back at it, but did not retreat. Instead, it squatted on its ten legs and continued to stare at him while emitting a remarkable sequence of electronic *squirps* and moans.

"You're even weirder than the rest of the fractal fauna, aren't you?" Evan said to it. "You're not after my bones, but you're not in any particular hurry to leave either."

Surely there must be variations in intelligence among the local lifeforms, he mused as he continued drying himself. Perhaps this one stood at the pinnacle of Prismatic evolution. It might even approach the domestic dog in intelligence and reasoning power. Lingering in his vicinity implied territoriality, or curiosity, or both. Could it be tamed? It would be nice to have some sort of companion for the duration of his stay, assuming that Martine Ophemert had gone the way of the rest of the research staff. And if he could tame it, it would make a wonderful presentation when he returned home and gave his first report to the company. It would certainly put Machoka's living bracelet to shame.

He sat down by the water's edge and stirred the surface with his staff. None of the organosilicates which had pro-

vided his previous night's supper appeared. Apparently
they were nocturnal. Probably stayed buried safely in the
soft sand that lined the bottom of the pool.

His stomach would not leave him alone, so he reluctantly dug into a pack of concentrated food. A tug on the
tab opened it and he waited for the contents to cook
themselves. While the food began to steam, he settled
back against a comfortable boulder and regarded his beep-
ing, humming companion thoughtfully.

"I wish you'd announced yourself." He spoke for the
pleasure of hearing his own voice rise above the alien
cacophony of the forest. "You scared the crap out of me."
The creature's head dipped and bobbed several times, like
that of a lizard surveying its surroundings. It continued
to emit its amazing variety of sounds.

Evan recalled his earlier thought, about heat raising
the conductivity of silicon. "Is that why you joined me?
Not for the protection of the cave but for my body heat?
Did I enable you to stay powered up for an extra hour or
two?"

He shrugged, ate his breakfast, and then carefully
washed out the foil packet it had come in. The foil would
make a serviceable cup to complement his broken piece
of bubble grass. After stowing the makeshift utensils in
his pack, he donned his crude sunshade. The throbbing
which the rising sun had induced behind his eyes began
to fade as the reflective glare from the surrounding growth
was reduced.

Odd, but he felt he could see the bizarre shapes a little
more clearly now, could perceive the fractal surfaces in
greater detail—though he still had trouble telling where
some ended and others began.

Throughout his breakfast his alien companion had neither moved nor displayed anything resembling intelligence. Idiot, he chided himself. If anything on Prism had
the brains of a rat it would be a scientific revelation. His
desires and emotions had momentarily overcome his good

sense. There was nothing on this sterile world to keep him company, even inadvertently. Out of a desire for companionship he was ascribing characteristics to this particular creature which it did not possess. The inhabitants of this world were as much machine as animal.

You couldn't even say that such an automaton was alive, in the normal sense of the term. Was a solar-powered surveyor alive? Did it have a soul? True, other worlds had provided some extreme examples of divergent intelligent evolution, but however outré their basic design, all such examples of known lifeforms were fashioned of flesh and blood.

Time enough for such speculation when he'd completed his current search. If he located the Ophemert beacon within the next couple of days, all well and good. If not, he intended to start back toward the station to begin the serious business of somehow getting in touch with his rescue team.

Checking his position by the sun, he chose a course and started off into the fantastically colored forest. As he did so the giant blue caterpillar behind him generated a series of loud buzzes and ambled off in his wake. After walking a dozen meters or so and noting that this peculiar silicate shadow was no coincidence, Evan halted. So did the caterpillar. Raised up off its first two pairs of legs, it regarded him out of cold glass eyes, apparently waiting for him to resume his march. The yellow cilia on its back swung around to face the sun.

Was it following him because it was attracted to him, or in hopes he would die and provide it with a harmless source of rare minerals? He shrugged. "All right, tag along if you want, but give me my room." It pleased him to talk at the creature if not to it. Understanding was a moot point. The caterpillar had no ears.

It couldn't match his stride, but with five times as many legs it managed to keep up with him. Gradually it drew nearer, until it was paralleling instead of following him.

Most of the time it kept its gaze fastened to its own course, but from time to time it would glance up and over to check his position to make sure he was still there.

It occurred to Evan that it might be waiting for nightfall again, and the comfort of his body heat. Well, he had no objection to sharing his sleep with the creature. By now he was pretty much convinced of its harmlessness.

A bed warmer, he mused. That's what my status has been reduced to on this crazy world. A simple heat engine.

Any kind of benign company was welcome. Besides, if something dangerous prowled these glass woods at night, perhaps his new companion would react to its presence and awaken him.

The heat engine and the caterpillar alarm. Better material for a poem than a dissertation on xenobiology.

 **7**

THE LONG DAY WENDED ITS WAY TOWARD EVE-
ning. Nothing plunged from the sky or the cascalarians
and condarites to smash him flat. Nothing charged from
the forest to crush him beneath massive silicate paws.
The acid-spitters left him alone; the quartz-eaters ignored
him as they browsed contentedly on fields of citrine and
chalcedony.

His initial terror at moving about without the protection of a proper suit had almost vanished. He was more
confident than ever. All you had to do to avoid harm on
this world, he decided, was simply to exercise a little
prudent judgment and work to stay out of trouble's way,
and you would be left in peace to continue your journey.
Traveling without the encumbrances of an MHW was not
only possible; it could be educational and invigorating.
He wasn't dead, had no prospects of immediately entering
that state, and was making good progress toward the location of the beacon.

As he walked he tried to estimate the distance he'd

covered since abandoning his suit. It was impressive, if he did say so himself. So pleased was he that he decided to treat himself to an early supper of real food.

Neither pool nor stream was close at hand, but he wasn't especially thirsty. A brief search for a place to relax turned up a shallow depression beneath an entirely new growth.

Instead of branches or leaves or the torus of the cascalarians, this new plant consisted of broad pink plates growing from the ends of short, thick stems. Each plate was about four centimeters thick and more than two meters in diameter. They grew one atop the other, competing for space and for access to sunlight. This particular growth had opted for several large photoreceptors instead of hundreds of smaller ones.

Evan scrunched down into the shade they provided and took his time with his food. When he'd finished he packed away the debris and lay down beneath the translucent pink plates. With the sun behind them, he found he could now make out the delicate tracery of individual substructures within each plate, the network that drew energy from the sun and delivered it to the thick stems rooted in the ground.

Rose-colored glasses, he thought, recalling an ancient rhyme. He was looking at the whole world through gigantic rose-colored glasses. The plates provided so much shade that he found he was able to remove his effective but uncomfortable sunshade. Thus screened, he was able to see around him so long as he was careful not to look directly at any of the highly reflective growths that ringed his resting place. It was a relief to get the knot of plastic off the back of his head.

He lay there, content and confident, while his food was digested. An hour's siesta didn't seem out of the question.

When the hour was up he prepared to resume his trek. The only trouble was that he couldn't. He twisted hard.

His legs wouldn't budge. It was all he could do to sit up. He looked down at his suddenly immobile legs. What he saw made him want to vomit.

Something, or rather some *things*, were moving about beneath his pants legs. It was a sinuous, rippling motion, smooth and supple. As he stared, little dots of red began to stain the beige of his lower clothing. Blood.

His blood. It had to be, because he'd seen nothing to indicate that any of Prism's inhabitants possessed anything in their bodies like that rich red, unmistakable fluid. He felt no pain.

Reaching out and down, he slapped at his right leg. Several twisting, curling shapes burst through the thin material of his pants. None was thicker around than his little finger.

The worms were the same color as the sandy soil he was lying on. Indeed, they were composed of the same elements as that soil. Half a dozen of them were snaking up each leg of his pants, linked to one another head to tail by means of powerful little suckers. Two were linked head to side.

He leaned over and looked at his left side. More worms there, dozens more, fastened tightly to one another in a living net that was binding him with increasing strength to his place of rest. And more of them emerging to join their brethren every minute.

The soil all around and beneath him was alive, rippling with the movements of hundreds of anxious, hungry shapes.

Horror lent strength to his efforts. He gave a tremendous jerk with his legs and succeeded in wrenching the left one free. Linked worms flew in all directions. As soon as they struck the ground they began crawling back toward him, joining in lengths of twos and threes in expectation of re-forming the cocoon around him.

Yet Evan couldn't pull his right leg free of the ground. Twisting around onto his belly, he scrabbled at the earth, trying to reach the nearest stem of the plants shading him. His tranquil resting place had all the hallmarks of becoming his coffin, and a particularly revolting one at that, unless he could pull or push himself loose.

The stem was far out of reach. Sitting up again, he tried to grab one of the overhanging plates, just did manage to grasp the lowest. Hope turned to powder along with the plate, however, as it disintegrated in his hand. Like so much of Prism's flora it was far more fragile than it appeared. Frantic now, he started looking for a rock, wishing he'd kept one in his pack. Nothing was within reach but fine sand.

His silent attackers re-established their grip on his freed leg, and this time it didn't seem likely he'd be able to pull it free. From the knees down both of his legs were stained with blood. It suddenly occurred to him that the mineral salts in his blood were what the worms were after. He'd be willing enough to share it with them if they'd just let him go. But why should they have to share, he thought wildly, when they could have it all? They would pin him down until they'd drained him of the last drop and then abandon him to the scavengers. First his skin would be dissolved and digested, then the calcium-rich bones.

He found a small rock, began battering away at the living chains encircling his thighs. But the worms were made of stronger stuff than their terrestrial cousins. They were neither soft and pulpy nor brittle like the growth beneath which he was being patiently devoured. They were flexible, rubbery, and tough as bundles of silicate fibers. When he finally did manage to kill one by smashing its head, two more appeared to take the dead worm's place.

Evan was leaning on his left arm, flailing away with the rock in his right hand, when three worms popped out of the ground, linked together, and encircled the thumb of his supporting hand. With a cry, he turned and pounded them back into the soil. More appeared in the wake of the initial trio. It dawned on him that he'd chosen to lie down in a hive or nest of the loathsome creatures. The commotion caused by his resistance was awakening more and more of them, excited by the activity and the taste of fresh food. If they managed to tie his hands down he'd be utterly helpless.

Though he was losing blood slowly, the worms had been at it long enough to have drained a pint or more out of him. He was weakening just when he needed strength. Evan, however, was not the type to concede any argument, least of all that acknowledging his own demise. He kept bashing away with his wholly inadequate weapon.

Somehow he had to free his legs before he passed out. But with his increasing weakness, his aim and the force with which he delivered his blows were failing him and he was hitting himself as often as his targets. He put his left hand down to balance himself again, raised the rock high over his head, and promptly fell backward as his left arm was yanked out from under him. Thirty or more worms had formed a double-thick cable to pull him down.

He twisted onto his left side and tried to knock them away. On the third blow the rock slipped out of his hands. Exhausted, he lay there breathing hard and contemplating the tiny lifeform which had defeated the finest mind humanity had to offer. Not for Evan Orgell false modesty even in the face of imminent death.

Strange how calm he suddenly was. Composed. His greatest disappointment was that he wouldn't live long enough to study the exact nature of his passing.

What a stupid, ridiculous way to die, he thought tiredly. After surviving a broken MHW suit and a host of dangerous alien lifeforms. Brought down by a colony of communal worms. Food for worms, true enough. But that wasn't supposed to be the case until *after* you'd been dead for a while. The worms weren't supposed to hurry the inevitable. Of course, these weren't terran worms. They hadn't been instructed in their proper place in the scheme of things.

They had him pinned to the ground the way the Lilliputians had tried to pin Gulliver, and they'd done a much better job of it. He passed out.

The sun was high in the sky but in the wrong place when he opened his eyes again. He was excruciatingly tired, more than he'd ever imagined being. It went beyond exhaustion. There was about and throughout his body a numbness that belonged to inorganic things like rocks and metal, not poor flesh and blood.

And blood. He raised his head and looked down at himself. From the knees down his pants were gone, torn away by some agency unknown. He could see the worm scars clearly, long and thin and caked with dried blood. He had no idea how much they'd sucked out of him, but evidently not enough to kill him.

The pink photoreceptors that had shaded him were gone. His unprotected eyes squeezed together to shut out the unbearably bright light, but he could still make out things in his immediate vicinity. He was lying beneath a growth that looked very much like a normal tree. Closer inspection revealed it to be plated with long strips of brown silica, but it had a green heart. He tried hard to tell himself it was made of wood.

On both sides of him clumps of bright yellow flower shapes that resembled blue-and-green striped ultrasound projectors moved lazily in the gentle breeze—but not so lazily that they didn't keep themselves oriented to the sun. They might very well *be* ultrasound projectors, he told himself, given the insane world on which they grew.

The flowers and tree were comforting, but where were the worms? How long had he lain unconscious? Minutes, hours, longer still? His stomach felt empty but he wasn't starving, so it couldn't have been too many days, if days it had been. A single day or so, then. Thirty hours or more of unconsciousness while his body recuperated from the assault. He felt oddly lightheaded, and not just from loss of blood.

Then he remembered what he'd seen just before he'd blacked out. Or what he thought he'd seen.

The blue caterpillar, coming down the slight slope, wading into the milling worms and scattering them with swings of its legs, crunching them in its mouth and spraying them with the mysterious fluid from the hypodermic organ beneath its jaws. A drop of that liquid caused the worms to break their links, to contort violently as their bodies cracked open and they died.

Undoubtedly the caterpillar had been partaking of an unexpected abundance of prey, feasting on the worms even as they had been feasting on Evan. Perhaps that was why the creature had been following him all along. But that didn't seem right, he thought. Surely the caterpillar was a photovore, with all those light-gathering cilia on its back?

Even so, it probably required minerals. So it would take them, when the opportunity presented itself, from the small worm bodies in which the minerals had been concentrated. Sure. The caterpillar was after the same substances as the worms.

Then why hadn't it attacked Evan that night in the cave?

It didn't matter now. What mattered was that the caterpillar's unexpected assault had killed so many of the worms that the rest had given up and retreated to their underground sanctuary. Weak and barely conscious, Evan then must have managed to crawl out of the lethal depression to this place of safe rest, where his wounded body had taken the opportunity to repair itself.

Operating on instinct, then, the caterpillar had inadvertently done him a good turn. He hoped to encounter it again. Maybe, somehow, he'd have a chance to repay the favor. *If* his memory of events was correct and if that was truly what had happened. Perhaps it would turn up to follow him again. If he could entice it to follow him back to the station he'd feed it the remnants of the chemical lab until it couldn't consume any more. It could ingest rare minerals to its heart's content—assuming it had a heart instead of a collection of silicate batteries.

The lightheadedness wouldn't go away. His body had done its best, but now it needed more than rest to continue the rejuvenating process. His stomach insisted on it. As he tried to sit up, he found himself listing to his left. Something was tugging at his left ear. Frowning, he reached up to scratch the itch, to remove whatever loose bits of matter had fallen on him while he'd slept.

His fingers contacted two extremely thin tendrils dangling from his head. They were not wrapped around his ear, entwined in his hair, or stuck to his sideburns. They hung from the ear itself. Out of it.

He looked sharply to his left. A pair of bright green glassy orbs stared back into his own from a distance of a few centimeters. It was the caterpillar.

It was sitting on his shoulders, curled around the back of his neck like a silicate stole. The legs gripped his clavicle and shoulder muscles, digging in lightly but firmly. Those jaws, which were capable of shredding rock, rested lightly against the flesh of his upper arm.

The two thin tendrils emerged from its head to enter Evan's ear, in their penetration bypassing the tympanum without damaging it and slipping deeper into the skull. Something tickled Evan's brain. It was as though he'd been given a slight shock.

What happened next was that he blacked out without losing consciousness. To put it another way, he went slightly mad for a while, jumping to his feet and running and twisting in circles, bouncing off the glassy growths around him, all the while trying to dislodge the creature on his shoulders and the tendrils it had inserted into his brain. He pulled and tugged and yanked at the thin filaments. They would not break, and even at full strength it's doubtful he could have broken that ten-legged grip.

Throughout it all, the caterpillar did not move, did not utter a sound. Only its black eyelids reacted, closing to protect the green lenses from Evan's desperately stabbing fingers. It was like jabbing a mirror. He did more harm to himself by banging into trees and rocks than he did to the caterpillar.

When he pulled at the filaments dangling from his ear he only succeeded in causing himself the most excruciating pain.

His throat gave out first, raw from nonstop screaming. During his wild dash through the forest he'd sloughed off the last vestiges of confidence that he'd succeeded in building up since he'd abandoned his suit, along with much of what would be called civilized behavior. First the worms, then seeming salvation, and now this. Only an unshakable confidence in his ability to survive, somehow, kept him from going completely insane. Others might have called it arrogance.

Eventually the exhaustion reached his legs and he dropped to his knees. He cupped his face in his hands and sobbed uncontrollably. Throughout, the caterpillar clung to his shoulders, glassy and imperturbable, as unaffected by his emotional breakdown as it had been by his hysterical attempts to dislodge it from its perch.

Evan collapsed on his right side. He lay there, shuddering, trying to shut out the thought of what had happened to him, of what might yet happen to him. Far better to have died painlessly from the attentions of the worms. Worst of all, he had no idea what the thing was doing to him. Feeding on him somehow? Preparing his brain as a repository for its young?

Since he could no longer run or scream, all he could do was lie still and contemplate. Contemplate and think. It was taking him apart from the inside out. Yes, dissolving his brain tissue and extracting it bit by bit through those two tendrils. He'd lose control slowly at first. There would be only the pain of knowing.

A fresh attempt to loosen the tendrils only produced a resurgence of the sharp pain that previous tries had generated. A dull throbbing had begun near the back of his skull. The first signs, he thought. He was too tired to yell anymore. It alleviated nothing anyway. His situation was utterly hopeless.

Yes, it was destroying him from within. He'd already seen what the creature could do with that hypodermic organ beneath its mouth. Was it injecting that or some similar fluid into his head even now? It seemed strange there should be no pain, but as long as he didn't pull on the tendrils, there was only the slight throbbing sensation, a throbbing which rose and fell, went away without warning and returned without hurt. He was so tired of hurting.

The throbbing was like waves beating on a beach. Soft and pulsing, not painful at all. Just as the words weren't painful.

"I am sorry, Soft Thing," went the throbbing, "that it took so long to mesh with you, but your plug was hard to find."

Evan rolled over and sat up, swayed for a moment before steadying himself to listen to the echo of the word throbs rattling around inside his brain. More was to come.

"Are you understanding me? I feel that you must be receiving but you do not broadcast."

So this is what it's like to be mad, Evan thought quietly.

"You are not mentally unbalanced," the voice informed him confidently. "Confused and tired, yes, but I believe sane. Your impulses are properly organized. They were utterly alien to me at first but conceptually they translate very well."

"What translates very well?" Evan became aware that he only thought the question. He hadn't opened his mouth since he'd stopped screaming and was afraid to do so lest he start again. He didn't want to do that. Raving was counterproductive.

"The communication impulses your brain generates. Somewhat confusing, but that is to be expected. All communications impulses produced by soft-tissue minds are slightly disorganized."

"You don't say," Evan muttered, aloud this time. The sound of his nonshrieking voice was comforting. Crazed he might be, but still in control of himself.

He forced himself to turn to stare directly at the blue and green and yellow apparition that had stepped out of the Looking Glass onto his shoulders.

"What are you doing to me?"

"I am conversing with you. Accept reality." By way of further proof the caterpillar winked at him.

Gingerly this time, Evan reached up to feel of the thin silvery tendrils running from the top of the creature's head into his left ear. Mesh? Plug?

"I don't have a plug inside my head," he mumbled.

"Of course you do." The caterpillar sounded absolutely sure of itself. "Every intelligent being has a plug. Yours was difficult for me to locate. Amazing as it seems, it has never been used before. As a result, it has atrophied and changed. To make a proper connection required some modifications, which I performed while you recovered from the depredations of the syaruzi."

Evan took long, regular breaths. It kept him from shaking. "What are you talking about, 'modification'? You did something inside my head? *What have you done to me?*"

"Merely cleaned up some overgrowth and allowed your natural organs to function properly so as to facilitate normal meshing." The caterpillar managed to sound puzzled. "I should think you would be grateful."

"I'm sure as hell grateful to you for pulling me away from those worm-things. Anything else I'm reserving judgment on. How come I can understand you so clearly?"

"Clarity is a consequence of meshing. It is only to be

expected when two intelligent beings are plugged into each other. All communications impulses are similar."

Impulses. The caterpillar was deciphering the electrical impulses which together formed rational thoughts in Evan's mind. Just as he must be doing with the caterpillar's impulses. But how? Through "plugs"? Was this fantasy or physiology?

Whatever it was, it seemed to work.

"The sequence and intensity of impulses varies," the caterpillar told him helpfully, "but within specific limits. With care, all are eventually comprehensible. I did not think you were intelligent when I first encountered you in the cave. I was attracted by the astonishing amount of waste heat your body generates. In any event, you did not demonstrate the ability to communicate. I called out to you many times, without ever receiving a response."

"You mean, all those buzzes and chirps? That was just so much noise to me."

"As were your modulated sound waves to me. You are generating them now in conjunction with your thoughts, but I could not understand a single concept were we unmeshed.

"When you did not respond to my signals, I more or less decided there was nothing to communicate with. I did find your new form interesting, however, despite what I thought was your demonstrable stupidity."

Evan bristled slightly, but on reflection found himself agreeing with the caterpillar's assessment. Sprawling out atop a syaruzi community, after all, would not be perceived by a local intelligence as the action of a particularly bright individual.

"What made you change your mind?"

"The methodical way in which you attempted to free yourself from the syaruzi's clutches. I thought that an attempt at a more intimate means of communication was worth a try. So I made the effort, which was considerable, to locate and modify your plug so that it could be utilized for proper meshing. And how were my attempts rewarded? The first thing you tried to do was break the connection. Hardly the reaction of an intelligent creature."

Evan's pulse had dropped to something like normal. "I'm sorry. I didn't know what was happening to me. I vaguely recalled your attacking the syaruzi, though I didn't know it was on my behalf. I—my species, my kind aren't familiar with this method of communication you call meshing. My plug, as you call it, is something in my own brain that I'm not familiar with. I never heard of it before. And when you call this method of communication intimate, as far as my kind is concerned, that's one hell of an understatement. The thought of something inserting itself into our heads is, well, not pleasant." After a pause he added, "Listen, are you sure I have this plug organ or whatever it is inside my skull, or have you added something and you're not telling me the truth about it?"

"I only modified what already exists in your mind. When you panicked I thought of breaking the connection and leaving you alone. But your distress was so obvious and your ignorance so extreme that I did not see how you could survive for long without help. So I persisted until you calmed down long enough to permit another serious attempt at rational conversation."

"Again, I'm sorry. I'm not used to walking around like this. Ever since I had to abandon my suit—"

"Suit?"

Evan described the MHW and its functions, trying to make as clear a mental picture of it for the caterpillar as possible.

"Ah. So you do have a hard exoskeleton like so many other soft things, but you were forced to slough it off."

"No, no." Evan contained his impatience. "It's a *suit*. It's not natural, not a normal part of our bodies. It's a manufactured item, something fashioned out of raw metals and chemicals."

"So is an exoskeleton."

"But an exoskeleton is made by one's body. A suit is built up with tools, by machines."

"What are tools?"

Evan was taken aback. A highly intelligent alien completely ignorant of tools?

"We can discuss it later." He was searching the ground nearby anxiously. The caterpillar had thoughtfully recovered his pack, which lay nearby, apparently undamaged. Either the scavengers hadn't discovered its contents yet or else his alien rescuer had frightened them off.

Food packets lay scattered about where they had fallen out of the pack. He rose, doing his best to ignore the weight on his shoulders, walked over, and began restocking the pack.

"What are those things?"

"Food."

"Really? There is no brightness to them at all."

"They contain stored chemical energy. I'm not a photovore like you. My body produces energy by oxydizing certain chemical compounds and breaking them down into sugars and other substances which—well, we can go into organic chemistry later."

"I know that soft forms draw energy from consuming other soft forms, but I have never seen them reduced to such a state. I knew that you had to be a soft-form consumer because you sought shade when all other intelligent creatures instinctively seek the light."

"I don't need sunlight to live," Evan started to say, then corrected himself, "except for an occasional slight dose so my body can produce certain vitamins. I can't convert it to direct energy like you."

"And so, like other soft-form consumers, you must spend much of your time searching for chemical combinations to eat. What a terrible waste of precious life time."

"I agree. On the other hand, I can carry food with me into total darkness and live there for a long period of time."

"Who would want to?" The caterpillar gave a mental shudder at the thought.

The tendrils brushed lightly against Evan's neck as he bent to retrieve his belongings. "Listen, do you think we could maybe do without this meshing-plug business and learn to talk by means of modulated sound waves?"

"I tried that at first, as I said. I do not think it would ever be feasible. Your modulations are so much pure noise. Furthermore, much was generated at a frequency so low as to be almost indetectable. Is the meshing causing you pain?"

"No, no—not anymore. It's just that I'm not used to the idea yet, I guess."

"I still find it hard to believe you are in possession of a proper plug without being aware of its existence in your own body."

"Believe it. Yours is the first indication of its presence I've ever had. My kind communicate only by speaking."

"More and more extraordinary. How do you hold simultaneous group conversations?"

"We don't. One person talks and everyone else listens."

"That is sad. It must greatly slow your communications, your exchange of information. It must be difficult for you to work in harmonious groups."

"Sometimes," Evan admitted, thinking back to the endless arguments he'd had with fellow workers. "We're an argumentative lot, we humans."

Evan found himself beginning to relax despite the presence in his head of alien tendrils. Not only was his new-found friend curious and startlingly intelligent; it was also compassionate. And it had rescued him from the bloodsuckers. True, it had invaded his body without his permission, but it had only done so as a last resort to facilitate communication. Within its own ethical parameters it had acted properly. Evan knew full well that he never would have allowed the meshing to take place had he been conscious and aware of what was going on.

"Do you have an individuality or are you just part of a composite?"

"I beg your pardon? I mean, I don't understand."

"Among my kind each individual is identified by a descriptive term appropriate to the individual alone. I, for example, am A Surface of Fine Azure-Tinted Reflection With Pyroxin Dendritic Inclusions."

Evan mulled that over. "How about if I just call you Azure?"

The caterpillar sounded disappointed. "That is not properly descriptive."

"It's a lot better than mine. I'm called Evan."

"Ev-an. Is that descriptive of anything?"

"It's descriptive of me."

"You define yourself by yourself. Uninformative."

"It's an abstract."

"I'm not good with abstracts," Azure confessed. "They are the business of philosophers and teachers. I am only a scout."

"That's your profession?"

"Profession?" More confusion. "It is what I am. A teacher is a teacher. A warrior is a warrior. A scout is a scout. Everyone is what they are."

"That's not the case with us. We can switch between occupations whenever we want to."

"Now I am truly puzzled. For an intelligent being you are afflicted by the most bizarre notions."

"That's quite an assumption for a glass caterpillar to make," Evan shot back.

Azure was not offended. "A more descriptive image, though imprecise and based on an obscure alien reference."

Evan let his fingers trace the path taken by the tendrils. "You're positive you haven't done any permanent damage to my mind or ear or anything?"

"I proceeded only where I was confident," Azure assured him. "I did not attempt to proceed where there was no reaction."

"Reaction?"

"Impulse response. The output of your own brain guided me along the correct route to the plug. You can imagine my astonishment when I finally made contact, only to find the organ shrunken and unused. I had never before attempted to mesh with another mind possessing a previously unutilized plug, but the reactions of your mind and body were so smooth that I determined to proceed. Now that the necessary modifications have been made, it will be easy for you to mesh with anyone else in the future."

Except that it will never be needed again, Evan told himself. He was able to keep the thought private, not wishing to insult his friend's delicate handiwork. He was able to do so, because in order to communicate he had to think *at* the alien.

He wished for a mirror, though if he wanted to see himself badly enough, the forest was rich with reflective surfaces. He tugged gently on the tendrils, was rewarded with a brief stab of pain.

"Do you wish me to break the connection?" Azure asked quickly. "I can sense your discomfort."

"It's all right. I just can't keep my hands to myself. It's the kind of reality that requires constant reassurance for continued belief. There's no pain when I leave them alone. Besides, this is the biggest news in interpersonal communication in the last three centuries."

"You are a library, then?"

"A what?"

"A library. A repositor and collector of knowledge, fed by scouts." The little alien seemed unusually excited. "No wonder I had such an easy time making the connection. You were designed to accept it."

"Now wait a minute. I'm no library—librarian, I mean.

I'm a research engineer specializing in macroconcepts who—but we're arguing descriptions again. Yes, it is part of my job to acquire and store knowledge, but that's not all I do."

"Of course it is not, but everyone is designed to carry out a primary function, and yours is that of library. Your plug design confirms it."

"I wish you'd quit talking about that." He was trying to keep from thinking about the particulars of the place where the pair of alien probes actually pierced his brain.

Were all humans like that? Was everyone walking around unknowingly in possession of a tiny, unused organ designed for intimate communication with individuals of other species? If so, what did that say about convergent evolution, not to mention the potential theological implications? Had all intelligent life, even the utterly alien silicon-based life of Prism, come from some primeval basic design? Did the thranx and the AAnn possess similar organs?

If so, it pointed toward revelations so immense as to barely be imagined. If confirmed it would be a discovery vast enough to overwhelm everything else that had been learned since man had taken his first tentative step outward from the home world.

He couldn't deal with it. He was too busy just trying to live through the day. If this caterpillar, this Azure, could facilitate survival by sticking a couple of glass fibers into his ear, then he would gladly accept the intrusion.

"What does a scout do?"

"Like anything else, it defines itself, but since you desire elaboration: a scout ranges far from the Associative on its behalf. My task is to gather knowledge of the world that surrounds the Associative, of good places to mine the minerals and the metals necessary to our health, and to keep watch out for and provide warning of potential dangers."

"This Associative, it's like a town, a community? So there are others like you?"

"There are a few other scouts, of course."

"No, I didn't mean that." Evan tried to think of another way to phrase the question. "I mean, there's a larger grouping of you, some of whom perform other functions on behalf of the community?"

"Certainly. What else would an Associative consist of? Are not your own Associatives comprised of individuals who specialize?"

"That's right. I'm a specialist myself. A specialist in generalities, if that's not too confusing. Though I'm not getting a clear picture of what you mean when you say specialize. It seems to mean something more than what I think of when I use the same term." He paused to rub his forehead.

"More pain?"

"Not really. It's just a dull throbbing when you talk at me, like a weak headache."

"That sounds like an affliction peculiar to soft forms."

"You don't experience mental stress to the point of discomfort?"

"Not physically. A soft-form conception." Azure was silent for a long moment before announcing brightly, "I have come up with a descriptive for you. I will call you Flexible Modular Argumentative Random-Motion Carbon Concentrate."

"Evan will do nicely."

"You have this preference for nondescriptive identification," the alien grumbled disappointedly.

"We have enough trouble making ourselves understood to one another. Look on it as a communications saver."

"If it will make you feel more comfortable." Azure still didn't sound convinced.

"It will. Let me ask you something." Evan turned to point back toward the distant but still identifiable depression where he'd nearly been bled to death. "The syaruzi, as you call them, were after the trace elements in my blood."

"The metals and minerals in the liquid part of your body, yes."

"They don't interest you? These fibers you've got stuck in my head, they're only there for communications purposes? You're not having this nice, polite conversation with me and simultaneously draining me of some vital trace substance like zinc, are you?"

Azure's shock was almost palpable. "Certainly not! Some creatures obtain what they need of important elements by stealing them from the bodies of others, but the majority extract them directly from the ground. I will unplug and show you."

"All right."

He braced himself, but there was no pain as the alien broke the connection. The two tendrils slipped cleanly and bloodlessly out his ear. Azure released his grasp on Evan's shoulders and jumped to the ground, absorbing the shock easily through his ten legs.

Finding a suitable patch of ground, he cleared away the bubble grass, lowered his head, and began sucking up the sandy soil beneath through a short, flexible snout. He kept at it for a couple of minutes, then looked back up at Evan and buzzed. Despite the warning, Evan flinched when the alien jumped back onto his shoulders. The alien. It had a name, didn't it? It was intelligent, wasn't it?

It was much harder and required a supreme effort of will for Evan to stand motionless with his hands at his sides while Azure reinserted the communications tendrils into his skull.

 8

Iᴛ ᴅɪᴅɴ'ᴛ ʜᴇʟᴘ ᴛʜᴀᴛ ʜᴇ ᴡᴀs ғᴜʟʟʏ ᴄᴏɴsᴄɪᴏᴜs while the procedure was being carried out. He could feel the slick fibers sliding smoothly into his ear, past the tympanum and farther into his head. Again, there was no pain, only a faint coolness. There was no feeling of being "plugged in." But when the tendrils had ceased moving, the throbbing voice returned.

"I sense your unease," Azure murmured. "There is no reason for such discomfort. The plug is there because it is meant to be used."

"I know a surgeon who'd like to talk to you about that."

"A surgeon? You mean, a physician? Perhaps you can talk to mine."

Evan was immediately interested. What revelations could a silicate shaman provide? How did one go about repairing damage to creatures composed of silicon and beryllium and boron alloys?

"I have never encountered anything like you," Azure said.

Evan smiled slightly. "I have a number of acquaintances who've said more or less the same thing to me."

"You must come from a place," and here he (Evan had come to think of his friend as a "he," though from all indications thus far Azure was quite asexual) used a term which did not translate well, "far away."

"Farther than you can imagine." Finding a comfortable place, Evan sat down and did his best to explain himself, his origins, and his reason for being on Azure's world.

The alien responded quickly when Evan had finished. "Fascinatinger and fascinatinger! You must come back to the Associative with me and tell all this to the libraries."

"You have more than one?"

"Certainly. Ours is a progressive Associative."

"You must have acquired a lot of books."

"What are books?"

Now it was Evan's turn to be confused. "Books, and tapes, and related storage materials are what go into a library."

"Storage materials. That much I understand."

"I can't go with you just now, Azure. Much as I'd like to, I can't." He displayed his wrist, with the steadily glowing beacon. "I have to try and find this other human. I told you about that."

Azure considered. "But you are not certain as to your colleague's location?"

"No. I can only use this to take me into her general vicinity. Then I have to make a visual search and hope I get lucky."

"Perhaps we can help. There is nothing unusual about the frequency of your little broadcasting unit." He indicated the beacon with a pair of legs. "Come back with me and I will put your problem to our talkers. They can accurately locate anyone broadcasting."

Evan frowned. It seemed highly unlikely that Azure's people possessed anything as sophisticated as a directional locator—hadn't he already confessed an ignorance of tools? And what was a talker? Still, if there was anything to what his friend claimed, it could lead him directly to Ophemert's body and save him days of wandering around in the glittering, hostile forest.

"All right. Let's see what these 'talkers' of yours can do."

"Excellent! Most pleasuring." Azure gave a twist to show his delight. The bright green eyes passed several times over Evan's form. "But first we must do something about your vulnerability. We must try to get you an exoskeleton of sorts. You cannot go walking about as you are, soft-bodied and defenseless. You say that your own exoskeleton, this suit or whatever it is, is now of no use to you?"

"I'm afraid so. With its systems dead there's no way I could move it under my own power."

"Another strange concept." He rose on his rear six legs and surveyed the surrounding flora, finally gesturing with his mouthparts. "First we must do something about your sensitive vision. This way."

Evan followed the alien a short distance into a thick clump of trees. They halted before a growth almost worthy of the name. Brown globes grew directly upon a gray brown trunk. There were no leaves or branches, but neither did Evan see any of the ubiquitous photoreceptors. This was a carbon-based structure, the nearest thing to a real tree he'd seen since setting down on Prism.

A mound of broken globes had accumulated around the base of the tree. "Kneel, please," Azure said. Evan did so. As he bent, the alien reached up and pulled the strip of flimsy plastic from Evan's eyes.

"Hey, I need that!"

"Not any longer, I hope." Azure disconnected, still holding on to the plastic film, and dropped to the ground.

Already Prism's overpowering light was starting tears from Evan's eyes. He squinted hard, trying to follow the alien's actions. "Come on, give it back." Useless admonition. He was unplugged.

Azure appeared to be doing something with the silicate

debris, glancing occasionally back at the crouching human, then sorting through fragments of shattered globe. Eventually selecting a couple of choice shards, he began trimming and adjusting them. Evan watched as the alien's mouthparts cut through the tough material as though it was paper. He could easily imagine what they could do to his own flesh if Azure took a sudden dislike to him.

More speculative glances in Evan's direction. The globular fragments had been cut and glued into four sections, two straight and curved, two round and bubblelike. These four became one under Azure's skillful claws.

When he was finished the result was handed to Evan. It was a remarkably polished piece of work and might have come out of a machine instead of an alien mouth. Evan slipped the straight bars over his ears and hooked them together in back of his head. The twin hemispheres they were connected to in front fit neatly over his eyes. They were a bit large and probably gave him the aspect of a giant bug, but he wasn't much interested in appearances.

The brown silicate screened out most of the sun's rays and the painful reflections of the surrounding growths. For the first time since he'd been forced to abandon the MHW, he could see clearly and without difficulty. A light, warm rain began to fall.

"How did you know?" He bent again and allowed Azure to climb back onto his shoulders and remesh. "How did you know?"

"The purpose of the thin material wrapped around your face was self-evident and obviously inefficient," Azure replied. He gestured toward the strip of plastic now lying crumpled on the ground. "I thought pieces of *Eria* fruit would serve better. It is better?"

"It's wonderful. Can't thank you enough." He surveyed the terrain, luxuriating in being able to open his eyes fully for the first time in days. "Which way now?"

"We are not finished here yet."

"Whatever you say." What else did Azure have in mind for him? Another pair of glasses, perhaps, fashioned from some darker material?

Azure directed him through the forest until they were confronted by a small pool. This one stood by itself, with no visible outlet. As might be expected, the water was murky and rich with diatomous swarms.

"Get in," Azure told him.

"What?" Evan eyed the soupy broth uncertainly.

"Immerse yourself—and be sure to keep your head above water."

"Why? What's the danger?"

"No danger. Just a precaution a soft form needs to take."

Evan leaned over and tried to penetrate the mystery of the pool. "What's going to happen to me?"

"You need protection. The pool will provide it." When Evan continued to hesitate, Azure added, with a hint of exasperation, "Have I done anything to cause you harm?"

"No-o-o-o." Evan considered. It was only water. He could always get out fast if that seemed necessary.

He stepped in and slowly assumed a supine position, his head resting on the dry bank. Warm water began to leak in around his light clothing. Something began to irritate his legs.

He reached down to scratch but was forestalled by Azure, who had crawled onto the shore near his head, still plugged in to his tall soft friend.

"Don't do that. Relax and let the froporia do its work."

Evan did as he was told, though the crawling sensation intensified and it was an effort to keep his hands at his sides. It wasn't painful; merely uncomfortable. He lifted his head to look down at himself.

A thin layer of silica was forming on his body. As it took hold, his clothing was split and torn from beneath. The loss of the light undersuit didn't upset him too much. It was frayed and torn already anyway. The process was fascinating to observe. Millions of microscopic creatures were cementing themselves together no more than a centimeter above his skin, in much the same way corals form barrier reefs, only the process was occurring infinitely faster.

He twisted and turned slightly. Where there was resistance, the froporia allowed more room for movement. He began to work his way down his own body, moving the thickening formation farther from his skin at joints and creases, flexing his muscles individually where possible. When the coating was a centimeter or so thick, growth ceased.

Obeying Azure's instructions, he lay as still as he could for several hours, whereupon his friend said, "You may get up now."

Evan glanced down at the creamy white wrapping encasing him, tried to bend his legs. The formation was as unyielding as metal. "How?"

"How indeed? I forgot."

"You forgot?" Evan fought to keep any suggestion of panic out of his thoughts. If he'd been deceived all this time and had gone and packaged himself for leisurely consumption...

Azure trundled forward and grasped Evan by the shoulders. With unexpected strength, he pulled the encased human clear of the pool. Then he began working on Evan's body, cutting and secreting fluid at the joints. As soon as Evan divined what he was doing, he offered suggestions and instructions.

First the right arm was loosened at shoulder, elbow, and wrist, then the left. The fingers were last and Azure moved on to work on the torso. Eventually the work was completed and the alien resumed its position on Evan's shoulders.

"I'm going to stand up now," he informed his segmented friend. It took a little work, as stiff as his new suit was. Prism had provided him with new armor. It was creamy white and light as a graphite composite. He wondered if it was as tough as it seemed.

"The froporia are strong indeed," Azure assured him. "That is how they protect themselves, by encasing those who would eat them. Out of the water, they die. We have fashioned you a new exoskeleton out of many smaller ones."

A walking graveyard, Evan mused. Not a pretty thought, but he wasn't about to give up his new armor out of sorrow. Besides, the pool appeared as full of life now as it had been when he'd first lain down in it.

Not that he doubted Azure, but he was curious to see just what his new suit was capable of. He found a rock that weighed a good five kilos and with some trepidation dropped it on his right foot. It bounced off without so much as scratching the smooth white surface. A good beginning. He picked up the rock a second time, raised it over his head, and slammed it down on his big toe as hard as he could. His wince was purely mental. Once again the rock bounced harmlessly away. Whatever the white substance was composed of, it had very little give. He stared down at his uninjured foot, wondering what other surprises his primitive friend held in store. Perhaps even something like a "talker" that could pinpoint the location of the Ophemert beacon. He fingered his new silicate sunshades and grinned.

Inside the safety of a suit again Evan felt more like his old confident self, even if that suit had been grown in an alien pond by diatomous fauna instead of having rolled off the assembly line of one of Samstead's factories.

"There are those dangerous creatures which can penetrate a froporia shell," Azure informed him, "but they are not common. I regret having to leave your head exposed, but being a soft thing I assume you require the constant ingestion of gas to sustain life."

"I have to breathe, if that's what you mean." He tapped his armored chest. "This will do nicely, thanks."

He flexed his left hand, enjoying the free play of his fingers where Azure had softened the joints. Having destroyed his original suit, Prism had thoughtfully provided him with a new one. Best of all, after the dark brown sunshades Azure had fashioned for him, were his pure white "boots." Now he could stride with indifference through piles of razor-sharp silicate fragments and sword-like growths.

A part of his anatomy higher than his feet gave a twinge, warning him of one area that still had to be dealt with. He explained it to Azure, who listened thoughtfully. After all, he was familiar with waste products even if his were of a far more solid composition than those of purely organic lifeforms.

Disconnecting temporarily, he made the necessary modifications. Evan experimented with both and was relieved to find that they worked as smoothly as the rest of his suit, and he marveled yet again at the tower of bright golden crystals which sprang from the ground several minutes after he'd concluded.

The patient organisms living in Prism's soil had pounced upon the unexpected uric bonanza to utilize the valuable salts contained therein. The delicate crystalline structure which had risen in the wake of his twinge was the result.

He rose and let Azure plug in. "Let's go find your village and see what these 'talkers' of yours can do."

"It is not a village, if I understand the term correctly," Azure replied primly even as he gestured to the west. Evan started off in the indicated direction, striding confidently through the glittering forest. "It is an association of free specialized individuals. An Associative."

"All right then, an Associative." As he walked, Evan searched the forest floor for something that would make a better weapon than his silica staff. "Tell me something. You're completely independent. You get your energy directly from the sun, so there's no need to cooperate in hunting. Why bother with an association? Seems to me that you don't need anyone but yourself. Why live together with others of your kind? Just for company?"

"There are many reasons for emphasizing gregariousness over solitude. Surely as an independent organism you must recognize some of them yourself. There is more to life than food gathering. For example, there are common dangers which can better be dealt with on a cooperative rather than an individual basis."

So even as seemingly indestructible a creature as Azure felt threatened by the unseen and still unexperienced dangers of the forest. That was a sobering thought for something as fragile as a human being to mull over. Perhaps Prism was home to things even more lethal than the acid-spitters and ultrasound generators. The course of adaptive evolution on Prism had run no more smoothly or politely than on any other world, for all its divergence into the world of silicon.

He looked down at the bubble grass crunching beneath his feet. Here even the simplest, lowliest lifeforms sported protective shells. Where did something like Azure fit into such an environment? Were his kind at the top of the food chain? But photovores stood outside the food chain, independent of it. Yet he had expressed fear of attack. It distressed Evan to think of larger, more powerful creatures preying on a being as intelligent and, yes, sympathetic as Azure. But hadn't there been a time, eons ago, when man himself had been forced to settle for a position in the middle of the food chain? It gave him plenty to ponder as he carried his newfound friend through the forest of wonders and astonishments.

The whole world grated on his senses. Wherever he looked were hard, unyielding shapes. Beautiful and exotic they might be, but there was no tenderness to any of them. Even the silica fibers which simulated the appearance of plant fronds and stems were rough to the touch and would cut bare skin if pressed against it. He thought again of the syaruzi and how easily they had pierced his flesh and was more grateful than ever for the armor which Azure had provided.

They'd chosen a place to spend the night and Evan had drifted to sleep when he was awakened by a soft buzzing in his right ear. Dancing jewels darted about overhead, though not in the profusion of several nights before.

The buzzing came again. He sat up and stared into the darkness, all of Azure's warnings coming back to him with a rush.

"There's something moving out there," he thought to his friend.

"I know." The reply was slow and sleepy, as though Azure couldn't shake himself awake. Come to think of it, he'd never discussed the matter of sleep with the little alien.

He wasn't going to now, either. He was too busy trying to penetrate the surrounding darkness. The moonlight added eerie shadows to the already disquieting silhouette of the forest. Other night sounds filled the air. They weren't loud enough to drown out that steady, monotonous buzzing.

"I don't see anything."

"Nor do I," Azure murmured. Why did he sound so tired? Evan wondered. Hadn't he ridden all day on Evan's shoulders?

A form separated itself from the trees and came toward them. It was slightly larger than a dog and took the shape of a smooth hemisphere that traveled on four stumpy brown legs. A pair of bright red eyes peeped out at the world from just beneath the fore edge of the glassy dome. There were two more eyes on each side and a pair facing backward, but he didn't notice them until later. It was moving with ponderous deliberation, displayed nothing in the way of fang or claw, and looked anything but threatening.

Azure saw it and panicked.

"A busck! I have to disconnect. Run, Evan, and don't look back! I will try to find you later."

"Hey, wait a minute!" Evan shouted, but Azure had already pulled the communications tendrils free from his ear and dropped to the ground.

The busck continued to lumber toward them at glacial speed, buzzing excitedly. Evan was convinced he could outrun it by hopping on one leg, much less two good ones. He studied intently, searching in vain for any sign of offensive armament. If it was an acid-spitter the telltale hypo organ was completely hidden from view. In any case, Azure had assured him his suit should be capable of resisting the effects of all but the most powerful acids.

He reached down to try and restrain his friend, for the first time feeling awkward and alone during a disconnect. But Azure seemed interested only in flight.

Maybe the approaching creature outmassed him, but not Evan, who was several times its size. "What's wrong? It doesn't look very—"

The ball of light that filled the campsite was as intense as it was unexpected. It was as if someone had set off a dozen magnesium flares at their feet. Evan was temporarily blinded, having doffed his sunshades for the night. The effect was magnified by the reflective surfaces of the forest growth.

He staggered backward, rubbing at his outraged eyes with both hands until he bumped into the solid mass of a big condarite. Instantly the trunk behind him began to vibrate and he stumbled away. Through vibration, a condarite could generate quite a bit of heat. It was a defensive reaction designed to discourage browsers, whose conductivity would be thrown off balance by the internal heat. It's hard to gnaw on something if it burns your mouth.

Gradually the plethora of tiny novas began to disappear from the backside of his eyelids. Just as he was able to see again the burst of light was repeated. But this time he was turned away from the busck. Shielding his eyes with one arm, he felt of his supplies until he recovered his sunshades. They should offer some protection.

He was able to time and thus forecast when the busck was going to flare, since its pulses came at regular intervals. It had started toward him, but when he'd backed away it had turned its attention to Azure. To Evan's shock and surprise, instead of fleeing as he'd announced his intention to do, the little alien was standing motionless where he'd landed.

"Azure, run! Why don't you run?" Idiot! he admonished himself. You're not plugged in. His companion's lack of movement was a complete mystery.

Especially since it was quite clear that the busck was making straight for him. As it drew near it slowly began to rise on its four legs. They seemed to extend themselves like hydraulic pillars instead of unfolding or unwinding. Every couple of minutes it would generate another intense flash of light, the hemispherical body acting like an enormous omnidirectional lens.

You didn't have to be a biologist to divine the predator's intent. It was going to lift itself until it was high enough off the ground to clear Azure's body and then drop down to cover him completely. Evan didn't care to visualize the sucking, tearing mouthparts that must be concealed beneath the glassy dome, mouthparts which would rip Azure apart at their leisure.

Still his friend didn't move. Logic drew a quick connection between Azure's immobility and the periodic bursts of light. The wavelengths involved were of a type sufficient to paralyze his companion, penetrating the silicate optics to numb the brain beyond. Evan had heard of animals which could paralyze by the use of sound, but this was the first time he'd encountered a predator which employed light to immobilize its prey.

The busck had reached a position immediately above the senseless Azure and was beginning to descend. Like its walk, the descent of that glassy dome was slow, so slow. The bursts of light hurt, but Evan's optics were not as sensitized to their wavelength as were the inhabitants of this world. He moved fast.

Feeling uncomfortably like someone sticking his hand beneath a hydraulic press, he reached forward between the busck's legs. Grabbing Azure by two of his ten legs, he pulled him clear. The busck made no attempt to interfere with this brazen rescue effort, though for all Evan knew it might be emitting screams of outrage on frequencies beyond his range of hearing.

What it finally did do was cease lowering its body toward the ground, turn, and start stalking the bipedal interloper, pulsing intensely. The light had no effect on Evan at all.

He had plenty of time to pick up his staff and pack and walk away into the night. Turning occasionally he could still make out the intermittent pulses of light the pursuing busck was generating. It continued to follow even after Evan was safely beyond its range, unable to believe its prey had escaped. Evan sympathized briefly with its confusion. It wasn't designed for chasing but rather for making a leisurely meal of completely paralyzed victims, the way a starfish would digest an oyster. Evan's flight was beyond its experience.

Despite its demonstrated snaillike gait, Evan didn't pause until the last vestige of light had been swallowed up by the forest behind him.

Azure hadn't stirred during the escape. Not knowing what else to do, Evan set him down gently and sprawled out nearby to wait. He couldn't very well pick up the curled communications tendrils and insert them in his own ear any more than he could administer first aid. For that matter, he couldn't tell if his companion was paralyzed or dead. All he could do was wait, hope, and provide residual heat.

He tried to sleep but could not, and his patience was rewarded the following morning when first the legs and then Azure's mouthparts began to move. So that his friend would not have to make the considerable leap from ground to shoulder, Evan moved as close as possible to the limp silicate form.

The tendrils uncurled and extended toward his head. Halfway inside there was a sharp stab of pain, but Evan ground his teeth and held his position. A moment later and the mesh was complete again.

"I hurt you," were Azure's first words since the night before.

"It's all right, it's nothing." Evan ignored the few drops of blood that spilled from his ear.

"What happened? When we did not run in time I thought all was lost. Busck light penetrates even solid lids." He blinked by way of emphasis. "I did not expect consciousness to return."

"It didn't affect me the same way," Evan explained. "It blinded me for a moment, but there was no paralysis. It was just about to start dining on you when I yanked you clear and walked off into the forest. I didn't have to move very fast."

"The busck does not rely on speed."

"Conveniently. Don't worry. It's a long way behind us now."

"Yes, it is easy to run away from the busck. The danger lies in its seeing you before you see it. I owe you my life. If not for you I would be powder by now."

Azure's effusive thanks didn't embarrass Evan. He thoroughly enjoyed such accolades, whether they came from colleagues or a silicate alien lifeform.

"You've done a lot for me. I'm just glad I was able to repay the favors."

"To be unaffected by busck light. That is a fine ability to have. It compensates somewhat for your delicate body. If you will excuse me, I must now . . ."

"I know." Evan smiled. He made himself a quick breakfast while Azure lay in the sun recharging his severely depleted system. The reason for his friend's unaccountable exhaustion the night before was brought out in discussion when Evan mentioned the business of sleeping.

It developed that Azure did not "sleep" in the same sense as a human being did. The state was more akin to hibernation. As its supply of solar energy was depleted, a diurnal lifeform like Azure gradually shut down all internal systems save those required to maintain memory and other brain functions. In such a state it was at the mercy of nocturnal organosilicate predators and scavengers, who instead of the sun relied on a round-the-clock production of chemical energy. No wonder Azure had taken the time to seal himself in the cave he'd shared with Evan.

Evan did not go on to explain that he was as able as any busck to function continuously during the long Prismatic night. Let Azure surmise what he might about his tall companion's sleeping habits. Despite all the alien had done for him, Evan still couldn't bring himself to trust it completely. No doubt he was being unfair to Azure, but when one's very survival is at stake it's not the time to make assumptions about the motivations of aliens or to take chances. So that one little secret he kept to himself, for the time being.

Nothing else sprang out at them to interrupt their journey, and they reached Azure's Associative the following day. It was not what Evan had envisioned. He'd imagined Azure and his friends living in a larger cave or some kind of crude stone enclosure or community hut. He certainly didn't expect them to dwell within a cathedral.

Much less a living one.

 9

"Is that what I think it is?"

Azure sounded pleased. "Home. The Associative."

Evan reached up to push back his specially made shades. He wanted a clear look at this miracle even if it did make his eyes water.

Someone had taken a thousand rainbows, frozen the lot, and thrown them together in a bowl filled with a thousand gallons of transparent glue. Smooth curving walls were topped with intricate curlicues and spikes as sharp as they were beautiful. It glistened in the sunlight, a radiant testament to the architectural abilities of a race that could hardly be called primitive any longer.

As it turned out, he was completely wrong, and for all the wrong reasons.

"Wonderful," he murmured as he slipped his shades back down over his eyes and resumed his stride. "Who designed and built it?"

"Designed? Built? You are confused. No one built it. It is the Associative."

"We're not communicating." Evan couldn't take his eyes from the mirrored rainbow ramparts. In places the wall rose eight meters above the forest floor. "Someone built this structure for your friends and you to live within, right?"

"I believe I see the cause of your confusion. The Associative not only lives within; the within itself is part of the Associative."

"That doesn't clear it up," Evan replied dubiously. He slowed. Two creatures had abruptly appeared in front of them.

They came up to Evan's waist. Both were jet black with crimson streaks running through them. They were thick, squat, heavily built, and their legs were concealed beneath the curving black shield that protected their flanks. Barbed spikes covered their sides and backs. Each held out a pair of arms ending in four-fingered hands. The fingers were triangular and each side was as sharp as a scalpel. In each jaw a pair of sawtoothed disks rotated at high speed and produced a threatening whine.

"Warriors. I will greet them."

Evan nodded, waited patiently while his friend communicated in high-pitched squeals and hums to the two intimidating guards. Tiny well-armored eyes regarded him emotionlessly.

For a moment the two appeared to consult each other. Then they stepped aside. Evan glanced back and noted that they continued to observe his progress as he resumed his march toward the rainbow wall, but they did not follow.

"Their station is behind us," Azure explained.

"A different tribe allied to your own? They're certainly well equipped for fighting."

"Different? No, they are the same. They are members of the Associative. Warriors, as I am a scout."

"But you don't look anything like them."

Azure stared up at his friend in confusion. "What does appearance have to do with anything?"

Evan forbore from answering as he stopped before the wall. The brilliant highly reflective surface was composed of hexagonal shapes tightly interlocked.

"Where's the gate?"

"Gate? Oh, an opening. I was beginning to think we had lost the ability to understand one another's concepts." He broke off to emit a rapid high-pitched series of beeps.

Eyes appeared in the upper sections of several dozen blocks. Short, stubby hands emerged from the seams where the blocks joined. Incredibly strong grips were released. Like so many acrobats, the blocks unlinked and lowered themselves to the ground, forming a double line framing the newly created entrance. A gaping Evan strode through the magically formed gap, whereupon the blocks crawled and jumped back into position behind him. The wall was solid once again.

"What were those?" He kept glancing back at the barrier. Here and there the seemingly solid structure would twist as one or two of the blocks tried to get a better look at the alien visitor without breaking ranks.

"The walls, of course." Azure gestured forward with his front set of legs. "Here are the other members of the Associative."

The spacious enclosure provided by the walls was filled with dozens of radically different lifeforms, each busy with its life task. The number of utterly alien shapes and colors took Evan's breath away. It was a xenobiologist's paradise. Azure guided him through the milling mass toward a definite destination.

Each creature was as different from its neighbor as it was from Evan. Each specialized in providing a particular service to the Associative as a whole. All were true individuals, Azure assured him, though some were more independent than others. Walls, for example, became paranoid if deprived for long of the company of other walls. So did the conduits, long brown tubular shapes linked together by short tentacles, whose job it was to carry excess rainwater away from the rest of the Associative.

High above the community rose sweeping mirrored surfaces composed of slim polished bodies called flects. Their job it was to follow the sun's path across the sky and concentrate as much of its life-giving energy as possible on their fellow associates below.

They were heading for the low hillock which dominated the center of the Associative. It was hollowed out by gatherers, Azure explained, who then filled it with those rare earths and minerals necessary to continued silicate good health. Processors refined these valuable substances according to the needs of the community, reducing and purifying them in their tough multiple gullets.

A few hailed Azure curiously. Some he replied to, others he ignored. Walls were curious but stupid, he explained, while processors were interested in little but their work.

They passed a creature which towered above the highest of the community walls. It consisted of a spiral shell nearly ten meters tall, which ended in a crown composed of dozens of beautifully curved silicate projections. Evan saw no arms, but the base of the creature was rimmed with several dozen legs.

"Talker," Azure said tersely, and went on to explain that the living switchboards enabled members of the Associative to stay in touch with each other over considerable distances.

"Mobile relay stations," Evan murmured.

"I don't know what that is. Talkers talk, that's all."

Evan watched as scanners scrambled up and down walls and talkers to study the terrain outside the Associative. They consisted almost entirely of enormous multiple lenses mounted on short afterthought bodies. Silicate tentacles enabled them to climb sheer smooth surfaces. Scanners, Azure explained, always tried to stay close to talkers in case some threat manifested itself close to the Associative.

An injured flect lay on the ground with a smaller creature standing over it. The busy one was a physician, Azure informed him. It had been provided with an array of specialized forelimbs and a highly sensitive touch.

"Who runs all this?" Evan made a sweeping gesture with one hand. "Who tells the walls when to rise and the warriors where to position themselves? Where are your rulers?"

"Rulers?"

"Yes. Isn't someone in charge here? Don't you have a chief or king or premier or something who tells everyone else what to do?"

Azure's response was full of surprise and confusion. As he replied Evan noted that they had acquired a small entourage consisting of a couple of off-duty walls, several gatherers, one lumbering processor, and a physician.

"The Associative makes all its own decisions," Azure summed up finally.

"Yes, of course, but who makes the final decisions for all the Associative? I'm afraid I still don't understand."

"You are not paying attention. New information is collected by scouts and scanners, who relay it to the talkers. The talkers inform all the rest of the Associative simultaneously. Discussion follows until a consensus is reached."

"Does everyone's opinion carry the same weight? You said the walls were pretty dumb. Does a wall's opinion have the same weight as that of a physician?"

"Naturally not, but there are few physicians and many walls. Everyone's opinion is taken into consideration before a decision affecting the Associative is made."

"So instead of hierarchy you have anarchy."

"I understand the term and it does not apply to the Associative. There can be no anarchy where there is reason."

This is swell, Evan thought. I'm standing here debating political philosophy with a glass caterpillar by means of antenna stuck into my feeble mind. Furthermore, I am enjoying it.

The Associative, he decided, had been responsible for the development of intelligent life on Prism. Creatures like walls and flects, who could survive but not progress on their own beyond a certain point, made great strides mentally when they functioned in harmony with and close proximity to more intelligent individuals like physicians. For their part, the more fragile and vulnerable physicians and processors survived and prospered and developed their brains under the protection afforded by more primitive types like the walls.

Did such a cooperative facilitate reproduction? Though he referred to Azure as a "he," it was a facile more than a descriptive term. Azure was distinctly asexual in attitude. What of creatures like the flects and conduits?

"What do you do when someone dies?"

"You mean, when a member of the Associative loses mind function? When that occurs a relative is designated to produce another of its own kind." Azure had them detour long enough for Evan to see a wall in the process of growing a replica of itself. Sure enough, a tiny hexagon was emerging from the back side of its mature parent. The process was more like budding than any other reproductive process he could think of.

"How shall I describe you to others?" Azure asked him when they'd resumed their previous course. "You carry out multiple functions. That is a difficult concept for many to grasp. A wall or digger could not empathize."

Evan considered, said finally, "In function I suppose I'm closest to you. Just call me a scout." Azure was delighted. "It's not all that farfetched," Evan went on. "I belong to an organization similar to an Associative back home, and it's my job to move about and make useful new discoveries for it." They were approaching the far side of the central hillock. He could make out a dark opening set in bare rock.

"Where are we going, anyway?"

"You need to be studied. I found you and brought you back, but I am not equipped to make suggestions about you nor to decide how to proceed."

"Oh, so?" Evan was suddenly wary. "Studied by whom?" Visions of extensive if oh-so-polite vivisection filled his thoughts. There wasn't much he could do to prevent the Associative from taking such actions, not now. He couldn't scale the glassy barrier enclosing the community and he doubted the walls would step aside to let him through.

"By the libraries, of course."

"Ah." He relaxed a little. If Azure had referred to the physicians or the warriors, Evan's apprehension would have intensified, but there's something innocuous and reassuring about a creature called a library.

"Under here." Azure directed him to the shallow cave, more of a stone overhang really, that was filled with bright light thanks to the efforts of dozens of nearby flects. A talker stood patiently nearby.

The opening was barely high enough for a stooping Evan to enter. The floor had been lined with clean white sand. The flects immediately realigned themselves to bounce the light around his bulk.

Squatting in the center of that waterfall of sunlight were three figures. Their six legs looked too thin and weak to support their rounded, pebbled bodies. Eighteen eyes of varying size stared up at him. From the front of each head, several long hornlike organs swept up and back to rest on the rear of each two-meter-long torso. Evan wondered at their function. Not sexual ornamentation, obviously, and since it seemed unlikely that libraries would be expected to defend themselves, probably not weapons either. Some kind of storage facility? He would have to ask Azure.

He sat down and waited. One of the trio was munching on a pile of what looked like copper shavings. It was connected to the other two by tendrils similar to the pair dangling from Evan's left ear. For private conversation, Azure explained.

Was he expected to make the first gesture? No clue was forthcoming from Azure. So Evan leaned forward slightly and extended an open hand in what he hoped was a universally reassuring gesture.

"Hello." He was well aware the word would mean nothing to these three, but he was offering friendship and greetings the only way he knew how.

The nearest library flinched from the extended limb while the third in line emitted a burst of noise.

"Second Library says for you to make no more unannounced movements," Azure informed him hastily. "Do nothing until it has been decided what to do about you."

"All right." Evan drew back his hand. Only then did he notice the line of warriors that had materialized outside the cave, sitting there like so many black bombs. If the libraries directed them to do so, he didn't have the slightest doubt they would dismember him in a minute.

Apparently Azure sensed his nervousness. "Do not worry. I know that you are not dangerous and that you mean only well."

"Yeah, but you're not giving the orders here."

"Need I remind you no one gives orders here? Remember that any decision must be arrived at through collective agreement."

"Even those that have to be made in a hurry?"

"That is a simple matter when all are in touch through the talkers."

"But no one's paying any attention to what's going on in here," Evan protested, nodding back out to where diggers and gatherers and the rest were going about their daily chores.

"On the contrary. Everyone is aware of this meeting.

They are being informed by the talkers' broadcasts. It is possible to listen, to decide, and to work at the same time."

"I see," Evan muttered, but he still didn't feel completely comfortable. Not with all those warriors and their buzzsaw mouths waiting anxiously just outside.

More beeps arose from the first library as he resumed his former position. It would help if they had normal eyes, Evan mused. The eyes were the windows to the soul, but he could see nothing behind those bright green and blue multiple lenses. They were no more revealing than the business end of a camera.

"They're afraid of me, aren't they? Haven't you told them there's no reason to be afraid of me?"

"I have been telling them just that, as well as how we came to meet in the forest and what transpired there between us. They are not afraid of you, Evan. They are merely cautious. That is the nature of libraries."

"The feeling's mutual." More beeps and buzzes. Then it was Azure's turn to sound hesitant.

"It is not that they don't believe me. They have accepted that you are intelligent despite the fact that you are purely organic, but they will not grant you equal intelligence on my word alone."

"So what do we do?"

"They want to communicate with you directly."

"Now wait a minute." He jerked backward, bumping his head good and hard against the unyielding ceiling. He tapped the left side of his skull. "There's barely enough room in here for you to plug in."

"It is not that complicated. There is room enough for a talker tendril. With you connected to a talker communication will be possible with the rest of the Associative."

Evan glanced at the tall spiral-bodied creature standing outside. Already a single incredibly thin fiber was wending its way over the sand toward him.

"I have already instructed it how to best make the connection," Azure said, trying to reassure his friend.

"Well—if you're sure there won't be any problem..."

"It is the best way."

"All right then." Still, Evan tried not to look at the tendril as it snaked up his chest. It was much longer than Azure's, but thinner. He could feel it enter his ear. There was no pain.

Until the connection was made.

His hands clapped the sides of his head. His skull had been turned into an amphitheater. He was an actor facing a shouting audience of hundreds, all demanding that he reply to them at once. The furious babble of thoughts threatened to overwhelm him.

He screamed back at them. "It's not the connection! Everyone's talking to me at once. Please, it's too much, I can't—!"

A new voice, more powerful than Azure's, overrode the mob. "This is not a general conference."

A single vast sigh of acquiescence arose, and the voices vanished. Evan blinked, let out a relieved wheeze.

The voice came again. "Is that better?"

Evan glanced down. The thoughts came from the spindly library in the middle. They were powerful thoughts, full of confidence, indicative of their progenitor's mental abilities. He saw the library for what it was: not a multihorned crystalline alien but an old and wise intelligence. He was not intimidated by it, though. Evan Orgell thought too highly of himself to be intimidated by anything.

One thin leg gestured toward Azure. "The scout has explained how you came to meet. He has told us that you are not of our universe."

"Your world," Evan corrected it, whereupon he launched into a brief discourse on basic astronomy. The libraries listened intently. They had little knowledge of the galaxy beyond Prism, since they were forced into hibernation not long after nightfall. Hard to study the stars when one only sees them for an hour or two after sunset. Evan already understood why Azure held such fear of the night. During that time, he and his kind were utterly helpless.

When he'd finished, the three libraries caucused to a consensus. "You are welcome among us," the second library informed him. At the same time the warriors who had surrounded the meeting place began to disperse, returning to their usual duty stations. None displayed an inclination to linger. Evan wondered if they were actively repelled by the alien soft thing which had entered their midst.

"We have little contact with organics," the third library said. "It is hard for us to imagine intelligence arising in such a fragile creature. I cannot imagine how you survived before our scout was able to aid you."

Evan tried to explain the concept of a manufactured suit. He got no further with the wizened libraries than he had with Azure.

"This beacon you spoke of earlier," the third library said. "You believe it indicates the presence of another of your own kind?"

"Or of her body. I'm hoping she has somehow survived the catastrophe which destroyed our research sta . . . our associative and all its members. You wouldn't by any chance have any idea how that might have happened, would you?"

"The world is a dangerous place," the first library solemnly declared. "Only the members of the most alert Associatives can survive in it. Your warriors must not have been attending to their duties."

"We don't have specialized warriors. At least, none were assigned to the station. Everyone stationed there was trained to carry out more than one function."

You could almost see the libraries shaking their heads dolefully as they digested this astonishing information.

"Multiple functions! How inefficient. The very idea suggests self-induced paranoid complications."

"Many things could have devastated your Associative," the first library said gently, the only one of the three more interested in providing sympathy than criticism. "You say it has gone away now?"

"Well, I wasn't bothered. I think whatever destroyed the camp had moved on by the time I arrived."

"Perhaps your kin will know."

"If she's still alive. She may have fled into the forest to escape the danger, or maybe she was working there when whatever it was struck the station."

"You say 'if,'" the second library said. "How can she be broadcasting if she is dead?"

"We don't actually broadcast ourselves. We have artificial, manufactured beacons implanted in our arms. These operate whether or not their owner is alive. They're activated only in an emergency and can be used to locate one another. See?" He stuck out his arm and showed them the steadily glowing chip embedded in his wrist.

"I knew I heard something," the third library declared. "Such a low frequency!"

"Almost inaudible," the second agreed. "I can barely hear it."

"Our talkers are more versatile," the first said.

"So Azure told me. I was hoping you might be able to place the beacon precisely for me. It would save me a lot of valuable time. Also, if you'd be willing to let Azure come with me I could certainly use his help."

Again the libraries conferred. Privately, connected to one another by the familiar double tendrils. Finally the first library replied via the talker outside. "We will try to help you, soft thing Evan."

"I appreciate it. Maybe I can do something in return. When I'm picked up and contact with your people expands, there are many devices which—"

"We are not interested in devices," the third library

announced. "We are libraries. We are interested in knowledge. What you called astronomy: we would know more of it. And organic lifeforms like you, we would know more of their workings. You are full of wonderful new concepts. We would become conversant with them all. Such knowledge deserves to be stored for future study, and to be shared among Associatives."

"Be glad to. But first, if you don't mind, I've got to have something to eat."

Mealtime didn't slow the endlessly inquisitive libraries down. Between bites, Evan was compelled to explain in great detail the process by which his body converted solid organic matter into chemical energy. The subject was a source of unending fascination to the libraries and he could hardly get a mouthful down before he was bombarded by another half-dozen questions.

By early evening everything had been settled. Not only would the Associative's talkers try to triangulate the position of Ophemert's beacon; Azure would be permitted to accompany Evan for the remainder of his journey. The Associative would also send along a number of additional members to ensure the success of his search. The enthusiastic response to his requests was more than Evan dared hope for. He went to sleep feeling better about his situation than he had at any time since abandoning the MHW.

One friend accidentally found had led him to a community of allies. Their efforts would save him days of useless crisscrossing back and forth over Prism's dangerous surface. If Ophemert turned out to be dead, as he expected, he might be able to convince his newfound friends to convoy him all the way back to the station.

He curled up within the temporary shelter a pair of diggers had prepared for him. Azure lay nearby, disconnected so Evan could toss and turn unencumbered in his sleep. Half a dozen flects assembled outside to make sure the last rays of the sun penetrated the excavation. A conduit wandered over and treated Evan to a long drink of water from which the last trace of minerals had been filtered, then scampered off to accept the waste from a laggard gatherer.

Evan fully intended to sleep the entire long night, but Prism had other plans in store.

The sounds were raucous, harsh, and quite unlike anything he'd heard so far. They woke him instantly. He experienced that long moment of complete disorientation one suffers upon awakening in a strange place before he recognized the smooth curve of stone overhead, the arch of linked flects sleeping nearby. Light from all three of the planet's moons illuminated the motionless form of Azure. His coiled communications tendrils glistened in the light.

The sounds came again. Evan wasn't surprised. Unlike Azure and his friends, unlike the busck and the dancing jewels, there were creatures who could move about Prism's forests all night long—the organosilicates, hybrid creatures with silicate shells and body parts but protein innards. He'd encountered several of them already. The smaller ones he'd eaten.

The noise continued. Evan crawled out and rose. Within the walls of the Associative nothing else moved. The members had shut down for the night, waiting patiently for the sun to repower their photovoltaic hearts.

Evan strode out into the moonlight. It didn't take him long to locate the source of the noise.

Several pieces of wall were lying scattered across the ground, their shells cracked and internal fluids spilled out upon the sand. One of them twitched feebly, its short arms and legs rotating as they sought the familiar interlocking grasp of its fellows, spending what remained of its stored life force in futile, instinctive flailing.

A gap had been torn in the barrier, the walls ripped away, and several things were marching through the opening. Each was half as tall as Evan but considerably more massive. They moved slowly on four stubby, thick tentacles, the tip of each of which curled backward. Four slimmer tentacles, likewise short and powerful, were held in readiness in front of each invader. A pair of eyes, large to facilitate night vision, stared out at the world. They were normal eyes, shockingly ordinary, not glassy pupilless lenses of the type employed by Azure and his kind.

They were completely organic excepting the gleaming shells that protected them.

There were more than a dozen, and the first ones in began gathering up the bodies of the dead walls, slipping them into baskets. The next half dozen headed straight for the center of the Associative, where a cylindrical conclave of walls housed the rare earths and mineral salts vital to silicate health and growth. Organosilicates required regular doses of such substances also, to ensure the steady health and growth of their silicate shells.

The invaders' intentions were quite clear. They were taking advantage of their ability to move about during the night in order to perpetrate a bit of murder and thievery.

They didn't appear to be in any hurry, though their pace may not have been a matter of choice. While thick and powerful, the bent-back tentacles on which they walked were not designed for speed.

Evan almost tripped over a comatose wall. Seeing that it was still largely intact, he took the time to move it out of the path of the other invaders. There was no point in trying to restore it to its original resting place. It didn't have the energy to relink with its kin.

An Associative warrior stood in the way of the raiders. One of the intruders reached out with a pair of tentacles and gave it a contemptuous shove. The immobile warrior, so impressive and invulnerable during the day, simply fell over on its side. Its assailant began pulling its legs off, using two tentacles to hold it in place while the other pair twisted and wrenched until the limb came free. Each limb was then tossed into the invaders' basket. Oily internal fluids spilled from the joints.

As this carnage proceeded quietly and unopposed, Evan was desperately looking for some kind of weapon. He ran past motionless flects and silent physicians, wondering if they were even aware that an attack was taking place even as he wandered how often such nocturnal invasions occurred.

Near the center of the Associative stood the silicate stump of a cascalarian. It had been torn down by the diggers to eliminate its unwanted shade. Now the stump stood alone, full of splinters and fragments. Evan chose a meter-long chunk of quartzlike material with ragged edges, hefted it in both hands. It was solid and heavy.

The first raiders had nearly reached the storehouse. All that stood in their way was a trio of immobile warriors. The invader in the forefront shoved two of them aside. One warrior broke an eye lens when he struck the ground.

Evan let out a yell and brought the quartz club around in a sweeping arc, aiming for the face beneath the silicate shield that covered the head. It was strange to see flesh give on this world, to witness the flow of real blood.

Tentacles flailing the air, the invader fell sideways and began clawing at its ruined face. Its companions shifted their attention to this unexpected wraith, but their tentacles moved so slowly that Evan was able to dodge them with ease. He attacked both simultaneously, bashing at limbs and bodies unscientifically but with great enthusiasm.

In the face of this furious defense the invaders retreated, uttering calls like anxious coughs, calls that were produced by vocal cords and fleshy throats instead of peculiar inorganic cells. The rest of the raiding party, baskets half full of dismembered members of the Associative, hurried to help.

But they were *so* slow. Even when it appeared they had him encircled, all he had to do was jump over the nearest individual. Jumping was another talent none of them possessed. Come to think of it, Azure was the only one of his kind who had demonstrated any kind of leaping ability. These inhabitants of Prism, silicate and organo-silicate alike, were largely earthbound.

Even as they wheeled around he was behind them, swinging his club energetically and generally wreaking havoc. It made no impression on their silicate armor, but limbs and skulls were not as well protected as the rest of the squat bodies. Whenever he struck a soft area he was rewarded with a cough of discomfort.

Faced with the relentless assault of the alien demon who had suddenly materialized in their midst, the invaders abandoned their attack on the storehouse. Carrying what loot they could, they began their slow retreat. Evan harried them mercilessly all the way. He had the satisfaction of killing two of them: the one whose eye he'd struck with his first blow and another whose tentacles he battered to a pulp while the others put on a burst of real speed.

Finally the last of them had disappeared back through the gap in the walls. Evan stood there, staring through it into the surrounding forest and panting heavily. The club hung from his right hand. He did not look much like the ultimate product of a highly evolved civilization just then. Not that he gave a damn. There'd been no question of his trying to help, and not just because Azure and the libraries and the others had agreed to help him. A fair fight was one thing, and far be it from him to render judgment on hereditary alien feuds, but to attack and dismember an enemy while it was locked, helpless, in hibernation was something else again. Evan might be more closely related to the invaders than to Azure and his kind, but there was no question in his mind which group was more deserving of his friendship. Mankind had learned soon after leaving its home system that civilization and civilized behavior was not a function of shape or composition.

The ease with which the invaders had gone about their

plundering had shocked him. If he hadn't been there to intervene he had no doubt they would have emptied the storehouse at their leisure in addition to decimating the population of the Associative. There had to be some way for Azure and his kind to mount a defense against such nocturnal assaults, but how?

Tired as he was, he didn't sleep any more that night.

10

THE FLECTS STIRRED FIRST, SENSITIVE TO THE
first rays of the rising sun. Powered up, they turned to
the business of pouring light on their still somnolent companions. Next into action were the warriors. They immediately took note of what had occurred while they'd slept
and began the sad task of supervising the cleanup. The
walls hurried to repair the gap in the community's protective barrier.

Evan wished he could listen in to their conversation,
but he had no way of deciphering the cacophony of buzzes,
squeaks, and hums that filled the morning air. He had to
wait for Azure to wake. Plugged in both to him and to
the tower, they waited together on the lingering libraries,
who remained motionless longest of all. Perhaps they
required more energy to become active because of their
prodigious memories.

"Vwacorites," muttered the first library when the corpse
of one Evan had killed was displayed by a pair of warriors.
"A periodic curse. Nothing we can do about them, unfor-

tunately, except hope that the walls will hold through the night. In this instance it's clear they did not, though they are not to blame. We encounter the creatures during the day sometimes. When we do, our warriors kill all they can find. They cannot stand against us during the day. The world is nothing if not equitable, however. The night belongs to them. Then they take their revenge."

"It is not equitable," the third library insisted. "They can run or fight during the day. We can do neither during the long darkness."

"A fact which I particularly regretted last night," the second declared. "It would have been a grand sight to watch our alien friend drive them away. They cannot know that you are a pure organic and that your exoskeleton is a product of the froporia and not your own body. Such knowledge would shock them even more."

"Do they form communities too, like your Associative?"

"None that we have ever encountered." There was sorrow in the third library's tone. "The Vwacorites are not the only ones we have to fear during the long darkness, but they are the worst because they work together."

"It's so damned unfair," Evan mumbled. "There must be some way for you to defend yourself at night."

"Would that there were. In most instances the solidity of the walls is sufficient. Very few creatures have the strength to break through healthy walls before we awaken. Only the Vwacorites are a persistent problem." Evan received the impression of a sigh. "Intelligence carries with it corresponding curses. Surely it's the same with your own kind."

Evan mulled that one over. He was still outraged by what he'd witnessed the night before. The grounds of the Associative were full of busy gatherers patiently recovering the fragments of walls and warriors and the others who'd been killed. Once more the storehouse was defended by three warriors. A physician was working to repair the lens of the one who was missing an eye.

"Naturally there is no way for us to thank you appropriately for what you have done for us."

"Any civilized individual would have done the same."

"There is no need for false modesty."

Evan smiled faintly. "That's something I've never been guilty of. Listen, when I get back in touch with my people we're going to take care of this problem for you, somehow. We have developed defenses, weapons, that function just as well at night as they do during the day."

"These defenses would operate forever, without your supervision?"

"Well, not forever, no, but..." He hesitated, struck by a sudden thought. "What you need, of course, is something you can maintain and repair yourselves. Maybe what you really need isn't something new at all. It's always more practical to modify an existing device than to replace it."

"We do not understand your meaning." The three libraries spoke in concert.

"It may not be worth anything. My idea, that is. But I would like to suggest it."

"Go ahead and suggest," said the third library.

"I need something first." He was glad they could not interpret the expression on his face. They owed him for what he'd done last night, but still, there was no accounting for alien reactions. They seemed sensible, highly logical folk, but how could you guess at customs as yet unobserved?

He'd gone too far to back out. "I need," he said evenly, "one of your cadavers."

A pause while he waited tensely. The libraries conversed among themselves. They must have passed on their conclusion to the talker standing outside because two gatherers appeared shortly thereafter. They carried a dead warrior between them.

Evan moved to examine the corpse. It lay on its back

and though the bright colors hadn't changed, they had become duller somehow; the red lenses were dark. Several of the limbs were missing, carried off by the Vwacorites. Around the body lingered the vinegary smell of dried internal fluids.

The heavy armor was cracked in several places, but Evan couldn't see inside. He explained his requirements to Azure, who passed them on to the libraries. Evan waited and hoped he wasn't stepping on any local superstitions. But the corpse had to be opened up.

While they waited the flects shifted their stances periodically to ensure that those at the meeting place received maximum sunshine. Occasionally one would have to be reminded to turn away from Evan, who had less need of their attentions.

Eventually they were joined by four physicians. Together they represented more than half of the medical complement of the Associative. Their names were far longer and more complex than Azure's. Evan satisfied himself by identifying them with numbers, as he had the libraries.

Once the request was explained to them they went to work quickly. They looked much like the libraries, though not as large and without the distinctive backward-facing horns. By way of compensation they boasted the most extraordinary array of fine tentacles, fingers, and cilia, along with more specialized limbs, that Evan had ever seen attached to a single being. These they employed on the warrior's corpse with marvelous efficiency.

The dissection was not ignored by the other members of the Associative. While they continued about their daily tasks, those who passed the meeting ground glanced curiously at the activities taking place there, wondering what the libraries and the strange alien were up to. Only the less intelligent, more prosaic individuals like the conduits and walls ignored the goings-on.

Evan watched intently and tried to make sense out of

the warrior's insides. He wasn't having too much luck. It was more like looking at a machine than a living creature, and an alien machine at that. With neither metal nor plastic in its body.

It was left to the physicians, communicating with him through the good offices of the talker, to enlighten him. The third gestured with a delicate tentacle.

"Here is the organ you expressed an interest in seeing."

Evan leaned over the opened body. The physician was indicating a cylindrical silicate shape full of fine striations and subtle inclusions. It was light yellow and mildly translucent. Evan could see where the striations connected up with filaments that ran through the rest of the body.

Despite the absence of blood and flesh, he had to steady himself while the physician, at his request, removed the organ in question. It was handed to Evan, who tried to examine it with the scientific detachment he tried to convince himself he possessed. Bundles of filaments protruded from both ends. It was not very heavy.

When he asked the physicians what the organ was called, he was not surprised when the mind picture they gave him was translated as heart.

"I've watched you replacing legs and eyes. Why can't you simply enlarge these organs? Is this beyond your skills?"

"We are not ignorant," the second physician replied. "The same line of thinking has occurred to us also. But no matter how much we increase the size of the heart, it does not seem capable of generating additional energy."

So much for that bright idea, Evan thought disconsolately. He studied the organ closely. It was dry to the touch. Evidently it could not store solar power for very long. A few hours of darkness depleted its reserves.

If it could be supercooled it might provide enough power to last someone like Azure through the long night. He was dreaming. Encasing the organ in a bath of liquid nitrogen would likely have other, less efficacious effects on the rest of the body. Gently he placed the organ back in the warrior's body and stepped clear.

It had been a worthwhile idea, though, even if it hadn't panned out. It seemed that Azure and his kin were destined to remain at the mercy of night-roaming organosilicates.

From what the libraries had told him the Vwacorites were likely to return, perhaps more heavily armed this time and prepared to deal even with alien interlopers.

"It's not fair," he said again, without thinking that it would be picked up by the talker and relayed to those around him.

"Who ever said life was?" quipped the fourth physician. "There is nothing to be done for it. When the sun goes down, we go down with it."

"Your bodies are so well designed, so efficiently put together. This is all that's holding you back. Maybe one day you'll have access to my people's advanced technology. You're such natural biosilicate engineers now, I can see you someday producing something as advanced as this without the need for machines." He showed them the emergency beacon that pulsed in his wrist.

"This is the device that produces the signal that we're going to try to trace. It's a small transmitter, homing unit, and identity generator all in one, powered by a tiny lithium battery."

One of the libraries perked up. "Battery? That sounds like heart."

"No, they're not the same." He found himself frowning as he thought furiously. What a crazy idea! "They're not the same at all."

One of the physicians crawled nearer. Multiple lenses focused on the softly pulsing beacon. "Might I see that a little more closely?"

"Well—be careful with it."

"We are careful with everything," came the slightly insulted reply.

They had trusted him. Could he do less, even with his last link to a possible survivor of the station catastrophe? Surely they would handle it with great care. He used thumb and forefinger to remove it from its aseptic receptacle in his wrist and handed it to the curious alien. Physicians crowded around the strange artifact. Peculiar limbs and structures felt of it constantly.

"Interesting flavor," the first physician murmured.

"Miorian, yancoth, seririgia," the fourth added. "What of the internal structure?"

Evan winced as the cap on the back of the unit was pried open, but he held his peace.

"Fascinating. See here?" the third said. "Different but not complex."

"The purpose is clearly divined via the structure," the first commented.

Eventually they handed it back to Evan.

"I believe," the first physician said solemnly, "that we can duplicate this and apply it to our own bodies."

Evan snapped it back into his wrist, smiled gently. "I don't mean to denigrate your abilities, but I don't think you can. The beacon is the product of a fully equipped modern factory. You don't just grow one like a flower."

"Not the entire organ. We are interested only in its heart."

"Even that. There's lithium involved. You can't toss that stuff around in a free state. It's too volatile."

"What is he talking about?" the second physician muttered.

"I think he refers to bequanel," the third said.

"Oh. Is that all?"

The four physicians conferred. A discussion involving the libraries followed. Two of the physicians disappeared, to return moments later with a pair of processors in tow. The meeting place became a hive of activity. For the moment, Evan's presence was forgotten.

"What are they doing?"

"Trying, I think, to build a little heart like the one in your wrist," Azure informed him.

"I was afraid of that. I didn't mean to raise false hopes. I was hoping your own hearts could be modified to store more energy. You can't just add another organ to your bodies, even if it could be duplicated without the use of sophisticated microprocessor-controlled machine tools."

Azure looked up at him innocently. "Why not?"

"Well—because."

"I am no physician or library, but that does not strike me as a reasonable explanation. You must not underestimate the skill of the physicians. They can rebuild almost any part of a body. Except the mind, of course. You cannot rebuild memories."

"I don't think you can handle lithium in a free state either, but it looks like they're going to have to find that out for themselves." When final discouragement set in, he decided, he didn't want to be around to witness it. He rose. The others ignored him. "I'd like to see the rest of the Associative at work. I've still got a lot to learn about it."

"Truly," agreed Azure ambiguously.

He spent most of the remainder of the day watching the inhabitants of the community go about their daily tasks, marveling at the skill of the gatherers, exchanging stares with the big-eyed scanners, chatting with other scouts. It was late afternoon when he and Azure returned to the meeting place. He sat down and hardly took notice when the talker outside plugged itself in.

"You see," he said as gently as possible, "there are some substances that just can't be manipulated by hand. Or any other kind of limb."

The first physician sounded apologetic. "Actually, we have already placed the newly grown organs within ourselves and the libraries. We will be working on the warriors next."

Evan frowned. "New organs?"

"Similar to the storage organ you showed us. Very ingeniously constructed. We had to make certain modifications—we are not keen on metal, for example. It makes us itch."

"Look, you can't grow batteries the way you raise wheat. They have to be—"

"Yes, that is what we will call them." Ignoring their confused guest, the physicians exchanged a brief flurry of information. The second looked up at him.

"Would you like to see one?"

Evan said nothing. The physicians construed his silence as acceptance.

A line of warriors was waiting outside the meeting place. One entered and lay down between the physicians. In a minute it was stiff and immobile, though whether the coma was self-induced or a result of some medical sleight-of-hand by the physicians Evan couldn't tell.

They went to work silently. Two linked themselves directly to the motionless form by means of tubular limbs. The other pair peeled back strips and plates of silicate material, exposing the interior structure of their guardian. Throughout the operation the warrior never stirred.

The two physicians doing the delicate work turned to face each other. Substances began to appear from the tips of organs, to be formed into a tiny shape as the viscous matter solidified. The finished product was a little larger than Evan's fist. It was a dull gray except for the numerous thin glassy fibers that protruded from both ends. It looked like nothing he'd ever seen before.

They turned back to their patient and delved still deeper, until they had exposed a yellowish organ shaped like a pipe. Evan recognized the silicate heart. It did not beat, of course. Unlike a mammalian heart it delivered its steady flow of energy to its owner quietly and without visible movement.

As he stared, the physicians disconnected several small bundles of the fibers emerging from one end of the organ.

A hollow was carved out and the newly formed mass of silicon carefully emplaced. Fibers were connected and sealed. Then the body cavity was closed back up.

The other pair of physicians disconnected themselves, leaving the warrior to function on his own. One touched a thin limb to the heavily armored skull. Black lenses clicked together over red eyes. Another minute and the patient was back on its many feet. Evan watched in amazement as it thanked the physicians before turning to depart. Outside, its comrades were waiting to question it. A second warrior moved forward in anticipation of its own operation.

"Don't you feel pain?"

"Usually it can be restricted by shutting down certain parts of the body," the first physician informed him. "It depends on how extensive the damage is and how large the area to be repaired. We thank you for the gift of this wondrous new organ."

"But it's not an organ," Evan protested. "It's a battery, and you don't just make one out of regurgitated goo."

"What do you consider to be an organ?"

"Well, it's a part of the body, the overall structure, that performs a clearly defined function contributing to that body's continued healthy operation."

"I could not have defined it better myself. The compounds and structure involved are quite simple. We are simply improving on nature. Do you never do this to your own bodies?"

"No. I mean it's different." Well, was it? How many people back on Samstead did he know who had artificial organs or limbs of one kind or another? No, it wasn't the thought of placing an artificial organ in a member of the Associative that challenged conventional thought, Evan decided. It was the method of manufacture that seemed so outrageous. It *couldn't* work. You couldn't just slap together a lithium battery because its design was...

Very simple, wasn't it?

Could it actually work? And if it did, what other machine-manufactured devices could the physicians of Prism mimic?

"If this functions as it should," the third physician told him with barely concealed glee, "the Vwacorites are going to be in for quite a shock."

"We'll know tonight," the fourth added. "By then we should have all the warriors modified."

"Not to mention the scouts," Azure added.

The Vwacorites did indeed return late that night. This time they came armed with weapons that resembled bows of blue glass that could fire many-pointed shards of silica. They could have cut Evan and any other interfering organic to ribbons. But Evan had no intention of exposing himself to those quartz arrows, nor did he have to. The warriors held their positions until a signal launched them at the invaders. So overwhelming and unexpected was the counterattack that the raiders offered no resistance. They simply could not believe what was happening. Something had turned the natural order of things on its figurative ear. The Vwacorites were unable to adjust.

Powerful limbs and jaws took the more vulnerable invaders apart. Buzzsawlike teeth and jaws ripped through silicate exoskeletons to make short work of the soft flesh inside.

The surviving Vwacorites had barely enough sense to retreat back into the forest. If it had been left to the warriors none would have escaped the ambush, but the libraries had decreed that some should live so that they might inform others of their kind that this Associative, at least, ought to be left alone at night as well as during the day. No longer would the members of the community greet the darkness in fear. No longer would the hard-won booty of the gatherers and processors be carried off with impunity by unseen thieves.

In showing them the lithium wafer battery Evan had

done more than demonstrate one small aspect of humanx technology. He had given back the night to the most intelligent inhabitants of Prism.

He had already surmised that the members of the Associative were not given to effusive displays of emotion, but that didn't prevent their taking time off the following day for a brief celebration. Many invocations were made to the sun, that source of all life. Evan approved, for like all living things he too drew his strength from the sun, if rather less directly than his newfound friends. There was also something akin to a concert, with the libraries generating (via the talkers) a great deal of amplified noise that closely resembled electronic music.

"I've been thinking," Evan started to tell the first physician during a lull in the cacophony.

"A laudable enterprise."

He smiled. "If you can analyze the structure of and then duplicate naturally something as simple as a wafer battery, I wonder what you'd do with a more complex energy-storage system. You might be able to mimic a unit that would enable you to function for several days of continuous darkness."

"That thought has occurred to us already," said Azure. "The physicians are working on it now." A hint of pride reverberated in his mental voice.

Evan hoped he didn't come across as condescending. "Duplicating an existing design is one thing, but I'm not sure you have the wherewithal to make improvements. You don't have any background in microengineering or manufacture, for one thing."

"You may be right," the first physician conceded. "I do not understand the meaning of those terms. All we know how to do is repair our own bodies. But it is fun to try."

"Well, you know what can hurt you and what can't."

"Yes, that is so."

Evan had the most peculiar feeling that the physician was trying hard not to sound condescending to *him*.

"Actually," the alien continued, "we have been considering the possibility of building an improved battery organ for you."

Evan tapped his wrist below the glowing emergency beacon. "That's all right. There's plenty of power left in this one yet. I just activated it recently."

"No, you misunderstand." The physician waddled forward and traced a circle over Evan's chest. "For *you*."

The range of expressions that played over Evan's face would have been fascinating to another human observer. "You don't understand," he said finally, speaking slowly and clearly with his mind. "I run on chemical energy, not solar. I don't have a battery. My heart doesn't store energy the way yours does, and there's no way to supplement its supply. I have millions of much smaller batteries called cells."

"I see," said the physician after a moment of careful deliberation. "There is much about organics we do not know, though we have studied them at every opportunity."

I am not a new opportunity, Evan felt like informing them brusquely, but it shouldn't be necessary to point that out. "I appreciate the thought, really. A battery wouldn't be a bad idea. Maybe I wouldn't get hungry as often as I have been here lately. But I'm afraid the analogy doesn't hold up where my body is concerned."

"What a pity," murmured the fourth physician. "You don't mind if we continue to discuss the concept, though. Purely for our own amusement."

"Not at all." He was curious to see what bizarre ideas they might come up with. Maybe one of them would suggest building him a second stomach.

Yes, he was curious, because he'd seen what they could do, and it implied opportunities for profit no one could have foreseen. These natives were evidently able to synthesize complex structures from raw materials. Imagine several of them assigned to a company starship. He wondered about their tolerances for extremes of heat and cold. They did not breathe. He envisioned several trained physicians living on the skin of a ship, attending to dangerous and complex repairs without the encumbrances of suits or tools, growing the necessary replacement parts within their own bodies.

Farfetched? Certainly, but no more extreme than what he'd already seen on Prism. Exploration of such possibilities required that several things come to pass first, however. Not the least of these was that he return safely to the station in the company of Martine Ophemert, if possible, without her if not.

The Associative's talkers easily triangulated the rapidly weakening beacon, and the expedition to accompany Evan was decided upon. It would consist of a gatherer and processor, two of the physicians, an appropriate number of warriors, and, of course, Azure. After some discussion it was determined that the first library should also go. Not so much to aid Evan in his purpose as to ensure that whatever knowledge the group gleaned would be preserved for the edification of the community.

Evan was repacking his supplies on the morning set for departure while the rest of the group assembled outside the meeting place. "Why not bring along a talker?" he asked Azure. "That way we could all stay in touch with the rest of the Associative."

"It would take ten times longer to reach your friend," the scout explained, "and you have indicated it is important to find her as quickly as possible. Talkers are not very mobile. They prefer to remain in one place and move only when the entire Associative moves to a new location." Azure seemed to hesitate a moment, then added, "The question of talking has provoked much discussion these past several days. It has also engendered an experiment, of sorts. Physicians, processors, and the libraries have collaborated on it."

"Really?" Almost through with his repacking, Evan looked up curiously at the glassy face only centimeters from his own. "What kind of experiment?"

Again the hesitation before replying. "It is in the nature of a present."

"You don't say?" Evan hadn't noticed much in the way of arts and crafts within the Associative, but out of politeness if naught else he'd certainly accept whatever bauble or trinket they'd decided to bestow on him.

While he waited, a solemn procession entered the meeting place and lined up to face him. The first physician stepped forward. Evan extended a hand to accept the gift. The physician eyed the limb, then turned to speak rapidly at Azure.

"It is not something you carry with you," the scout tried to explain. "It is something you carry *with* you."

"Well, that clarifies it," Evan said dryly.

Azure elaborated. "It is an insertion."

Evan frowned, withdrew his hand. "A whaaat?"

"We have studied organic forms intensively and have accumulated a great deal of knowledge about their design. The libraries and physicians retain all such information. In addition, I have been able to study your particular anatomy intimately these past many days. Particularly while you slept. This learning I passed on to the libraries."

Evan felt himself tensing. "You studied me while I was asleep? Without my knowledge?"

"It did not seem to trouble you."

"It troubles me now!" Evan had visions of alien limbs probing his motionless body, of pains and discomforts barely sensed. It wasn't that he found the revelation revolting—after all, the probing had never even awakened him from a sound sleep. It was just that it was, well, discourteous. A man's body is his castle.

But not to Azure's kin. To them it was a new book, to

be read and studied. "I am sorry for that. What will you do with the present?"

He held up both hands. "Nobody's sticking anything in me, no matter how well intentioned."

"Your pardon, but you have accepted communications tendrils from the talker and myself, without injury or hurt."

Evan lowered his hands. He was not xenophobic, and he *was* curious. "Let's see the damn thing, anyway."

After a brief conversation the third physician stepped forward and held out a hand. The entire hand was no larger than the nail on Evan's small finger. The open palm was ringed by minuscule digits. Within the center of the palm was what looked like a splinter of brown crystal. Evan had to lean close and squint to make it out. He had expected something considerably larger.

"That's the present?" Azure said yes. "Where is it supposed to go—assuming I'd allow it to go anywhere—and what's it supposed to do?"

"It will fit in your empty plug," Azure informed him slowly, "and will enable you to communicate not just with me but with any member of the Associative, without the complication of communications tendrils. It will permit you to talk as we talk. For private conversation tendrils must still be employed, but we have nothing to hide from you and you have no tendrils of your own in any case."

Evan gazed at the minuscule fragment in fascination. It had been manufactured—no, grown—by the members of the Associative. Specifically for him. To fit his plug. Was it possible? And if it was possible, what of the unreal possibility it raised? To wit: if two humans were equipped with such a device, would it permit mind-to-mind communication between them?

The advent of one of mankind's most cherished and ancient dreams, here, on this primitive, berserk world? Telepathy?

Well, no, he told himself. Not telepathy. A kind of radio to radio to mind broadcasting. The appearance of telepathy without the substance. Dare he let these hard-bodied aliens monkey with his mind?

Hadn't they already?

"You must trust the physicians," Azure implored him. "They know exactly what they are about, and can draw on the knowledge of the libraries for confirmation. They would not attempt anything they did not think they could carry out."

Evan took a deep breath. "How much cutting is involved?"

"No cutting. Only connecting."

That was something. Since the transplant was not composed of organic materials, his body's immune system ought to ignore it. "What about pain?"

The first physician addressed him via the talker outside, and sounded offended. "We are physicians!"

Everything the members of the Associative had done thus far had been on the up and up. They had helped him without being asked, and he had reciprocated as best as he'd been able. Every dealing to date between man and members had been of mutual benefit. It would be wonderful, of course, to be able to make the forthcoming journey without Azure draped around his neck, and to be able to talk directly to any one of his companions-to-be.

When he finally consented, however, it was not to gain those very real advantages. He did it because of what its success would imply for the future. "What do I do?" I am completely out of my mind, he thought.

"Lie down," Azure instructed him.

Evan complied, closing his eyes and removing his crystal sunshades. He had accepted those and the suit of white armor readily enough, but that was very different from having something inserted inside his body. He could sense shapes surrounding his head, moving close. Azure's tendrils were withdrawn. He felt oddly light-headed, a condition that commonly affects those on the verge of a great discovery—or a sea change. With Azure unplugged, would any of them understand the meaning of a human scream?

Touches at his left ear, so faint and delicate it might have been nothing more than a light breeze. A soft humming sound, pleasant and relaxing. It must have been some kind of sonic anaesthetic, for he felt no pain. He thought of music and to keep his mind busy and content he tried to recall special works of art and match them mentally to different compositions. A dim, distant part of him shouted desperately, *What are you doing?* He ignored it, preferring instead to concentrate on the gentle susurration washing over his mind.

He was about to gesture for Azure to plug back in so he could ask what the delay was when a familiar voice said softly, "It's already over, Evan. The installation is complete."

Installation. Appropriate. He opened his eyes and sat up slowly, his muscles stiff and tired. He'd been half-conscious for more than the couple of minutes he'd envisioned. A few drops of blood stained his hand when he put it to his ear, but no more. And still there was no pain.

"It seems to have gone well," another mental voice said, deeper and more resonant than the scout's. He looked down and saw the first physician eying him speculatively. "How do you feel?"

"Like I just took a giant step into a vast empty place," the still numb Evan murmured. Gingerly he felt of the area around his ear. He had received an implant tuned to the broadcast and receive frequencies of these creatures, though whether his mind or the device was doing the actual translating of words he couldn't tell. He was involved with aspects of science that were beyond him.

Intimately involved, now.

The primitive physicians of Prism had just done something no human medical lab could have accomplished. They had done it naturally, without the aid of complex machines, unless you regarded them as machines. Aren't we all machines? he mused. Change the arrangement of atoms within molecules and you have metal instead of flesh. Life defines itself. The rest is nothing more than cosmetics.

The rest of the Associative went about its daily business as the search party departed, though it still received something of a triumphal send-off. Instead of merely parting to let the travelers out, the walls formed a temporary arch of majestic proportions, while the flects produced a dazzling display of rainbows and beams of light. Then the walls closed the gap behind them, and the little expedition was on its own, following the course defined by the talkers. Evan's beacon grew brighter as they marched, confirming the accuracy of the talkers' triangulation.

Evan thought he'd seen the only intelligent lifeforms on Prism when the Vwacorites had fought his friends. The second day out showed him otherwise. Prism was home to several intelligent species, all of them battling the inimical forest forms while competing for dominance among themselves.

They heard the sounds of battle before they found the source. The noise rose from a valley beyond the ridge they were ascending. As they reached the crest, the battlefield came into view, but it was distant and far below. He couldn't make out individuals clearly, nor could his companions. Except for Azure, who provided a running description for the rest of them. Acute vision was vital to a scout.

While Azure described, the library recorded for posterity. There was nothing unique about the conflict, Evan was told. This sort of thing went on among the Qwacolia all the time.

From what little Evan could see, the members of this third intelligent race closely resembled the Vwacorites who had attacked the Associative. Organosilicates, their hard exteriors protected softer insides. They fought with spears and clubs fashioned of complex silicate compounds. Even at a distance many of the weapons were beautiful to look upon, though their purpose was not.

"What are they fighting about?"

"Who knows what soft ones fight over?" the library replied. "Territory? Food? This peculiar drive involving reproduction? All of it is irrational, since any of it could be better achieved by cooperation instead of fighting. But that is not the way of soft things." Evan felt vitreous lenses focused on him, and not only those of the library. "Is it the same with your own kind?"

"Sometimes. We've learned to cooperate a lot better these past several hundred years, and the thranx have helped a lot, but we still have many conflicts over petty things. As you say, nothing that couldn't be better solved through cooperation."

"See." The library turned back to survey the ongoing battle. "The soft ones of the nearer tribe are driving the others back."

As some of the dust settled Evan could make out individual corpses littering the ground. Azure resumed his commentary.

"They are all so similar in form. They may differ in external ornamentation, but they have the same number and kinds of limbs, of eyes and other sensory organs. Yet they fight one another while we, who are as different as can be, do not."

All true, Evan mused. Difficult to imagine two more different beings than a library and a warrior, or flect and physician.

"Specialization seems to compel harmony," he commented, "whereas each of us combines in ourselves aspects of warrior and physician, library and gatherer, processor and scanner. It appears that versatility engenders hostility instead of cooperation."

"Except in your case," the library observed cogently.

"Perhaps we are more advanced in the hierarchy of

soft things. We have used our minds to overcome many of our ancient instincts. Though physically I'm probably more closely related to those combatants down there, in every other way I have far more in common with you, mentally and morally."

"I have seen enough." The library was unable to keep the disgust out of his voice. "We don't want to tarry here."

As they marched on Evan considered what had just been seen and said. Did the device they had implanted in his head do more than just facilitate communication? Had they decided to work on his mind instead of his body? Distorting his perspective in order to guarantee his friendship?

No, that was nonsense. His opinions remained his own, formed strictly on the basis of cool observations of his surroundings. He was still the same Evan Orgell. A broadcast-and-receive unit inside his head and a suit of organic armor hadn't changed that. He hadn't said what he'd said because it was what his new friends wanted to hear. He'd said it because it was the truth.

He glanced down at his gleaming white froporia armor. Clothing, nothing more. He could remove it at his leisure. He just didn't want to, that's all. It was beautiful as well as utilitarian. He was simply being practical.

They pushed their way through what looked like a grove of giant asparagus fashioned of solid emerald. Evan declared his intention to take a sample from one of the magnificent growths. His companions were willing enough to assist in this peculiar request but the trunks resisted even the cutting power of the warrior's jaws. This despite the fact that the boles were hollow. Minute creatures of red and blue lived inside, scampering up and down the inner corridors. Another relationship Evan didn't have time to explore.

As the hours passed he became aware of the changes within his own body. Working behind a desk does little for the muscles. The long walks he took had helped, but not to the extent of his past days on Prism. The slight potbelly he'd acquired over the past five years had vanished. Legs and stomach alike had firmed up considerably, responding to the recent unusual demands he'd put on the rarely used tissue. He felt stronger and healthier than he had in a decade. All that as a result of having abandoned his suit.

But he hadn't really gone suitless. He'd merely traded in the MHW for a local, primitive analog, one which encouraged rather than suppressed the body's own development. The froporia exoskeleton could not begin to duplicate what the MHW could do, but on the other hand his body was now capable of much more than it had been while he'd been encased in that supreme product of Samsteadian technology. Which combination was the more practical for traveling about on an alien world: superior suit and weaker body, or better body and primitive suit?

Not that he'd been given a choice in the matter.

The equation was slightly tilted when he awoke the next morning. He was more surprised than startled to see one of the warriors standing over him. The physicians were nearby, watching.

"We have made some improvements to your exoskeleton," the warrior informed him in its gruff fashion. The mere fact of the announcement itself was unusual. Conversation was not the warriors' strong suit.

Evan sat up, blinking and still sleepy. "Improvements ... what?" He looked over toward the physicians, who voiced concurrence.

"What kind of 'improvements'?"

"It is not enough to be able to withstand an attack. Sometimes vigorous methods of defense must be employed. The other fighters and I have noted you did not possess the facilities for such. We offered suggestions. The physicians agreed with them. Together we oversaw the improvements while you slept."

"That was very considerate of you." Evan eyed the

fighting machine warily. "Uh, how do I make use of these improvements?" He stood, feeling perversely more confident now that the warrior was forced to look up at him.

"Clench tightly the fingers of your right hand."

Evan complied with the order, jumped slightly in spite of himself when the action caused four ten-centimeter-long spikes to emerge from his armor just above the knuckles. Flexing his fingers, he observed that the spikes withdrew and re-emerged like the claws of a cat. His left hand was similarly equipped. The silicate stilettos fit perfectly into the armor that covered his wrist and the back of his hand.

Springs of some kind activated the weapons, cued to the contractions of his own tendons. Making a tight fist, he examined the spikes on his right hand closely. They were perfectly transparent. Each ended in a sharp point. They were impressive enough to fend off many silicate lifeforms and were capable of devastating anything organic.

"Thank you." He spoke directly to the warrior. "It's nice to have weapons of one's own. I've been feeling pretty helpless ever since I had to give up my first suit. It's been embarrassing, having to rely on you for my protection all the time."

"Why?" the library asked him. "We all rely on warriors for protection. None of us is equipped to defend ourselves. Only warriors."

"And scouts," Azure chipped in, "which is why the warriors felt you would feel more confident with devices of your own. I agreed." He turned and gestured. "I have been ahead, as is my job. There is another canyon to negotiate."

11

THE SECOND SURPRISE OF THE MORNING greeted Evan when they broke through the forest and had their first sight of Azure's canyon. Technically the scout's description had been accurate. He had neglected to mention one additional fact, however.

The canyon was full of water.

"That's a river," Evan exclaimed. Not a stream this time, but a wide, slowly flowing watercourse of considerable dimensions.

His companions hadn't stopped to stare. Azure turned to look back at him, wondering at his friend's hesitation. "A canyon filled with denser air, yes. What is the problem?"

"I can't just walk through it, you know."

Azure eyed him blankly. "You can't?"

"We are forgetting the nature of our companion's energy system," the library declared. "Soft things require the constant ingestion of gas, not liquid, in order to power their bodies. It is therefore apparent that submergence in heavier liquids would prevent the gas from entering properly."

"Certain soft things can make use of the denser air," one of the physicians pointed out.

"I'm not a fish, if that's what you mean," Evan informed it. "I'm afraid I can only make use of the thinner gas."

"Can't you just shut down for a while? We'll carry you across," one warrior suggested.

Evan shook his head. "Sorry. When my kind shut down completely, the condition is irreversible."

"Inconvenient," another warrior muttered.

"I agree, but I'm afraid that's the way it is."

"I have seen this before." Azure was considering the breadth of the river. "If the flow of gas to an organosilicate is cut off for even a short while, it dies. I should have thought of that."

"Organosilicates do not possess nonvolatile memories as we do," the library added. "To them, shut-down and death are one and the same."

Everyone considered the problem. It was Evan's alone, he knew. Having no use or need for a steady supply of oxygen in the first place, his companions could and doubtless would simply march right across the riverbed, ignoring the water as if it weren't there. To them it was simply a denser part of the atmosphere.

"If I were in my MHW," he murmured, "I'd just swim across."

"Swim." Azure turned the concept over in his mind. "Like the amarex." He pointed upstream.

Coming toward them and drifting to an unknown destination was a long line of rhomboidal shapes. Each consisted of a bright olive green pad about a meter across that was filled with an exquisite array of pink and white flowers. Here and there a larger blossom of deep purple announced itself with an explosion of breathtakingly large petals. Transparent floats hung from the underside of each pad, supporting the heavy load of flowers. From the center of the pads a single thin silicate blade swept up and back, catching the wind to propel the amarex from side to side and bank to bank as well as downstream.

"Couldn't you gather a few amarex beneath you and use them to carry you to the far side?"

Evan considered carefully. The amarex looked stable enough, but a piece of log would do better. That was a laugh! Cellulose growths were in the minority on Prism. But if floating creatures like the amarex were common out in midstream, skeletons and shells of similarly buoyant creatures ought to be tossed up frequently on shore. Surely he could find something that would support him. His suit was not heavy.

That was not the real problem. The real problem was that he'd never really been swimming in his life and had only the vaguest notion of the mechanics involved. He knew enough, though, to realize that there were important and critical differences between swimming and wading. Floating like the amarex would not be sufficient. A river was not a lake. He would have to contend with a current of unknown strength. That meant propelling himself bodily through the water.

Not that he hadn't spent time in the water before. He'd taken numerous pleasure trips to the oceans of Samstead—usually within a self-contained sea suit which provided thrust, food, oxygen, and complete freedom of movement within its sealed environment. How else did one visit the ocean? The very idea of attempting to cross an open body of water higher than one's own head was appalling. He knew what swimming entailed. Tridees of sports competitions on other, less advanced worlds had supplied that vicarious thrill. The required movements were relatively simple. But he wouldn't dream of trying it without something to keep him afloat. Since there appeared no alternative he was perfectly willing to try swimming—so long as there was no chance of sinking.

He left his companions behind and started searching

the shoreline upstream. They awaited his return impatiently.

"What do you think of it?" the second physician asked.

"Quite intelligent and well intentioned." Library and physician spoke by means of communications tendrils so that their conversation would remain private. "Physically repellent. One would think it impossible for such a fragile lifeform to have achieved so much. I am fascinated by its dependence on artificial devices. It seems unaware of the inadequacies of its own body and how this in turn has affected its mental condition."

"Actually I am surprised at the degree of adaptability it has demonstrated." The physician was methodically cleaning several of its delicate extremities, a never-ending procedure. It was a matter of efficiency, not sanitation. Silicon is not subject to infection.

"Evan is more versatile than either of you think," put in Azure, having joined the discussion. "As he has yet to demonstrate. Look, he's returning, and he's found something to help him overcome his physical deficiency. Don't speak of it in his presence. It will upset him. I have found that he is very sensitive about such things. I suspect it is common among his kind."

"Sensitive about reality?" Clearly the physician had a difficult time accepting this odd concept.

"We are not dealing with a normal person." Azure hastened to disconnect. The second physician and the library simultaneously withdrew.

"I see what you intend," Azure said quickly to his friend.

"This ought to do the trick." Evan displayed the discarded exoskeleton of some unknown organosilicate. It consisted of a series of interconnected transparent ovoids which had washed up in a small cove. He'd tied several of them together with fibers taken from a willowy growth that grew from the riverbank.

First he placed his chest against the center of the bundle and practiced drifting in shallow water. When it became clear the ovoid structure would support him easily, he turned and pushed himself out into the river. He was inordinately pleased to find that kicking his legs did indeed propel him forward.

"About time," one of the warriors grumbled.

Evan not only could talk to his friends as they started across the river bottom; he could see them easily through the clear water. They marched forward beneath him, warriors surrounding the others save for Azure, who, as always, was out in front.

"Everything okay?" he thought at his friend.

"The bottom is a little soft. It is good that the water is so clear."

"So that you can see your way across?"

"No. So that we can still receive the sunlife."

All the advantages were not with his friends, then. Dark waters would not have troubled him at all—if he'd had gills.

We complement one another, he thought. Friends. And for how long? Age was a topic not yet touched upon. Did their internal components wear out like those of any living creature, or were they infinitely replaceable via the skills of the physicians? There was still the matter of memory retention, but he had no idea how long a silicate brain could function without degenerating.

It hit him suddenly that Azure, the library, the physicians, and the other senior members of the Associative might be thousands of years old. Unlikely, yes. Impossible, no. What if they did live two or three hundred years, though? What might happen if such intelligent, adaptable beings were given access to advanced technology? There was no telling what they might accomplish. If they could grow a mind-to-mind communications device using nothing more than their own specialized bodies, what else could they produce if given the right patterns? Could they grow a computer?

Evan saw that the introduction of Commonwealth technology to Prism was going to have to be carried out under the strictest supervision. Companionable but cautious would have to be the company's byword.

Meanwhile there was still more than half a river to cross and he'd best concentrate on his kicking or there'd be no exciting future to contemplate. It was quite a boost to his ego to know that he was actually driving himself across the water under his own power instead of having to rely on a suit motor. His leg muscles were doing all the work, muscles which would have been incapable of providing the exertion demanded when he'd first set down on this world but which had subsequently been strengthened beyond belief by days of strenuous hiking.

There was no need for the citizens of Samstead to exercise. Why waste time in expending calories on such primitive activities when there were few enough waking hours in the day to utilize the resources of one's mind? Anything you wanted to do, any variety of outdoor activity, was available without having to waste time on such absurdities. There were suits specialized for flying, for diving, for mountain-climbing and long-distance running. Exercise was for the feeble-minded.

No doubt that lack of physical conditioning had contributed to the disaster at the station. It was an interesting theory, one he would be sure to put to the company directors upon his return. In certain instances, it seemed, there were reasons for using your own body for something other than a mobile container for the brain.

Three quarters of the way across now and Evan had not only begun to relax but to enjoy the experience. Since his froporia suit was not watertight the river had long since seeped inside. The white suit held the same water next to his skin, where it attained a pleasing warmth. He felt as if he were swimming through a tepid body wash. So soothing was the warm water, the gentle movement of the river, and the soft breeze that barely stirred its surface that he nearly fell asleep. Azure woke him up in a hurry.

"Evan, we have a problem down here. Evan?"

He blinked. He'd been drifting mentally as well as with the current. "What kind of problem?" He peered downward as he asked the question.

The bright colors of his companions were no longer visible beneath him. There was only the sandy bottom some six meters beneath his dangling feet.

"Where are you? I can't see you anymore."

"Behind you, I think."

Evan managed to turn, taking pride in executing the necessary nautical maneuver, and kicked back toward the middle of the river. From time to time he would check the bottom. On the fourth check he stopped kicking and froze.

The bottom had vanished.

In its place was something huge and black. The current rippled its flanks but it held its position by moving cilia that lined its side. It curved out and down like an enormous black blanket.

"There's something below me now," he thought loudly, "covering a lot of riverbed. If it's a silicate lifeform it's the most flexible I've seen yet."

"It is a soft thing like you, without even a hard shell. It carries its skeleton within," Azure informed him. Apparently the creature's substance was no barrier to communication. "We have seen them washed up on beaches."

"This is the first grampion I have ever seen alive," the library added. "We were always curious how they hunted, since it was clear even in death they did not live on the sun. Now it is obvious. It simply covers its prey and shuts out the light until they die."

"It doesn't look very tough. Can't you cut your way through it?"

"Its inside is very tough." One of the warriors was speaking. "It will not cut. Our teeth slide off."

"It's waiting for us to become still," Azure informed him, "and it is watching us."

"It's watching me too," Evan replied. "Interesting arrangement of eyes. Very flexible."

Disconcertingly flexible, he thought as a second and then a third eye emerged from the blackness to gaze limpidly up at him. They were dark gold against the rippling black sheet of flesh. As Evan kicked and circled above it, the grampion's eyes migrated across the black surface to follow his progress.

It was at least twenty meters across, not counting any unseen portions that might be closing in around his friends. It would be patient, slowly suffocating them. Suffocate seemed the right description to use even though in this case it referred to deprivation of sunlight and not air.

"We are limiting our activities as much as possible to conserve our strength," Azure told him. "If not for our new battery organs, we would be in great danger already."

"Maybe when it sees that you aren't going to go belly up it'll think you're not photovores and will move off and leave you alone."

"I think not. It seems in no hurry to depart and likely can remain in place for as long as is necessary. If we cannot escape before nightfall we will run out of stored energy sometime after dark. Then we will be at its mercy."

"Since we cannot do anything," the library solemnly said, "you must do something."

That much was clear, but what could he do? If the warriors couldn't break free, how could he trouble that enormous mass of flesh? He couldn't even swim without the aid of floats.

A solid blow might discourage it or upset it enough to leave in search of less resilient prey. Plenty of large stones lined the banks of the river, but Evan could not float one out into the middle of the current without sinking himself.

The library, however, thought the suggestion excellent. "It need not be a rock," it argued. "There is another, more flexible method of dealing the required blow. Something already available and easy to maneuver into position."

"What's that?"

"Yourself. You are quite large and heavier than any of us. If you were to hit the grampion solidly where it is not expecting resistance, on its outside, surely it would retreat, if only to locate the source of such an unexpected assault."

Evan considered. It was a good idea, a sound idea, and if it failed they could always try something else. There was only one drawback.

"That means," he said slowly, "I would have to put my head under the water. Without any kind of protection."

"Soft things can do that. I've seen them myself," Azure argued.

"For a minute or two, sure, but what happens if I succeed and instead of retreating the grampion decides to envelop me the way it has you? I can't sit on the bottom until it gets bored. I'll drown—that's what happens to us soft things if we're forced to ingest large quantities of water."

"The shock should be sufficient to induce it to flee," the library said.

"Should be. What if you're wrong?"

The library had no reply to that one, nor had Evan expected one. The elements of the equation were unchanged. If he somehow couldn't free his companions from the grampion's grasp, all of them would die.

Damn morality, anyway. Why did it always have to show its fatuous, grinning self and make garbage of otherwise simple decisions?

He kicked until he was floating directly over the center of the rippling black surface. How muscular was it? The more he thought about it the less sense the plan of action made.

"Get ready to divert it if it comes for me." Who said that? Not Evan Orgell, surely!

"We will do our utmost." That from all the warriors, speaking at him simultaneously. "As we would for any member of the Associative."

"I'm not a member of your Associative. I'm a carbon-based nonphotovore."

"What of that?" the library shot back. "An Associative is an organization of compatible minds, not superstructures."

Too much philosophy, wrong time and place. He considered how best to proceed, then let loose of the floats. His intention was to achieve the maximum possible impact on the grampion's dorsal side. He'd seen pictures of people diving, of the whales of Cachalot performing. The motion was not difficult.

Taking several deep breaths, he arched his back and kicked hard. The added weight of his froporia suit helped him gain momentum and he struck the grampion with both fists. Then he turned and kicked for the surface. In so doing he struck the creature with his feet far harder than he had with his hands.

The reaction was considerably more violent than he'd anticipated. There was an explosion of water and black flesh. He was tumbled over and over until he was completely disoriented. Instead of a black sheet he saw white sand beneath him.

Then the blackness was gone. He kicked out wildly with hands and feet, attacking the water and going nowhere until he remembered something read long ago. He forced himself to relax, and it worked. His body oriented itself properly and he began to drift upward. As soon as he was certain of the direction he began kicking furiously again. His chest threatened to explode.

Air then, filling his starved lungs with a painful rush. After taking several deep breaths he searched for his float. There was no sign of it, not even downriver.

He discovered that by continuing to kick he could not only move forward but could stay afloat. As he paddled with agonizing slowness toward the far bank he fought to shake the water out of his bulbous sunshades.

"What happened?"

"It's gone." There was excitement in Azure's voice. "It was above us and then it was as though a piece of the night was flying down the canyon. You're not injured?"

"Only mentally." Looking down, he could see them moving across the bottom beneath him. "I wonder why it didn't fight back."

"Surprise, for one thing. No claws or teeth for another, and it could not be sure of your weapons."

"Fortunately for me."

"Where is your float? You are not sinking."

"No. The suit forces me to work harder than I otherwise should have to, but we humans are a little lighter than water. We're mostly water ourselves. I'm managing. Don't ask me how, but I'm managing."

"We will stay close to you."

"Terrific. You can catch me when I sink." He didn't respond to any more questions, needing all his strength for the complex mechanics of swimming. No wonder the advanced citizens of Samstead had chosen to eschew its dubious delights. To think that the inhabitants of other worlds regarded it as recreation.

At the last he was sure he wasn't going to make the shore, that all his efforts were in vain and he was doomed to sink like a stone to the bottom of the river. But he didn't sink, because suddenly something was supporting him from below. Looking down he saw Azure. The scout was standing atop a warrior, who was standing atop another warrior, who stood atop yet a third. They carried him the rest of the way until the water was shallow enough for him to stand. Once he'd managed to assume an erect posture again, staggering the rest of the way to shore was easy. He let out a long sigh and collapsed onto the beach.

His companions gathered around him, watched silently as the water drained out of his suit. He lay still while the sun dried him. It was the first time since he'd set foot on Prism that he was glad of its undivided attention.

He remained in that position no longer than was necessary, for fear of burning his exposed face. To the suited inhabitants of Samstead, sunburn was an alien affliction. Evan had no desire to experience it firsthand.

"You did well," the library finally said.

"I was too busy to be afraid. It's amazing what the body can do without a suit if it has to. That makes no sense to you, of course. Your suits are your bodies. Or vice versa." He looked past the library and frowned. "What's wrong with the gatherer?"

"It was badly injured by the grampion when it fled. The rest of us were able to avoid contact. Gatherer was not."

Even to Evan's untrained eye the creature's injuries looked severe. Several limbs were missing completely. One side had been ripped open, exposing innards that would have confused a biologist and fascinated an engineer.

"What happens now? Is it going to die?" Without the gatherer the physicians would have a much more difficult time healing injuries.

"Of course not," Azure said.

The two physicians were conversing with the processor. Clearly they were going to attempt to repair their injured—damaged?—companion.

Evan directed his question toward the motionless, leaking gatherer. "Are you in pain?"

"Pain?" The voice was gentle, slower than that of library or scout.

"You don't feel pain? Discomfort?"

"There is an awareness of bodily damage. It can become serious if not attended to. There is distress at loss of function. Is that what you mean?"

Evan hesitated. "I'm not sure." Then, as the physicians were ready to begin, he put a question to Azure. "Listen, I don't want to intrude on anything personal. Should I move into the forest so you can have privacy?"

"Privacy from another member of the Associative? Why would we want that?"

"But I'm not a member of—"

"You are. You have been ever since the night your knowledge helped us to repel the Vwacorites."

"No one said anything to me."

"It should not have been necessary. We did not make you a member of the Associative. That you did yourself. We thought you would be conscious of this."

"I guess I'm a little slow."

Azure was watching the physician work. "Besides, part of us is in you now."

Evan touched his temple below his left ear. "What, you mean the communicator? That's nothing."

"It is enough. That, and what you feel, and what you think, as well as what you have done."

"I'm honored. I guess I should thank everyone."

"You should not," the first physician said without looking up from its work. "You should remain silent. We are consulting."

Abashed, Evan complied. A high-pitched whine tickled his ears and he wondered how much of what was going on he was actually overhearing. Gatherer lay down on its side. The whine continued, directed at their injured companion, and Evan surmised its purpose. He'd had a taste of electronic anaesthesia himself.

What was new and what he wished he could see better was the means by which each physician generated an intense and narrow beam of light from just above their mouthparts. He couldn't see the beams themselves clearly, only the brilliant reflections they produced inside the gatherer's body cavity. Somehow the light was collected on their backs and concentrated within their bodies.

They were hard at work, connected to one another by communications tendrils. Joining them in intimacy was processor, who provided them with the raw materials necessary for the production of replacement parts. All three worked as one, smoothly and efficiently going about their respective tasks.

Gradually the damage to gatherer was being repaired, the physicians producing the necessary new parts within their own bodies and then fitting them into place. A task which would have required the cooperative efforts of thousands of humans was being performed with near equal efficiency by a trio of primitive aliens, working without tools.

On into the afternoon they worked without moving more than a few centimeters from their original positions. Tired as he was, Evan could not turn away from the reconstruction. He found himself becoming sleepy and lay down on the sandy soil to watch. Perhaps it was the effort of swimming the river and driving off the grampion, or maybe there was some leakover from the soporific whine the physicians were generating, but whatever the cause, he soon fell into a sound, dreamless sleep.

Just before he drifted off he thought he saw Azure arguing with the first physician, but that might have been nothing more than his imagination.

12

HE AWOKE WITH A POUNDING HEADACHE WHICH drew his attention immediately to the center of his forehead. He'd slept far too long. The operation must be over and by the look of the sun he'd been out all night. It was midday again, not late afternoon. Too polite to wake him, his friends would be waiting patiently for him to recover so they could continue on their way.

He rolled over and got to his feet, stretched, and looked down at Azure.

Or was it Azure?

The outline matched, but other things did not. Azure was primarily a deep blue. Evan didn't remember those blobs of shifting red and green light that were now clinging to his friend's exterior. As he stared the red light shifted to yellow in places, fluctuating in intensity even as he looked.

"Azure, what's happened to you?"

"I told them." His friend's tone was mildly mournful. "I told them you wouldn't know how to react."

"React to what?" Evan turned toward the forest—and recoiled. It was alive with minute crawling things, tiny intensely colored shapes that hadn't been there the morning before. Strange linear forms appeared to grow from the edges of fractal surfaces, surfaces which had previously been nothing more than a blur to him. Even the air was alive with unsuspected life.

The headache worried him. He put his right hand to his forehead. It failed to make contact with his sunshades, the special glasses Azure had fashioned for him. And yet he found he could see clearly, unaffected by the overpowering light of Prism's star or the blinding reflections of its flora. It was as if there were no glare at all.

A particularly cloudy day, he told himself. But when he tilted his head back to survey the sky there wasn't a cloud to be seen. By rights he ought to be rolling on the ground by now with the tears streaming from his eyes. Instead, he found he was perfectly comfortable no matter where he looked.

He became aware he was the center of attention. The warriors, library, the physicians, even the newly repaired gatherer were eying him intently. Their silence was more eloquent than anything that could have been said.

He looked back down at Azure, spoke slowly. "What do you mean I wouldn't know how to react?" When no reply was forthcoming from his friend he turned his gaze on the staring physicians. "You've done something to me," he said tightly. *"What have you done to me?"* Like Azure, they did not reply.

He stalked past them, to the edge of the forest. Several small bushes grew in the shadow of larger growths. From the center of their transparent shells several glassy stalks emerged. At the tip of each was a plate-size organ that looked like a six-sided flect. Evan snapped one off and held the reflective side in front of his face.

He was clad in his froporia armor, as he had been when he'd fallen asleep the previous day, but there was no sign of his glasses. Excepting their absence everything looked normal. It was the face of Evan Orgell that gazed anxiously back at him, unaltered. Wasn't it? Something was wrong. Something was different, but for the life of him he couldn't tell what it was. Subtle and yet obvious, he was overlooking it while staring straight at it.

Of course. Evan Orgell had brown eyes. The face in the natural mirror had eyes of pale violet. That was impossible, of course, unless he had been given contact lenses. He started to smile. Leave it to the physicians never to be satisfied. They had replaced the crude shades forged by Azure with tiny contacts that performed the same chores more efficiently. So precisely had they fitted them to his eyes that he hadn't even felt their presence. He reached up carefully with a finger preparatory to removing one lens for closer inspection.

He blinked when he touched his eye. No lens rested on its surface. The headache wouldn't go away. It was joined by a gnawing suspicion. "What did you do to me?" he asked again, uneasier than ever. "You put something in my eyes, didn't you? Some kind of drops or something. That's why I can see without my sunshades. It changed the color of my eyes."

"Not exactly," the first physician said, moving nearer. "We just thought that as long as we were operating on gatherer we might as well work on you too. For some time now, we've been thinking about a way to free you from the ungainly apparatus you were forced to wear over your eyes."

Evan sat down, pulled his knees close to his chin and stared at the physician. "How did you do it?" He rubbed his hands over his eyes. Still no suggestion of newly inserted contacts. It *had* to have been some kind of drops, then. How long would they last before the effects wore off and he'd have to be redosed?

He looked past his companions, found he could see farther into the forest than ever. Intense bursts of colored light erupted from previously dead-looking growths. There was twice as much life in the forest as he'd suspected.

"Is this how you see? Into the ultraviolet and the infrared as well as throughout the normal spectrum?"

"I do not know what you mean by normal spectrum," the first physician replied, "but it was apparent from a cursory examination of your eyes that you were partially blind. We thought we could remedy this, as well as enable you to see in normal daylight without impairing your ability to see at night. You are pleased?"

"Of course I'm pleased, except for this damned headache. I guess it will go away. Must be from the initial effects of the drops."

The second physician spoke up. "Drops? What drops?"

Evan smiled. "The ones you used on me to produce this effect."

The physicians looked at each other. "We used no drops," the first said.

"You mean you built new lenses after all?" He frowned, rubbed at his eyes again. "I can't believe how tightly they fit. How do I get them out to clean them?"

"I told you," Azure said suddenly. "I told you."

"Your body will clean them," the second physician informed him. "That is how it should be."

"Not the back side. I don't care how tightly you managed to fit the new ones, microscopic dirt and grit can always slip between a contact lens and the cornea."

"Evan," Azure said evenly, "you can't get them out."

"Your old lenses were deficient, as I explained," the first physician reminded him. "There was no way to modify them to see properly. So we replaced them."

"I can see that." Evan pointed toward his old shades, lying nearby.

"No. Your old lenses are here." Reaching into a cavity within his own body, the first physician removed something small and shiny and held it out. Evan found himself staring transfixed at two small, glassy objects. They were oval when seen from the side, round when viewed from above. They quivered slightly in the physician's open hand.

Evan stared at them until he began to shake violently. Finally he turned away, unable to look any longer. Despite the bright sunlight he was suddenly cold. But the headache was beginning to fade and there was no pain, though he was more conscious of his eyes than he'd ever been in his life. He kept them tightly shut, afraid to open them again.

"It was not as difficult as one might suppose." Unaware of Evan's trauma, physician rambled on as though discussing the repair of a simple household utensil. "We have studied soft-bodied forms intensively. We simply replaced your original lenses with new ones and made some small adjustments to the interpretation mechanism behind them."

"You did something to the rods and cones," Evan mumbled. "Something that enables me to see beyond the normal visible spectrum in both directions as well as to interpret fractal shapes more clearly."

Gently he used the tips of his fingers to press all around the orbits of his eyes. "What if it hadn't worked? What if I'd woken up completely blind?"

"You must have more confidence." Library spoke for the first time since Evan had rejoined them. "These physicians are among the most artistic of their kind."

"Your eyes are simple in form and almost identical to many we have studied," the second physician said. "The modifications were not complex. And we can always replace your old lenses anytime you wish us to do so."

"Not complex. My God, what could you people do with access to a few basic biology texts? What other operations can you perform?"

The first physician took another step toward him. "We have devoted much speculation to that. If you would like, we can—"

Evan retreated hastily. "No, no, you've done more than enough!" He blinked at the wonderfully enhanced world around him. "You're sure you can restore my original sight if you have to?"

The physician displayed Evan's original lenses a second time. "Reasonably sure. That is why I will retain them." In a gesture worthy of the most accomplished surrealist he slipped them back into a small body cavity.

"I do hope you will elect to keep your new lenses," the second physician said. "It would be a shame to undo such a good piece of work."

"I'll think about it," Evan told it. "In the meantime, promise me you won't perform any more surprise operations? No matter how much you're convinced it will benefit me?" The physicians promised. Reluctantly, it seemed to Evan.

"If we had told you of our intentions beforehand, would you have permitted us to perform the operation?" asked the second physician.

Evan swallowed. "Look, I've been out for most of a day and a night. It's time we were moving on. And no modifications while I sleep, understand?"

They pushed through the forest, leaving the river far behind. It was late afternoon when Azure came running back to rejoin them from his forward position. Instead of speaking immediately he reared back on his hind legs and listened intently.

"What is it?" Library inquired impatiently.

"I wish we had a talker with us to confirm."

Wishful thinking indeed, Evan knew. The towering talkers had less mobility than any other member of the Associative, which was why none had come along in the first place.

"Confirm what?"

"Something is coming toward us. Very low-grade emanations. Not intelligent."

Suddenly Evan found himself joining his companions in scanning the surrounding growths. They were in a section of forest where the pure silicate flora had largely crowded out the organosilicates. Clusters of glassy pipes reached heavenward all around them save where they were shoved aside by thick brown arches. The crest of each arch was full of huge, weaving photoreceptors.

Evan turned sharply to his left. "Wait a minute, I think I hear something too." This announcement was followed by a loud, splintering crash.

The physician next to his legs looked around nervously. "I hear nothing."

It struck Evan that his friends might be deaf at the lower frequencies, attuned as they were to radio frequencies they utilized for interpersonal communication. Something sporting half a dozen delicate wings set three to a side along a slim silicate body flew out of the forest. It wasn't attacking and ignored the travelers completely. It boasted a long sharp bill and was bright pink with yellow stripes.

It was followed by half a dozen equally bizarre flying things. Then a veritable silicate zoo came swarming toward them, running, rolling, and crawling its way eastward. Evan barely had time to note the new species as they raced past.

They all had one thing in common: they were running from something. Azure had sensed it too.

"Maybe we'd better run also." Evan took a step backward. "Back to the river."

"Unreasoning flight is not the refuge of the intelligent," library pointed out. "We should not retreat until we have ascertained the nature of any potential danger." He didn't need to add that neither he nor the physicians were built for running.

Evan tried to see through the dense undergrowth. It couldn't be a fire. There was nothing there to burn. Besides, he saw neither smoke nor flame. Suddenly two huge silicate trees shattered directly off to his left. Syrupy liquid began to fountain from the broken trunks. Evan's eyes widened.

"A *shervan*!" the library shouted even as he turned to scramble for cover. But there was no cover from a shervan. One simply got out of its way.

Evan had encountered few large lifeforms since setting down on Prism and he could only gape in astonishment at this one, the most extraordinary by far. What he'd thought at first were long, thick tentacles sheathed in opaque glass revealed themselves on closer inspection to be mouths on the ends of muscular necks. Each maw was lined with a splendid array of rotating serrated teeth and appeared capable of functioning independent of its neighbors. He counted twelve snapping, voracious sets of jaws growing from a massive gray lump of body without visible eyes, ears, or anything resembling a sensory organ. It traveled on a series of flat plates that ran in a continuous band around its entire body, which propelled the entire organism forward with startling speed.

Before Evan and his companions could scatter, one of the warriors was grasped by a powerful mouth. Two more mouths immediately attacked it from both sides while it squirmed desperately in the crushing grip of the first. Dismemberment occurred rapidly, but not before the doomed warrior had succeeded in damaging one neck with its own buzzsawlike teeth.

Evan dodged around a tree, looking backward instead of where he was going. So he didn't see the mouth that was waiting for him until he felt the pain. The shervan teeth went right through his froporia armor and pulled away with most of the lower section. It also tore out a substantial chunk of his abdomen. He staggered backward, staring down at his exposed intestines.

Another warrior jumped in and clamped its jaws on the neck, the sound of its rotating teeth harsh in Evan's ears. Flesh and silicate shards went flying. The mouth turned its attention to this new threat.

Somehow he ran on despite the gaping hole in his gut. The shervan pursued with demonic speed. It bit again, at his chest this time, spinning Evan completely around. Bones splintered as pressure was applied. The warrior who had freed him once leaped to the attack again and this time succeeded in cutting completely through the neck.

A human body can cope with only so much damage before the brain begins to shut it down. The last thing Evan remembered was a feeling of falling backward. Then he lay there, still half-conscious, and tried to follow the progress of the battle.

The shervan seemed to be turning away. Having lost one mouth completely with two more badly injured it had apparently decided to seek less resilient prey. Evan could see first physician attending to various wounds. One warrior at least had been killed and consumed, but by and large, his companions had survived the attack.

Unfortunately, he thought as he passed out, he was only made of flesh and blood.

They found him lying motionless in the patch of quick-weed where he'd fallen. In order to determine the full extent of his wounds the physicians hurriedly cut away what remained of his froporia armor. From what they knew of organic construction, it was clear that the damage was extensive.

In order to prevent the kind of decay and infection soft things were heir to, second physician immediately sealed the damaged areas with a thin, aseptic transparent film. Blood quickly began to fill the two raw cavities. It was clear even to the warriors that if drastic surgery wasn't performed soon, their strange otherworldly visitor would not last until nightfall.

The physicians were consulting nonstop. That peculiar pumping device which pushed red fluid through the entire system, for example, was badly damaged and functioning only fitfully. The same could be said for the twin gas bellows which lay over the pump and to the side, and for the chemical processing organs lying shredded in the main body cavity below. It was just as well Evan had passed out before becoming aware of the extent of his injuries. Had he known he undoubtedly would have given up on the spot.

His companions, however, were appraising the situation dispassionately.

"It will be interesting," library said. "We have never before undertaken to repair such an extensively damaged organic form."

"He won't like it." Azure glanced from processor, already working furiously, to the two physicians.

"He has no choice," library pointed out, "and neither do we. The life will leave him unless he can be repaired." It gestured with a thin tentacle. "Look at that mess. You know how fragile these organic systems are. Something must be done, and quickly."

"I am concerned about the shock when he regains consciousness," murmured the scout.

"Let us worry about that if and when he regains consciousness," the first physician said. "If we do not hasten to repair the damage, he will never regain consciousness long enough to experience shock." It turned its attention back to the soft body. "This is going to take some time. We will maintain necessary functions through the use of our own bodies where necessary. I hope this Evan form is possessed of a strong constitution. He is going to need it if he is to survive our work." It gestured, spoke to its colleague. "I think it best if we begin with that pump."

Second physician agreed. A tentacle reached toward that irregularly beating, pinkish-red organ. Its silicate tip was bright and sharp.

There was only the deep darkness. Then there was a distant, faint humming sound, soft and relaxing. Evan opened his eyes.

He was lying on his back, staring up at faces. Not faces exactly. More like the product of some busy abstract sculptor. The sculptures moved away until only two remained. He recognized Azure and first physician.

As he recognized he remembered: the terrible hot pain of the shervan's teeth cutting into him, ripping away huge gobbets of flesh, sending blood flying everywhere. He remembered gazing down at himself to see his guts hanging out of his belly like so many white ropes torn from a hidden spool. How detached his mind had been while considering his evisceration. It was as if he'd been only a witness to the disaster instead of an intimate participant.

In his mind he went over the long list of injuries he'd suffered. By any reasonable stretch of the imagination he ought to be stone cold dead. He was not. He did feel, though, as if he'd been run over several times by a large, heavy vehicle. His entire being ached, and he was glad of it. Another sign that he was alive. Everything seemed to be functioning properly, including the communications device the physicians had plugged into him. He was certain of the latter because he could clearly hear Azure addressing the rest of his companions.

"It works," the scout assured them.

"Yes, I still work," he mumbled mentally, "but I shouldn't. I shouldn't be talking to you now." He knew why he was alive, of course: the physicians had been at work. Somehow, they had taken the mess the shervan had made of him and put it back together. He was almost afraid to look down at himself for fear of what he might see. A foolish and unbecoming fear, he told himself. Whatever he saw could not be worse than being dead.

He sat up, noting that his newly modified eyes were functioning perfectly. Since he could now see well into the infrared he was not surprised to see that his lower abdomen was generating a substantial amount of heat. That was normal enough for a human body.

What was not was the transparent pane which had replaced his skin from the groin to just below his neck, much less the alien and unrecognizable shapes which lay behind it. He sat and stared, and stared.

"Shock?" the first physician wondered.

"I think not." The second stepped forward, rested a reassuring tentacle on Evan's right leg. "We were unable to repair the covering as it was too badly shredded. We cannot regenerate organic compounds such as those which comprise the covering you called skin. We haven't the necessary skills. So we repaired as best as we were able." Evan didn't comment. He was too engrossed in an intimate study of self.

First physician moved to stand alongside his colleague. "We had no choice. You would have died. You were dying as we worked on you. We did the best we could. We had no choice."

"I told you he'd be upset," Azure said.

"Upset?" Evan recognized the croak as his own voice. He raised his gaze to the physicians. "I know I was dying. Hell, I should be dead right now. That I'm not I know is due entirely to your skills and the work you did. I'm just not used to the *kind* of work you did." He looked thoughtful. "You know, we have an expression, something about a 'window onto the soul.'" Gingerly he pressed against the transparent skin, discovered that it was flexible and remarkably tough. Behind it, his insides hummed away at keeping him alive. And some of them literally hummed.

A lesser man might have fainted or gone mad. Not Evan Orgell. He was too conscious of his own invulnerable self. He wouldn't die because the universe obviously couldn't get along without him.

First physician extended a tendril. "We concluded that this was the most important organ of all, so we replaced it first."

"A good thing you were not struck in the head," second physician said. "That would have been beyond our skill."

Evan looked down into his chest, past the silvery balloons that were flexing in and out, out and in. Behind the one on the left was a mass of plastic and tubing that pulsed at a different rate.

"Two pumps. One for fluid, one for gas. That's all," first physician said.

"Yes, that's all."

"You can see where we bonded the replacement material to what remains of the original organic flesh. It was simpler than rebuilding the mess left behind. All that tubing, just to carry fluids, and so many small ones. Very inefficient. But we were too busy keeping you alive to worry about possible improvements."

Evan examined the new arteries and veins, flexible hoses fashioned of vitreous, gleaming material. They were translucent. If he looked hard he could make out the blood flowing through the largest.

"Actually, the pumps gave us less trouble than some of the less vital organs located farther down." Second physician gestured. "Those things there."

Evan looked off to one side. Lying on the ground, stacked neat as a roll of used cable, were his intestines. He swallowed, tried to view the sight clinically and from a distance. It was not easy.

His stomach had been repaired and put back in place. Protruding from it was a neat mass of tubing. Off to one side and slightly lower than the stomach was something that looked like a loaf of dried bread. As near as he could tell, his spleen and liver had survived intact.

Second physician turned back to him, occasionally referring to the pile of tattered intestines as he spoke. "Those were badly damaged. Repairing them properly would have taken too much time, and the entire arrangement struck us as a particularly bad example of internal organization. For one thing, they took up far more space than necessary." A tendril indicated the peculiar loaf shape. "We devised a storage facility for your body. It collects and distributes additional energy compounds as they are needed." The physician's voice was tinged with humor.

"You helped us create a battery for our own bodies. We thought it only fair to return the favor."

"This absurd business of metabolizing gas and the component parts of other soft things to power a body never ceases to amaze," library added.

"There is a simpler device for carrying off waste materials directly from the metabolizing units," first physician went on. "Less risk of contaminating the rest of the body. We also installed one venting device instead of the previous two. It struck us an utterly unnecessary duplication, in addition to which the vent now discarded appeared to possess the potential to interfere with organic reproductive methods. I'm sure you'll agree that this new arrangement is far more sensible and efficient."

"You know," the library said thoughtfully, "I really don't understand this need to kill and consume other organic forms when you can obtain all the same compounds directly from the ground. I think your modified metabolic system could process them directly. It would be much neater and save you a lot of light time."

"I don't think I could get used to eating dirt." At least there were no blinking lights inside his torso. He was still human—wasn't he? Or did Azure and the others now qualify as near relations instead of just friends?

"Are you ready to stand up?" asked Azure.

Evan nodded, put both palms against the ground, and pushed. He thought he rattled as he rose, but it was only his imagination. The remaining empty spaces within his body had been packed firm with an antiseptic, transparent gel. His immune system ignored all the replacements. There wasn't a "living" carbon-based device among them.

He wasn't the least bit hungry, nor was there reason for him to be, the physicians explained. They had helpfully tube-fed him while waiting for him to recover consciousness. Not only his stomach but his new storage organ should be full of glucose and other readily metabolized substances.

"How do you feel?" Azure asked him.

"Ten kilos lighter, but then I suppose I probably am." He did some twisting and bending. There was no pain. He touched his fingertips to his toes, bringing his face flat up against his transparent torso. Except for that vague, all-over ache, he felt hale and hearty.

"It was fortunate that your reproductive organs were below the highest blow the shervan delivered," second physician said. "As with your brain, our skills would not have been equal to the task of replacement."

"You're not half as glad as I am." Evan fought to keep the inevitable bizarre images out of his mind. "The rest of it strikes me as impossible anyway. You just don't throw away hearts and lungs and so forth and fashion new ones with your hands, like pottery."

"The design is complex," first physician agreed, "but no more so than similar organic systems we have studied. The body, any body, is only a mobile device for shuttling the brain about. The scout actually dissuaded us from attempting further improvements while we worked."

Evan threw Azure a grateful glance, wondering if it would be understood. "What sort of improvements?"

"For one thing," the second physician informed him, "we would like for you to consider the possibility at some future time of allowing us to replace that entire absurd oxydizing system with one similar to our own."

"Thanks," Evan told it, "but if I spend too much time out in the sun I'm likely to break out in hives." He glanced downward again. "Everything seems to be working. The toughest thing to get used to is the idea of being able to see inside myself."

"We could replace the covering with something opaque, perhaps even color it to match the rest of your skin."

"No. No, not now. Another time, perhaps."

"Everything is fashioned of the strongest materials," first physician said. "Processor saw to that. Strong yet soft, so as not to damage your remaining natural organs."

"You saved my life. Thank you. Even if this new life is going to take some getting used to."

"You really ought to let us replace that entire energy production system." Second physician was persistent.

Azure stepped between it and Evan. "Leave him alone. He's suffered enough shocks for one day, mental and physical. Consider his point of reference. How would you react if you awoke one morning to discover that your eyes had been replaced with orbs of organic matter floating in a loosely liquid socket?"

"A ghastly image."

The scout turned to look up at his newly repaired friend. "You came to study our home and it would seem you have become closer to your studies than you bargained for."

"Yeah. I had in mind a less intimate learning experience." He chuckled. The body ache was beginning to fade. "I'm going to be quite the center of attention when I return. Perhaps some of you would like to accompany me?" He could envision the physicians operating on a hopelessly injured human body, replacing damaged innards with smooth silicate replacements of their own manufacture and design.

"We must reach this beacon of yours first," Azure reminded him. "Or can it be that your priorities have changed along with your body?"

"No. I'm as human as I ever was." Only my perception has changed a little, he told himself confidently. Only the perception. There was nothing unusual about his new artificial heart or lungs. Different methods of installation and manufacture had been employed, that was all. A team of human surgeons trying to save his life would have dug into him with similar results in mind.

The lower portion of his froporia armor had survived and been recovered by the warriors, along with the arm pieces. Regretting the loss of the rest, he donned what was left. Perhaps they could locate another froporia pool and the missing sections could be regrown.

Somehow the process no longer struck him as threatening or repellent. He glanced down at his beacon. It was glowing very brightly indeed now. They didn't want to lose sight of where it was leading them.

Just as he would have to take pains not to lose sight of who he was.

"We must be very close." Azure looked excited in spite of himself. Looked rather than sounded. Evan had learned that when Azure or any of his kin became agitated, they tended to fluoresce slightly. "I can hear the signal myself now."

"So can I," library said, "though my hearing is not as acute as a scout's."

Apparently Evan wasn't the only one looking forward to the forthcoming reunion—assuming there was anything to reunion with.

Increasing their pace, they reached the crest of a steep hill, climbing through low flora fashioned from what looked like sheets of imperial topaz. From the ridge they could look down into a small valley. Martine Ophemert was nowhere in sight, but something else was.

"There lies your beacon," Azure said quietly, "but not your companion. I fear she has gone the way of all flesh."

"I have never seen anything like that in all my life." A profound confession, coming from library, who was after all the repository of every bit of knowledge the members of the Associative had ever accumulated. Not content to conclude with a single profundity, he added another.

"I think we'd better get away from this place."

Evan was gaping at the valley. It was completely bare of the normal profusion of silicate and organosilicate life. There wasn't any room for it because the valley was already occupied—by a single gargantuan, constantly shifting organism.

It was a crazy quilt of fractal shapes and projections, asymmetrical as a wild seashore. Even Evan's newly altered eyes failed to discern any unifying pattern. It was an uncontrolled explosion of life gone berserk, pulling and tearing at itself to form new combinations and shapes even as they watched. Antennae erupted from unpredictable sources, thrusting out of half-animal, half-inanimate bulges. Every type and kind of limb groped for a hold on the ground or the surviving valley flora which had not yet been overwhelmed: tentacles and hands, cilia and claw. Organic eyes competed with silicate lenses for viewing space.

Pink hemispheres hung in bloated bunches from the flanks of the abomination like bloody gas bags. One part decorated with delicate blue and green stripes ended abruptly where a massive red rhombohedral growth protruded from the monstrosity's back. The rhomboid was full of black inclusions and pulsed steadily in and out, like an enormous slab-sided lung. Limbs pushed and pulled without rhythm or pattern, with the result that the creature expended an enormous amount of energy in going nowhere.

"Chaos," muttered one of the physicians. "From what bud could such a horror spring? Randomness come to life. It is everything and yet it is nothing."

"What about the beacon?" Gazing down at the cancerous growth which filled the valley, Evan was afraid he already knew the answer.

Azure gestured toward the near end of the pulsating sea of life. "Down there."

"Your friend is dead, as you feared all along," said first physician. "Consumed along with dozens of other unlucky creatures."

"Yes. See there, the remains of several awarites." Library pointed to the back of the heaving mass, which rose a good thirty meters from the floor of the obliterated valley.

"Yes," physician agreed, "and over there the limbs of

cotars and eviols, still moving, still attempting to perform their natural functions."

"It does more than absorb its prey," library commented cautiously. "It keeps all or parts of them alive and makes use of them. That, I think, is the answer to your earlier question. This is not one creature but hundreds, all thrown and joined together by some unifying force. But there is no rhyme or reason to it, no design, no architecture. Chaos it is and chaos is its plan."

"You mean some of the other creatures that thing has consumed are still alive?" Evan was straining to follow library's train of thought.

"Alive perhaps. Alive as individuals, no. Perhaps the hundreds have not been consumed so much as co-opted."

"Then where is the being that began it all, that controls it—insofar as it's being controlled."

"Who knows? It must be greatly transformed from what it was originally. It must be buried deep within the anarchical self it has become." Library glanced up at Evan. "I say again we should leave this place. It is apparent that your friend is no longer alive. Her remains, by the location of the beacon that led us here, must lie somewhere within the mass. Look, the weight of it is so great the ground sags beneath it."

"Perhaps there is even more of it we cannot see," Azure suggested, "lying hidden beneath the surface."

Words too late to be dissected, alas, followed by proof all could have done without. Eight huge silicate tentacles broke the soil below them. Each ended in strong fingers of bright orange that clutched and grabbed.

Library and the physicians went up in coils of orange fibers, while the three warriors were pinned so tightly they couldn't bring their teeth to bear. Evan tried to run, was enveloped by a blast of sticky white fibers attached to the end of one tentacle. The soft, unbreakable fuzz tickled but he wasn't laughing. He felt himself being drawn down into the valley, kicking and shouting to his companions.

They were as helpless as ants in the hands of a giant, a giant that filled the entire valley.

"Co-opted!" library yelled at all of them as he fought against the entangling limbs. Did that mean dead or alive?

They were about to find out. A flap on the upper flank of the monster opened in expectation of their arrival. There were no visible teeth and it looked more like a door than a mouth. Meter-long cilia gripped him when the orange tentacle let go and withdrew. One by one, his friends joined him *inside*.

The outer flap closed and the roof began to descend. Evan fought hard. Suffocation was a particularly unpleasant form of death. The thin sheet of flesh pressed down tightly—and broke, to slide down around him and his friends. It halted near his waist, imprisoning him firmly. Like a bee floating in a bucket, a fist-size yellow-and-black eye popped out of the englobing ooze to stare briefly at him before moving on to inspect first physician.

Evan pressed against the material surrounding him. It was already hardening and held him tight. From below, a small wave of yellow slag was approaching, flowing upward in defiance of gravity. It reached him and began to crawl slowly up his sides, hardening as it advanced.

His friends were likewise imprisoned. If the rate of rise remained constant, all of them would be completely submerged before evening. By virtue of his greater height Evan might hold out for another day or so. Already he could feel the noisome stuff crawling over his chin, covering first his mouth, then plugging both nostrils, cutting off his air, his lungs bursting.

There was to be no placid period of extended contemplation, however. Thin waxy tendrils emerged from the fluid surface and tried to slither up his rib cage. He used his arms and hands to rip them away until something struck him from behind...

* * *

Night had fallen by the time he regained consciousness. The light from Prism's multiple moons cast a silvery gloss over the heaving, never still surface of which he was now a part. Both of his arms were imprisoned close to his ribs and the yellow syrup had risen to his sternum.

He was acutely conscious of the single tendril which had snaked its way up his shoulder to enter through his left ear. Once more he was plugged in, only this time the connection was involuntary.

A few lumpy silhouettes were visible off to his right, all that remained of his entombed companions. By this time tomorrow he too would have vanished. He could see library and Azure clearly beneath the layer of semitransparent material. Since they did not breathe they must still be alive. He could not decide if he envied them.

No point in screaming. He'd done enough screaming already on this world. He even managed a wry, private grin. Here he'd come all this way to find Martine Ophemert and now that he'd found her, he wasn't going to be allowed to leave. They were to be joined, as hundreds of other inhabitants of Prism had been joined, in a noxious and unholy congress.

He had come dozens of light-years to perish as part of an organic soup, an alien ollapodrida. All to no purpose.

"That is untrue," said an entirely new voice inside his head.

So the tendril reaching into his brain *was* a communications link, and not merely some forgotten animate independence acting out irresistible instincts.

"Each new acquisition contributes to the success of the whole."

Yes, a new voice, different from library's, different from Azure's. A vibrant, powerful voice walking the edge of nervous hysteria. The voice of a wholly confident mad thing. As unsettled verbally as it was physically.

"You have already absorbed another of my kind." It was intended as a statement of fact, not as a question.

The response was disconcerting. "I have seen another soft thing like yourself, but could not induce it to join me."

"That's not true. You have within you a device which was a part of this other individual, a device which emits light and sound."

"The thing you speak of, a most curious and fascinating artifact, is indeed within me. But I was not also able to cojoin with its originator. Sadly, it avoided my blandishments."

Anyone but Evan Orgell would have laughed. Or cried. He did neither, luxuriating in the delicious irony of the situation while retaining complete control of his churning emotions. How utterly perfect! How exquisitely droll! It was true, then, what the philosophers said: the universe was the biggest joker of all. He had walked, stumbled, and crawled across the hostile surface of an alien world in hopes of effecting a gallant rescue, only to end up in need of rescue by the one he sought.

But that thought was premature as well as unlikely. How this monstrosity had come into possession of Ophemert's beacon he could only surmise, but that didn't change the fact that she was probably dead. Consumed by some other voracious citizen of Prism, no doubt.

No wonder he'd been able to track her beacon so easily. No wonder the signal had remained in approximately the same place. The irony of it was marvelous.

What a shame he'd never have the opportunity to share it with anyone else.

"Why are you so despondent?" the voice wondered. "I mean you no harm."

Evan found that he was still able to laugh. He hoped his mental reply sounded sufficiently incredulous. "You mean us no harm? You attack and carry us off and then imprison us in this mass, which I presume is part of yourself, and you still claim to mean us no harm?"

"I mean you no harm. You are to become contributors to a great experiment."

"What kind of 'experiment'?"

"The experiment that is I. Me. Myself. I am the Integrator. I am you and you are me. All will become me and I will become all."

The philosophy is not new, Evan told himself. That was a cry common to many would-be tyrants and dictators stretching far back into the depths of human history. But he doubted it had ever been previously stated on a purely biological level. His demise was to be truly unique: he was going to be murdered by a megalomaniacal melanoma.

"All contribute. I especially value intelligence. You and your companions are intelligent. They come from an Associative, but I am the greatest Associative that has ever been or ever will be. I am the only true Associative."

"You are not an Associative because you are not organized." Evan was certain he recognized the voice of library, bitter and accusatory—and disturbingly weak.

"Organization follows form. I am the Integrator and my purpose is to link together as many lifeforms as possible, until I have become all the world and all the world has become me! One single immense organism, the logical end of all Associatives."

Though weakened and helpless, library would not concede. "You are not organized. There is no design to your growth, no rhythm to your expansion. It is as chaotic as your intentions. You are not an Associative. You are not integrated. You are an anarchy."

"Organization requires only the proper integration of a sufficient diversity of lifeforms. That has not yet been achieved."

"You don't understand yourself. You can continue to

grow in mass but not in mind. Organization does not occur on its own behalf."

"You are only a fragment," the Integrator replied contemptuously. "What can you know of destiny?"

Superficial as well as insane, Evan mused.

"You will see. There are several libraries within the Associative, each contributing its own store of knowledge to the greater whole that is I, Us, Me. See."

Quiet reigned while the Integrator put library in touch with others of his kind who had preceded him to oblivion. "You have their knowledge, their talents, yes. You have information without the ability to apply it, though, because you have stripped them of their individuality. They can no longer discuss, argue, and compare. They can only comply. You have destroyed that which is most useful about them."

"There can be no individuality within a true Associative. You will not miss yours, I assure you. Instead you will find far greater fulfillment as a library as part of a proper whole. It is how it was meant to be. Each contributes a specialization to the whole. Multiplicity is versatility."

"Not without individuality," library argued. "Without individuality there can be no innovation, and without innovation there can be no development. You can grow but you cannot mature. You can repeat but you cannot create. You will not be capable of an original thought."

"Ah, but that is where you are most wrong, for am I not the most original thought of all? Where but in me have you ever seen such originality before?"

"Only in nightmares," Evan murmured.

"You are mentally and physically insane," library added, "though I don't expect you to recognize that. Individuals cannot forcibly be integrated."

"Wrong, wrong, you are so wrong! It can be done. It *has* been done. I have done it. I *am* it." Around Evan the surface of the Integrator flared with an intense green light, an outpouring of uncontrolled emotion, a visual shout.

"You're right," Evan said quietly. "It can be done." He could sense the shock among his companions. "It can be done, and you are not proof of it—I am. Look closely at me. I am warrior, library, physician and scout, gatherer and scanner, all in one. You cannot integrate two Integrators."

"Yes, that's so," said Azure, quickly divining Evan's intent. "Let him go."

"No. I am not so easily tricked. Within myself are many purely organic lifeforms. Some contribute while others have proved useless, but I would not deny to any the fulfillment that comes from being wholly integrated. I will learn from this one as I did not have the chance to learn from the other."

"You won't learn a damn thing from me," Evan assured it. "I'm not a sun-eater. When this goo covers my head I'll die."

"It will not matter. I will learn from your parts, as I have learned from and made use of similar soft bodies." By way of illustration a dozen brown limbs emerged from the slick surface nearby and waved at him. They had been removed from a dozen unfortunate deceased owners. Evan was nearly sick.

"When you are fully integrated you will be more cooperative," the Integrator assured him blithely.

It veneers itself with reason, Evan told himself tiredly, much as a cheap piece of furniture is plated with expensive wood, and so it convinces itself it is sane. He wasn't going to be able to argue himself out of this deathtrap. The Integrator was composed of hundreds, thousands, of bodies of similar unfortunates, and Evan was going to join them. It would pick his imprisoned body apart, move his brain to the section reserved for brains, use his eyes and ears as it saw fit. And there was no reason to doubt that one day, unless it was stopped by some natural disaster, it would indeed have consumed every intelligent being on the planet. What would happen then, when it finally realized that it was no more successful than when it had begun? Would it finally recognize its own insanity?

An interesting and totally moot question, which Evan would not be around to learn the answer to. He and Azure and all the others were going to suffer the bliss of integration, whether they wanted to or not.

He could still broadcast to his friends by means of the device they had implanted in his head, but they did not reply to his repeated queries. Perhaps they were being blocked, or perhaps their own communications facilities had been taken over already. They might be able to hear him but not to respond. He was sure they were still alive. So long as sunlight reached their receptors and their bodies remained intact they would continue to live. Not like him, when his head was finally submerged. Heart pounding, lungs exploding. He wondered if his teeth would have any effect on the yellow silicate that was slowly entombing him and resolved come morning to find out.

And if he could hold it off, then what? Slow death from thirst or starvation? The alternatives were not promising.

The fear and tension, the worry and anxiety, combined to exhaust him. He welcomed the exhaustion, as he welcomed inevitable sleep. If he was extremely fortunate he might suffocate before he awoke.

13

Even that small favor was to be denied him. The rising sun woke him in time to discover that the enveloping yellow syrup had almost reached his chin. He was completely imprisoned now except for his head. Soon he was going to be able to try his teeth on the stuff. He thought of swallowing some. It might kill him a little quicker.

There was no response to his queries from Azure or any of his companions. Possibly the Integrator had begun to take control of their minds as well as their bodies. At least he could still see, thanks to the superb surgery of the physicians. He was facing toward the rising sun but was not blinded.

Unique discoveries which he had barely had time to enjoy. The Integrator heaved beneath him, a violent lurch that was as impressive as it was unexpected. Taking over another patch of ground, Evan told himself. He licked his lips, wondering what the yellow death would taste like.

An intense blast of rich red light that was brighter than

the sun caused the Integrator to convulse a second time. The light struck the curving bulk several meters below Evan's location. The yellow silicate began to melt and flow like hot butter.

"STOP—NOW!"

The deafening warning had no effect on the persistence of the red beam, which continued to slice across the surface of the Integrator. Huge tentacles and massive groping hands thrust out of the earth lining the valley, straining to rend the source of the annihilating light. They had no more effect on it than had the mental shout.

Unable to move, Evan could only pray the light would miss him. If it touched him he'd go up like a wick in a candle.

Library managed a frighteningly weak response to his query. "I can't imagine what the source is, but it can do no more harm to us than we have done to ourselves already. What damages the Integrator helps us—unless we are unlucky enough to be torched by the light as well."

"It is like a barrean." Evan had to strain to identify the source, finally recognized it as belonging to one of the surviving trio of warriors. "Very much like a barrean, though more powerful still."

"What the hell is a barrean?"

"A solitary and infrequently encountered creature which defends itself against its enemies by striking them with intense beams of colored light." Evan could sense library's frustration. "I wish I could see. As warrior observes, this is much like a barrean's work, except for its sense of purpose. There is a pattern to its destruction."

Evan had a much better view than any of them but could see little more. The source of the beam lay in the direction of the rising sun and despite his specially altered eyes, he could not see through the glare.

"Wait! I believe I can see something." Second physician, sounding tired and far away. "It is no larger than a

barrean, but differently shaped. When the sun rises higher
I may be able to make an identifica—"

The Integrator spasmed. A large section of the creature
broke away from the main body and slid to the ground.
It did not tumble, which was fortunate or Evan would
have been crushed between the excised material and the
unyielding gravel below.

The involuntary biopsy sent the Integrator into a frenzy.
Tentacles and cilia lashed the ground in all directions. The
earth shook as the entire enormous mass lifted and fell
back against the valley floor.

Evan saw the red beam swing toward him. He closed
his eyes. At least the end would be far quicker than if
he'd been left to suffocate. But the deadly light did not
touch him. Instead, it seemed to focus precisely on the
hardened silica in which he was encased. The stuff lique-
fied and ran. The beam was hellishly hot and some of the
heat was conducted to his body through the churning
silica, but sooner than he dared hope he was free of his
prison. Cramped from disuse, his leg muscles refused to
function and he fell over on his side.

His companions suffered no such lingering dysfunction
and hurried over to make certain he was all right. Two
warriors gripped his arms and began to haul him away
from the flailing Integrator. It ignored their flight, wholly
absorbed in trying to destroy its unreachable tormentor.

He was halfway up the hill and trying to stand when
he heard the voice. It came out of the rising sun, full of
impatience and self-assurance. It was startlingly clear.

"Hurry up! This way. The Integrator's truly dangerous
only when it has time to stop and think."

There were none of the shades of uncertainty which
marked the voices of his friends. It was almost as though
he was being addressed by—another human.

"'Yes, I'm Ophemert. Now get a move on."

Somehow she'd escaped with a station weapon, a survey laser or better. It might even be a component of an

undamaged survival suit. He struggled to his feet, forcing his agonized leg muscles to work, and staggered into the glare. Azure and the rest followed, their receptors straining thirstily toward the unscreened sunlight.

He half ran, half crawled, up the steep slope, shoving blindly through needlelike flora and ignoring the scratches they made on his face. His limbs were still protected by the remains of his froporia armor, and the transparent skin covering his torso did not bleed.

Finally they reached the top of the hill and were able to turn and gaze back down into the valley. The organosilicate ocean that was the Integrator was still thrashing about. No doubt it was roaring its defiance. Unlike Evan's companions, though, it could only communicate through tendrils. It had never learned how to communicate without intimate contact, just as it had not learned how to come to terms with its own insanity.

"Thanks." He squinted, trying to separate a mobile shape from the surrounding growths and the sunlight. "I thought my friends and I were dead. You saved our lives."

"The rest of you are welcome to your lives." What Evan hadn't had a moment to consider earlier struck him forcefully now: he was not hearing Martine Ophemert's speech. He was hearing her as he heard Azure and library and physician, through the device they had implanted in his brain. Somehow Martine Ophemert had also been given this gift. Another mystery to add to the top of a pile that Prism raised a little higher every day.

"You may leave, associatives. As for you, you must know that I am going to kill you." A stunned Evan realized immediately she must be talking about him. It was one comment he had no ready reply for. "You didn't think I'd let the Integrator have that pleasure, did you? I thought I'd watch you sweat for a while, though. But I couldn't see your face from here while you died. And I've been wanting to watch you die ever since"—Evan tasted of a mental sob—"what you did in camp. You rotten, sorry bastard, I'm so glad you came after me. Followed the beacon, didn't you? I hoped you would, oh, how I prayed you'd follow the beacon! You couldn't quit and leave any work undone, could you?"

Evan was stumbling backward, shielding his eyes and searching desperately for his unseen assassin-to-be. "But why do you want to kill me? I didn't do anything at the station! I'm here to rescue you." He tripped over a broken stump and fell backward onto the sand.

The red death was very close to his feet now. It had been tracking him ever since Ophemert had spoken. Now it moved away. The voice of Prism station's sole survivor suddenly sounded confused.

"You're not Humula. Where's Humula?"

Evan sat up and tried to see into the concealing forest. Even his newly modified eyes could not fight off every reflection, search out every possible hiding place. And what if they could? He had nothing to fight with.

"Hum-who? That name means nothing to me—no, wait a minute. Arin Humula, wasn't he a repair tech or something at the station?"

"Aram, not Arin," she corrected him. "That was his name, yes. I thought it was him, come to finish me off. Come to finish his work."

"Maybe we could have something like an intelligent conversation if you'd tell me what the hell you're talking about." He took a deep breath. "My name's Evan Orgell. I'm from company HQ on Samstead. I was put down here quietly to find out why there's been no report from the station for months."

"They put you down here by yourself—like that?" Her tone was disbelieving, understandably so. Evan didn't believe what had happened to him either.

"No. I had an MHW, the latest and best model available. Right out of the prototype lab. It wasn't good enough."

A light feminine chuckle. "Nothing is—for Prism."

"I decided to try and locate your beacon anyhow. I was fortunate enough to make some friends along the way"—he waved to where Azure and the others were cleaning yellow goo off themselves—"and when a choice specimen of local life tore me up, they fixed me up the best they knew how. I know it's a little hard to get used to, but—"

"Not at all." He felt he was being examined closely. "They seem to have done a fine job. Associative physicians are natural wonders. They're going to revolutionize the whole course of Commonwealth medicine."

"I followed your beacon. It led me to that." He nodded down into the valley. The Integrator already seemed but a distant nightmare, though if Ophemert was to be believed they weren't entirely out of danger.

"The Integrator tried to integrate me. I don't integrate easily."

"Well, you had a weapon. I'm unarmed."

"Yes, I have a weapon," she said strangely. "The Integrator sought to use me for its own purposes. I decided I could use it. I made it a gift of my beacon, knowing that in tracking me Humula would follow its signal. I'm sorry that you were almost sucked in instead of him. I couldn't imagine another single man coming after me. I was sure you were him, though I couldn't imagine why or how he'd come to have Associative members traveling with him. So you got down and came looking for me without running into Humula? I find that hard to believe."

"Oh, I found him. Dead, like everyone else at the station. You didn't know that?"

"I know everyone else is dead. Everyone but me. I didn't know he was, obviously, or I wouldn't have thought you were him. How did he die?"

Evan shrugged. "I can't give you any details. Prism killed him."

She was silent for a long time before replying. "First time a planet ever deprived me of an anticipated pleasure.

Somehow I don't feel cheated. I'm going to come out and join you now. Do you have a weak stomach, Evan Orgell?"

He frowned. What the devil was she talking about? "You think I'd have been given this assignment if I did?"

"I don't know. Here lately I don't have much confidence in the company's method of selecting offworld personnel."

A shape emerged from a stand of green crystalline growths and came toward Evan. He shaded his eyes with a hand just as it stopped and raised its right arm. Four fingers clustered together and from their tangent tips emerged that murderous shaft of red light.

Evan tried to dodge, falling to one side, while the two physicians who were resting behind him scattered. But the beam was not aimed at them. It thrust past him to slice into humping, twisting segments the two long tentacles which had crawled all the way up the slope from the valley below.

"I told you it was still dangerous here. The Integrator's persistent." The arm was lowered and the red light vanished. "I don't think it will try anything else for a while, but if we're going to talk there are safer places to do so." She half smiled at him.

It was only a half smile because she only had half a face.

Beautiful, she had been, in figure as well as face, and the sad dichotomy that was Martine Ophemert continued all the way down to her remaining foot. Only the left side was still fashioned of flesh and bone, and even it had been patched in several places. The color match of the patches was good, but the artificial skin was still painfully obvious.

The right side of her body was composed of an even deeper blue material than Azure's.

Something had rebuilt slightly more than half of Martine Ophemert. So deep was the royal blue that it was almost opaque. He could not see the artificial organs that lay inside. He did not have to see them to know they existed. Even the right half of the skull was of blue crystal, smooth and inflexible except for the lighter blue lens which substituted for the missing eye. It swiveled and rotated in tandem with its fleshy companion. He wondered how the brain correlated what must be two entirely different sets of visual messages. For that matter he wondered how much of the original brain was left.

Cosmetic detail had been attended to along with more practical concerns. From the right side of the head, long blue fibers trailed toward the ground. They were identical in length and diameter to Ophemert's natural black hair, except for their color—and the minute bit of light that danced at the tip of each fiber.

She stopped when she was barely a meter away and studied him as intently as he was studying her. What the physicians had done to him was wondrous, but Martine Ophemert was a miracle. A blue miracle.

His friends formed a curious circle around them both. "I see a couple of physicians. Did they do this work on you?" A hand of sapphire reached out to touch the transparent skin covering his abdomen.

"A necessary repair job." He was shaking his head in disbelief. "Nothing compared to what's been done to you. I wouldn't think that that much of human body could be rebuilt if I wasn't looking at the proof of it right now."

"Neither would I." Again that quirky yet charming half smile. The right side of her face did not move. Whoever had saved her had managed to give her a new heart, half a new body, and more. But they had not been able to rebuild her smile.

"I went racing through the forest to escape what happened back at the station. Had on my survival suit so I thought I was safe enough." Maybe she could manage only a half smile, but she could still produce a hearty laugh. "A top-heavy condarite fell on me. My right side was crushed. Members of an Associative found me and, well, you know how they work. They're as curious as they are skillful. In order to ask me questions they had to keep me alive.

"I can't claim to begin to understand the medical engineering that made it possible for me to live. All I can do is marvel at it."

"The light you used to save us," said library, "we thought it was barrean."

"Oh, that. They told me about the barrean. I was fascinated. That's part of my work. So they offered to make another modification." She turned and raised her right arm again.

As soon as the tips of all four fingers were brought into alignment the shaft of coherent red light reappeared. It vanished as quickly when she spread the fingers apart.

"My very own laser. I've got artificial rubies in my fingers and hand—it's just corundum to them—and argon gas in my arm. Something in my back collects and stores enough energy to make the whole setup lase when I bring all the elements into proper alignment. They did it because I kept expressing concern for my personal safety. Humula, you know." She lowered the arm and flexed shining blue fingers. "I can vary the intensity by moving my fingers slightly. It's funny. I've always been an admirer of bioengineering. Just never thought I'd experience it firsthand."

"Same here," Evan told her.

She glanced down into the valley. "The Integrator hasn't forgotten you. Let's take a walk." They turned and followed her down the other side of the ridge, leaving the baffling, maddening thing that was the Integrator to rage at their escape.

"I was sure you were Humula," she told him as they picked their way down the slope. "The only thing that made me hesitate was the presence of Associative members. I couldn't imagine how someone like him could induce physicians and a library to travel with him."

"What's the story with this Humula, anyway? I'm pretty sure I've got the basics puzzled out, but I'm still sketchy on the hows and whys."

"You saw what happened at the station. I imagine when you got over the initial shock you started imagining alien monstrosities running amok." He nodded. "It wasn't, of course, though something the size of the Integrator could have done it. It wasn't Prism's fault, though. We're so clever, we humans, we bring our own monstrosities with us.

"Naturally you wondered how anything could have surprised the staff, much less wiped it out, what with all the screens and weapons provided. It isn't difficult if all your attention is directed outward. Humula did it. He had it all figured out, disconnected alarms, went to work at night when everyone except the night watch was sleeping. He timed it perfectly." She spoke matter-of-factly, without bitterness. The bitterness had faded some time ago.

"Not quite perfectly," Evan pointed out. "He missed you."

"Saved by a whim. I couldn't sleep, so I went spargenox hunting." When he responded with a quizzical shake of his head, she explained. "From the old Latin; spargere for spark, nox for night. Night-sparks."

"I called them dancing jewels, I think."

She nodded. "I went collecting, didn't bother to tell anybody. The team leader, Jo Erlander, didn't approve of solo excursions beyond the perimeter, much less nocturnal ones. She's dead now too. Poor Mother Hen. We all loved her."

Evan waited quietly until the tears stopped. They fell only from one eye, of course.

"I saw Humula kill Eddie Chang myself. He had access to the armory and all I had were the defensive systems in my suit. I knew I didn't have a chance against him. So I ran. I ran like hell, because I knew he'd take a count and come after me when he found I wasn't anywhere in camp. I knew it would take him a while to go through every building and the grounds in detail, so I figured I'd have a pretty good head start. I did. I got away clean—and then a tree falls on me."

"He killed everyone?" Evan said slowly.

"All of them. Eddie, Mother Hen, Rajanshar—everyone. My friends. My family away from home. He murdered them, carefully and efficiently. I'm sure you can guess why as easily as I. He was working for another outfit, a rival concern. It would have to be a big one, big enough to want Prism's resources all to itself. Just like our company does.

"Once he'd taken care of the staff, Humula would have the station to himself. First he'd pirate the information we'd gathered and ship it off to his employers; then wait for 'rescue.' That would be you, Evan. He'd have a couple of options then. He could kill you and hope that would be enough to convince the company to abandon its interests here, or he could have dressed up a nice story about the invulnerable inimical lifeforms that would render any kind of colony here untenable, and how he'd barely managed to survive the attacks which had killed everyone else."

"And I probably would have believed him," Evan murmured softly.

"Why not? I would've believed him myself without anyone or anything to contradict him. That's why he had to come after me. I was the last witness, the last threat to his carefully thought out plan. But Prism got to him first." She shook her head. "If I'd known that I could've gone straight back and called in. I might—still be all me." She swallowed, sniffed once. "Hell with it. Half of me is history."

"This other Associative repaired you after the condarite fell on you?"

"Shock alone almost killed me. When I finally regained consciousness I was a long way from where the tree caught me. They'd carried me inside their wall and had gone to work. Gradually I got used to it—as used as anyone can to having half a new body, I guess. Just being alive makes all sorts of changes palatable.

"They'd saved the beacon, too. Naturally the falling condarite hadn't hurt it. That led to discussions of batteries and..."

"I did the same favor for my friends." Evan indicated the attentive circle of silicate faces surrounding them.

"So. There's nothing to stop us from going back to the station. That's not going to be easy for me."

"I'll help as much as I can. Getting a message out isn't going to be easy either, you know. I made a thorough tour of the station before I started following your beacon. The local scavengers have been pretty busy while you've been away."

"I can imagine. The native lifeforms treat rare earths, metals, and chemical compounds like candy." She sat down on the frozen skeleton of a yellow-pink tree. Evan marveled at her fluid movements. The master physicians who had repaired and replaced her crushed right side had done a remarkable job of duplicating human muscle and bone with entirely different materials.

"I don't know how to ask this," he said finally, "so I'll just ask it. Are you—comfortable, like that?"

"Like what? Oh." She laughed easily. "I've progressed beyond comfortable. Actually, I don't give it much thought. I'm not in pain, if that's what you mean. What matters is that I'm alive. In fact, I'm probably subject to less pain than before, since my doctors didn't try to duplicate the density of neural endings except where it really matters, like at the tips of my fingers. Talking is something else that's been hard for me to get used to. My half-new vocal cords don't mesh quite perfectly with what's left of the old ones, so I tend to whistle sometimes when I make s's. They were concentrating on saving the right side of my brain. Peripherals didn't receive as much attention.

"On the other hand, they made some improvements. My new right eye sees things the left never dreamed existed. I have a food storage system that lets me go without eating for quite a while. And then there's this little toy, courtesy of some intensive barrean study." She raised her right hand and brought her fingers halfway together, drew them over her left leg. The blue silicate skin picked up the light and dispersed it harmlessly.

She looked into his eyes. "So I guess you could say I'm comfortable with the way I turned out. Now, are *you* comfortable with the way I am?"

Evan licked his lips. "Blue becomes you."

She laughed harder than ever. Now that it had been mentioned, Evan noticed the faint whistling overtones. It didn't detract from the beauty of her laugh at all.

"A diplomat. I like you, Evan Orgell."

"Just Evan."

"Then, just Martine. Even if you aren't entirely human anymore."

He glanced down at his transparent torso. "Just missing some meat, and who's to say its replacement isn't more durable? The problem now is, do we wash or polish?" They laughed together.

"Prism has refashioned us in its own image. Partly, anyway." She turned serious. "You know, this world is going to make some wondrous things possible if the people who come here to learn approach what it has to offer with open minds. These changes have been forced on you and me by necessity, but there's no reason why they couldn't be performed on volunteers. Imagine what the physicians of the Associatives could do for severely deformed or damaged people if they were given access to Commonwealth medical technology. Look what they've done without it." She waved toward the now safely distant ridge.

"Even the Integrator has potential. Maybe a use can be found for it someday, if it can be contained and cured." Half her face was alive with excitement. "Evan, Prism's the most important discovery since mankind met up with the thranx!"

He shook his head slowly, wondering if he could have coped with such extensive changes as well as she had. "You're beautiful when you're half angry. All of you."

She grinned. "Maybe more than just a diplomat. You've either been away from women too long or else you're afflicted with a severe gemophilia fetish."

"Blue seems to be the predominant color here. I wonder why."

"Predominance of copper in the silicates. Preliminary research had time to confirm that much. Add minute amounts of chromium and you get bright red trees. Fascinating."

"It is nothing like that," Azure piped up. "It is just that the physicians who helped you clearly possessed a superior sense of design. You are blue because blue is by far the most attractive natural coloring."

That set off an argument between Azure and two of the black-sheened warriors. The warriors were outclassed but made up for it with sheer stubbornness. Gradually the rest of the party joined the discussion. Except for library, who remained aloof from such silliness.

"Tell me," Martine asked quietly during a lull in the sparring, "did you bury any of the staff?"

Evan shook his head. "I was too busy trying to find out if anyone was still alive to worry about the dead. We can bury them when we get back, if you want, and if we can get the remains away from the scavengers."

She nodded, sighed. The left side of her body heaved while the right gave a little twitch. She was all at once an alien, pitiable, and exotic figure.

"I've considered my own situation carefully. I've had plenty of time to think. I've been on my own here for some time now and I've gotten used to Prism. Comfortable, even. Once we contact the company and explain what's happened here I'm sure they'll want to stay and expand the station. The newcomers will need someone to explain things to them and keep them from making fools of themselves. For obvious reasons I don't think I'd be able to slip smoothly back into the everyday flow of life on Samstead—or anywhere else, for that matter. So— I'm thinking of staying here if the company will let me continue with my work."

"Staying. I think you're wrong about being able to fit in back home. That's just where you would be able to fit in, on Samstead. Because you'd be in a suit all the time. As for the right side of your face, there are ways to camouflage that."

"Word would leak out sooner or later. People, the media, would start seeking out the freak."

"You could be completely camouflaged. Syntheflesh everywhere and you'd look like everyone else. That's what I'm going to have done to me." He slapped his stomach.

"Maybe I could be fixed to look like everyone else, Evan, but I wouldn't *be* like everyone else. There's no way to fix that. And the media would still hunt me down. I couldn't cope with that. I'm a very private person, Evan. That's one reason why I chose the profession I did. I'm a loner, better at dealing with two people in a lab than two hundred at company offices. No, I made up my mind weeks ago, out in the forest. I'm staying here. I think the company will be delighted. Who else can work freely out in the wilds of this world without a suit? I'm adapted to this place, more so than any other human being."

She nearly left out the "other," Evan noticed.

"I'm not the girl down the street anymore. I never really was. Prism's made the condition permanent, that's all."

They were both silent for a long moment. Then that quirky smile returned. "As a loner I never dressed up much. I didn't care much for jewelry and now I can't leave it at home because it's become a part of me."

He smiled. "Once your friends armed you—pardon the pun—how come you never went looking for Humula?"

"Two reasons: I was afraid I'd never be able to surprise him if he stayed within the station's defensive perimeter, and I didn't know how to find my way back to the station without my suit."

"You couldn't judge from the position of the sun?"

"That may be part of your job. It wasn't part of mine. Who worried about such things inside a suit? Your survival suit took care of everything, including getting you home if you got lost. Hell, you couldn't get lost in a suit."

Evan nodded, remembering his own reliance on the MHW. Maybe it was time a few of Samstead's enlightened citizens considered doing without suits for a while. Maybe there was some basis to the criticism its citizens heard from the other inhabitants of the Commonwealth. Could one rely too heavily on technology to get through everyday life? A disturbing thought—and a promising one.

"You talk of returning to your Associative," a new voice said, unable to keep silent any longer.

"Excuse me." Evan gestured with his left hand. "This is my friend Azure."

"A Surface of Fine Azure-Tinted Reflection With Pyroxine Dendritic Inclusions—if you don't mind." Impressions of a mental sigh. "But since you humans have this inexplicable aversion to proper names, you may refer to me by the same stunted identification my companion uses."

"I am very pleased to make your acquaintance, scout."

Evan looked startled. "You know, Azure's the only one whose name I've bothered to ask." He looked back at the rest of his friends, who had ceased their arguing to watch and listen. "Library, what are you called?"

"'Library' will do, since it would take you until evening to hear my entire name. When we wish to pass such information among ourselves we can do so far faster than you can comprehend."

"If you want to return to your camp we can do that anytime," Azure informed his friend.

"How? Without my suit I'm all turned around. We'll have to rely on my sun sightings and go slowly and carefully so I don't lose my way. Even so, that'll only get us back to where my suit died. From there back to the station will take some guesswork."

Azure made a disgusted sound. "For you, perhaps. I do not function according to 'guesswork.' Why do you think I am called a scout?"

Evan smiled. "Do you remember every place you've ever been?"

"Certainly. It's my job."

"If you do not object the rest of us would like to accompany you." Evan turned to face library. "There is much to be learned from the continued study of human things."

"That's what the physicians who fixed me said," Martine commented, "but they were beginning a migratory and couldn't deviate from their planned course in any case."

"Of course you're welcome to join us," Evan told him. He shifted his attention back to Azure. "You think you can find your way from my suit back to the station?"

"You still do not fully comprehend the abilities of a scout. I will take you where we all wish to go."

"All right then. Let's go there."

14

THERE WAS PLENTY OF TIME FOR CONVERSA-
tion during the long march back to the Associative and a
great deal of information was exchanged between silicates
and organics. Their return was greeted quietly and without fanfare, the members of the Associative not being the
overly demonstrative type. But the presence of Martine,
who was as much silicate as soft, provoked so much comment that the work of the Associative suffered.

Farewells followed close upon greetings and they set
off in search of Evan's abandoned MHW, only by then
the travelers' numbers had been increased by the addition
of a dozen extra warriors. Thus protected, Evan found
time to delight in the wondrous sights and sensations that
had seemed so threatening on his way out.

Martine was continually pointing out some small silicate miracle Evan would otherwise have overlooked. At
times he didn't understand what she was talking about
even after long and detailed explanations. This bothered
her more than it did him because she was afraid it reflected

some loss of humanity within her. After several days she was moved to confess her innermost concern: that the physicians who had saved her life had been forced to modify some portions of her mind in order to keep her alive, and that they'd avoided telling her what they'd done to spare her further trauma.

He reassured her, without reassuring himself, that her heightened perceptions of the world around her were solely the result of modifications made to her eyes and ears, and that she was as human in her interpretation of her surroundings as he was. That prompted laughter from both of them and she never mentioned her fear again. But he knew it was still with her, would likely be with her always.

Azure fulfilled all his promises by leading them straight to the MHW, whose hollow interior had become home to half a dozen interesting local lifeforms, and thence to within sight of the research station's central observation tower. With one exception, everything looked as it had when Evan had left it in search of Humula and Martine. The exception, however, was a very large one.

Sitting at one end of the crude landing field was a gleaming, delta-winged shuttlecraft.

"I'll be dammed," Evan said excitedly. "They must have grown so worried about not hearing from me that they changed the plan and diverted a rescue ship!" He took a step forward, only to be restrained by a crystalline arm.

"Maybe." Martine was staring hard at the ship. "Don't forget, Humula's people have probably been waiting to hear from him, too."

Evan hesitated. "Surely they wouldn't risk a landing here until they'd received an all clear from their agent?"

"That would be the sensible approach, but people who authorize cold-blooded murders for the sake of money don't always act sensibly."

"We have to find out. We have to go in." He gazed anxiously, longingly, at where the shuttle squatted like a huge insect on the cleared strip next to the station. Whatever its origin, it represented the civilization he'd never thought he'd see again. Its lure was near irresistible.

"If it's from the company and they don't find me there," he told her anxiously, "they may give up and leave. Permanently."

Martine stood there vacillating, torn between common sense and uncommon emotions. "That's possible. I agree we have to check it out, but we have to exercise caution as well."

"Okay. You stay here and I'll go on in alone." He tapped the side of his head and grinned. "Thanks to the work of our friends I'll be able to tell you how we stand the instant I know."

"*If* these are our friends and not Humula's. No, I'm not staying behind even if that would be the right thing to do. Those are my friends lying dead in there. If that is a company ship, then they can help with the burying. If it's not—if it's not, I want to be in a position to deal with whoever it is in person. We'll both go."

"We understand," said library solemnly. "You have explained this all to us before, and we understand. We will wait here and prepare to do whatever it becomes necessary to do."

"I'm sure we'll just be a couple of minutes. Then you can come in." There was still no sign of life from the shuttle.

"Yes, Evan's probably right. I've spent so many days worrying that I've forgotten what's it like to live without being suspicious of everything that moves."

Together they started walking toward the station, crunching through the delicate bubble grass, trying to watch both the camp and the shuttle at the same time.

They were halfway to the station when Evan's face broke out in a big smile. He pointed toward the bow of the shuttle. "That settles it. You can relax now."

Sure enough, there on the bow was the company logo,

big and bright and sassy. Martine echoed his smile, but less certainly.

"I'm still surprised that they'd come looking for you before receiving a single report and without knowing what to expect. You must be a pretty important member of the corporate structure."

"Yes, I am," he replied blithely. "Obviously someone got nervous enough to take the risk and authorize the in-person check on my status. One of the original company scenarios postulated a station-wide communications failure. Probably they decided that was what's happened here, and that it subsequently also affected my ability to communicate. That's completely wrong, of course, but it would explain this unsolicited visit."

He wanted to let out a joyful shout when the first survival-suited figure appeared among the buildings. The woman was making a detailed inspection of the camp's nonfunctioning defensive perimeter, not attempting to fix it so much as trying to figure out what had caused it to fail. She was on her hands and knees, inspecting a relay pylon, and failed to notice their approach.

"Hi," Evan said. She didn't react, and it occurred to him that her external audio was probably turned off. The suit she was wearing was not nearly as massive or elaborately equipped as his abandoned MHW. Her tools were contained in an external belt.

She looked up then and her eyes widened at the sight of the two figures. Evan could sympathize with her reaction.

He waved. "Hello again!"

An audible click followed by a soft hum as she switched on her outside audio. "Who the hell are you?" She looked from Evan to his companion. "And what the hell is that?"

"I'm Evan Orgell. Senior company research, nonspecific. The troubleshooter who was shipped here to find out what happened? You know."

"Oh—yeah, right. I forgot." She waved toward his

transparent torso. "It's just that I wasn't expecting to run into you out here. Not to mention looking like that."

"Or like this," Martine added quietly.

The woman came close, eyed Evan's companion up and down. "What is she? Some kind of local hybrid?"

"Something like that," Evan told her hastily. "This is Martine Ophemert, the only surviving member of the original station staff. She knows what happened here, and why."

"We need to talk to whoever's in charge."

"Sure, sure. Tell me, what did happen here?"

"A bit more than your usual cut-and-dried industrial espionage. Some rival concern managed to slip an agent onto the station staff. He waited until the time was right, then killed everyone except me. *That's* what happened here."

The woman nodded thoughtfully. She was taking it well, Evan thought. "Yes, you could see it was something like that. We've been cleaning up the bodies. Hang on. I'll call in and tell them you're here."

Silence while she attended to in-suit communications. Eventually she looked up, chose to direct her attentions to Evan. He had the feeling that Martine's half-human, half-silicate stare made the other woman nervous. Well, that was understandable.

"What happened to the spy?"

"He started to come after me," Martine said, not caring whether the woman was looking at her or not, "but Prism took care of him. On this world the cocky don't live very long."

"We've seen what some of the local lifeforms are capable of," the woman replied uneasily. "We weren't expecting anything like what we found."

"No one was," Evan said easily. "There wasn't any reason to suppose that standard operational procedures would prove insufficient to protect the station and its staff.

I still think the staff here could have coped if this Humula hadn't intervened."

"You're probably right about that. Oh, my name's Winona. Winona Strand. Follow me. I've just been talking to Frazier and he said to bring you in straight away. Our temporary HQ's in the old administration building, what's left of it." She shook her head. "We're still clearing out native lifeforms. They're tough as hell. Trying to re-establish the perimeter, too, but we're having trouble bringing power back on line."

Evan chuckled. "Something's probably eaten half the wiring, not to mention the solar receptors."

"Eaten. Yeah." The woman kept glancing back at Martine, hurriedly turning away whenever her stare was noticed. Martine did not comment on the attention.

"The local silicate and organosilicate species have an insatiable appetite for rare-earth compounds. They have developed novel methods of extracting such elements from more complex compounds."

"I see," Winona murmured. "I'm sure the two of you have learned quite a lot since you've been stuck here. Our people are going to want to debrief you extensively. Your reports are going to be extremely valuable."

"Invaluable," Evan corrected her. "Who is this Frazier? I don't recognize the name."

"Not surprising. Strictly offworld operations. Hardly ever gets to Samstead, much less company central."

Now that they were in among the buildings they began to encounter other members of the shuttle crew. The expected expressions of astonishment and disbelief greeted them as they strode by. Evan was able to chat privately with Martine by means of the Associative transmitters.

"How does it feel to be back in camp?"

Martine's eyes were scanning the grounds, the structures she had helped raise. Half of them were overgrown with Prismatic flora.

"Different and yet the same. It's been a long time.

Nothing looks quite the way it did the last time I was here."

"Thank the physicians who altered your vision for that. It doesn't look the same anymore to me either, and I was here just recently."

She let out a resigned sigh. "I thought I'd feel more at home. I don't. I suppose I can thank my doctors for that, too. It isn't fair. You're supposed to feel alienated when you're away from your home, not when you come back to it. Perhaps it has nothing to do with my perception of the way things are. Maybe it's just all the undergrowth that's taken over." Blue light danced in her shoulder. "Maybe I'll feel differently once we're inside."

The administration building did look better. The rescue team had cleaned out the native intruders. Supplies were stacked against one wall and crated equipment lay nearby, but nothing to indicate that the newcomers planned to settle in for a long stay. That made sense. This was a search-and-rescue team, not a replacement crew. Rebuilding would have to await the arrival of a much larger and better equipped follow-up expedition.

One of the admin consoles had been cleared completely. One man was seated behind the curving desk while a man and woman stood staring at a nearby computer screen, arguing over adjustments. Safely inside, they wore standard duty suits instead of cumbersome survival outfits. Tools dangled from pockets and belt straps.

Winona led them forward, removed her suit and hood. Evan was beginning to get used to the stares. Their guide removed her suit hood, addressed the man behind the desk.

"Evan Orgell and Martine Ophemert, Mr. Frazier. She's original station staff; he was sent in subsequently to update station status."

"Right." Frazier inspected them each in turn, ended with his eyes fixed on Martine. "What about this Humula person, then?"

She repeated her story. He listened quietly, attentively, until she'd finished.

"I'm not going to ask how you were fixed. Time for that later. Suffice to say you're the most extraordinary-looking creature I've ever set eyes upon."

"I am conscious of my uniqueness," Martine replied dryly. "I'm sure you'll find the details of my sea change even more fascinating."

"No doubt." He shifted his gaze to Evan. "So you're the one who was sent here to find out what was going on. We thought you'd been killed along with everyone else."

"Not hardly."

The tall woman standing nearby spoke up. Her tone was demanding and harsh, unlike Frazier's. "What happened to your suits?"

"Martine's was smashed by a falling tree. Mine was—well, you've seen what the local lifeforms can do to alloys."

Frazier nodded. "We've hardly had a moment's peace since we set down here. I've had to mount a round-the-clock guard on everything: buildings, supplies, even the shuttle. There's some kind of subterranean slug that keeps trying to eat the landing struts." He shook his head. "What a world!"

"You're just not familiar with it," Martine told him.

"Hellish," the tall woman snapped, "but rife with potential."

"More than you can imagine," Evan assured her.

"Yes, I'm sure the company analysts will be slavering over your store of information for months, trying to decide which development to authorize first."

Frazier glanced up at Martine. "I'm sure you'll be able to point them in the most profitable direction."

She was staring hard at him. "I might. If you can explain one thing to me first."

Smiling, Frazier leaned forward. "Anything at all, Ms. Ophemert."

"When you were talking to Evan a minute ago you said, 'We thought you'd been killed along with everyone else.' The way in which you said it implies that you thought everyone had been killed *before you landed*. Why would you think everyone here was dead? The station might have suffered nothing more than a failure of its communications equipment."

Frazier shrugged. "The natural assumption, after such a long period of not hearing from you."

"Really? I'd think it more natural to assume a problem with communications before I'd assume there was no one left to communicate."

There was an uncomfortable silence. Evan was looking from Martine to Frazier, his thoughts churning. That smile—was it a bit forced?

"Who was your contact at Prism Project?" Martine asked him sharply. "Who authorized your trip here?"

"Houlton. Gabriel Houlton."

"Who told you about my visit?" Evan asked softly. "Who told you to come looking for me before you heard from me?"

Frazier glanced up at him. "Sumner."

Evan shook his head slowly. "Not good enough, Frazier. Sumner's a minor functionary, and a public one. Anybody could know his name. He's way down the ladder." When Frazier held his silence, Evan continued. "Fact is, hardly anybody knew about my visit. It was kept as quiet as possible. Only a few at the top knew I was coming here."

"She asked about Humula." Martine jerked a thumb in Winona's direction. "You asked about Humula. Not a word for the station commander, senior researchers—just your friendly assassin and mine, Aram Humula. A bit performer in our little play here—unless he was one of your own, and vice versa."

"I don't know what you're talking about, Ophemert."

"I'm afraid that you do. Come on, Evan. We need to talk." She turned to leave.

Winona stood between them and the two men who now guarded the exit. All three of them held needlers. "Sorry." She didn't sound sorry, Evan thought. He whirled on Frazier.

"Your shuttle displays the company logo."

"Naturally. No point in taking chances. As your half-human friend unfortunately noted, we assumed you'd all be dead when we got here, but when we didn't hear from Humula, we got nervous. We were confident of what to expect, but we couldn't be positive. If something had gone wrong, we didn't want to alarm any company survivors. Simple enough to acquire company-issue suits and mount the logo on our shuttle and ship. The latter is the *Sudaria*, by the way. She's awaiting our return a few planetary diameters out."

"I know the name." Evan's tone was grim. The concern which owned the *Sudaria* and its sister vessels was not renowned for its charity and kindness. He was disgusted at the situation. Mostly he was disgusted with himself, for having been taken in so completely by such a simple subterfuge. He'd been too excited by the prospect of rescue to think carefully.

"I thought you would, Orgell." He turned his attention back to Martine. "I know he's Evan Orgell. You say you're Martine Ophemert. I know who that *was*. I'm not convinced you're her. You look more like a local lifeform than a research scientist. For all I know you're a clever copy who's managed to dupe Orgell. You might be an original alien construction instead of a repaired human being. Frankly, you make me very nervous and I'm thinking of having you shot on the spot."

"I'm glad I make you nervous," Martine said dangerously, not helping the case for her survival one iota.

"She's Ophemert," Evan said hastily. "I can vouch for it."

"I'm going to assume that she is. Not because you vouch for it, Orgell, but because of what it means if she is human and has been repaired like this locally. Shame about Aram," he murmured to the tall woman. "He was a good man."

"He was a liar and a murderer," Martine said evenly.

"That sounds human enough." Frazier steepled his fingers, staring at her. "That's good. The information you've doubtless acquired during your extended sojourn out in that crystalline hades will be invaluable. It'll save us a great deal of legwork."

"If you think you can take over this station and claim by force—" Evan began.

Frazier cut him off with a laugh. "By force? Why should we have to use force, Orgell? Your company is famous for its conservatism. First they lose contact with their staff here, then they don't hear from the 'specialist' they sent in to find out what's wrong. I don't think they'll chance a third check. No, if your Board follows true to form, they'll simply vote not to throw good money after bad. They'll roll up this project and forget about it for a year or two, at least. By that time we'll be well established here."

"I wouldn't help you find your way to the toilet," Martine assured him.

The tall woman was smoking something that smelled like old roses. It tickled Evan's nostrils. "You'll cooperate—what's left of you. We have our own specialists, you know. Easier to pry information out of a person than a planet. I think enough of you is still human to respond to the right probes." She turned to look right through Evan. "I know that enough of your friend is."

"There isn't anything you or anyone else can do that would possibly induce me to tell you the least little thing about Prism," Martine said.

"Well, maybe you're right and I'm wrong. In that case I'm sure there's much to be learned from taking you apart."

"You're forgetting something," Evan put in. "It doesn't matter what you do to us. You can't build anything more elaborate than a research station on this world because Prism qualifies as Class A."

The woman's companion spoke for the first time. "What's that?" He looked anxiously over at Frazier. "He's lying. There's nothing in the station files about a sentient native lifeform."

"There are several." Evan was thoroughly enjoying their discomfiture. "Apparently you didn't pay close enough attention to Martine's story. She and I were repaired by natives acting from intelligence, not instinct. They're smart, smart enough to qualify as Class A inhabitants. You know what that means. Class A worlds are off-limits for development."

"I don't know what you're talking about." Frazier sounded bemused. "Since we've been here we've encountered nothing but the expected primitive lifeforms. Nice try, Orgell, but it won't work."

"You need proof? Who do you think did this surgery on us? Trees?"

"Maybe. Nothing about this world surprises me."

"If there are any 'intelligent' lifeforms here, they'll just have to keep out of our way," the tall woman added. "We've got a lot invested in this. Too much to be stopped by a story. For all we know you did the repair work on each other, or it was done by your surgeons before Humula got to them. If that's the case it'll turn up in the files when we've had time to run them all. I'll believe that a lot sooner than I'll believe you were rebuilt by some native lifeforms."

"You can't hide the existence of a new world forever. When the authorities find out what you're doing here that'll be the end of your whole Board of Directors."

"Maybe, but that might be a hundred years down the line," Frazier responded. "Our people can deal with it then. We won't have to worry about it. We'll have made and spent our fortunes by then and been laid to rest."

"There's some terrific stuff in here." The tall woman's

companion had turned back to the computer and was staring at the screen. "Nothing about them yet, though."

"It'll turn up, you'll see," the woman said confidently. "They're trying to buy a little independence with a story too crazy to be checked."

"What'll we do with them until then?" her companion asked.

Frazier leaned to his left, looked around Evan as he spoke to Winona. "Put these two up in the observation tower. They can't cause any trouble from up there. Tomorrow we'll run 'em up to the *Sudaria*. Nodaway and his people can get to work on them and we can get back to business down here." He looked back at his prisoners. "I'd advise you not to try anything. My people are very efficient. You can be more valuable to us alive, and it's better than being dead. You'll be well looked after." The smile that had greeted them earlier returned. "Nothing personal. This is just business."

"Yes." The tall woman moved closer. "We're just doing our jobs, just like you were doing yours. I'm sure our own people will make you a very handsome offer to ensure your cooperation. It doesn't make any difference in this lifetime who you work for, does it?"

Martine spat in her face. "No. But it does make a difference who I have to work *with*."

The woman slowly wiped the spittle from her cheek. "Maybe I'll get lucky. Maybe you'll keep refusing to cooperate. Wait till you meet Nodaway. Humula was a child compared to him."

Winona stepped forward, started to herd them out. Martine called back over a shoulder.

"I won't stand for any mistreatment of the natives."

"Natives?" Frazier looked amused. "You're really going to stick to that story, aren't you?" He looked up at the woman. "You seen any natives?"

"No, no natives." She spoke to one of the guards. "Either of you seen any natives out there?"

"No, ma'am. Nothing but that godawful stuff that tries to wrap itself around your leg and the little hard-shelled things that keep crawling all over you looking for a hole in your suit. But no natives."

"Then there's no one for us to mistreat, is there? Except you, if you persist in your stubbornness." Frazier turned to Winona. "See that they get anything they want in the way of food or drink." He looked back at Evan. "You must be ready for a regular meal after all those days out in the wilds. Maybe you'll feel more agreeable on a full belly."

They were marched across the station grounds. They had to climb to the platform atop the observation tower because power was still out to the lifts. The platform itself was deserted, its instruments sealed against dust and wind-borne lifeforms. The current occupants of the station were not interested in scientific observation.

Security bands were used to bind the prisoners' wrists and ankles. Evan and Martine were then made to sit against the wall. They did not look very threatening. Certainly it was a waste of manpower for three people to stand watch over two such helpless, unarmed intruders, so the guards chose among themselves to see which of their number would remain on duty.

Winona and one of the men departed, leaving their unlucky companion to grumble at his ill fortune. After a brief glance at his two motionless charges, he let his attention drift out over the glistening, fascinating alien landscape. What he did not know, could not know, was that his seemingly silent prisoners were conversing nonstop.

Evan nodded imperceptibly down toward the slim strap which bound his ankles together. "Self-sealing carbon-composite cuff. Same thing that's on your wrists. Ten men couldn't snap one."

"I could cut through it in a second, but I have to be able to straighten my arm in order to align the ulnar lenses properly."

"Which reminds me: why didn't you shoot a few people when you had the chance?"

"Too many guns around. I thought I'd wait for a better opportunity."

"I hope we get one." He tried to peer over the low inner wall, to see into the forest beyond. "I think we'll have to ask our friends to make one."

"I'd rather not drag the natives into human conflicts."

"They're already involved, whether we'd like them to be or not. They became involved when this world was discovered. If we don't do something to stop Frazier and his ilk, our friends will be the worse off for it."

Martine's tone was sardonic. "Will they? Is our company so altruistic?"

Evan resented having to admit it, but she had a point. Who was to say that their employers would deal any more fairly with Azure and his kin than Frazier's? He could simply have told her they'd worry about that later, but that wasn't Evan Orgell's style. He was constitutionally unable to leave a challenge unrefuted.

"No, it's not. If so, they'd have reported this discovery to the proper authorities immediately. They're after exclusive development rights for at least a year, you know that. And they haven't ordered anyone murdered. I can say for certain that you and I are better people than Frazier and that woman who was in the admin room with him."

She smiled ever so slightly. "You're sure of that?"

"Absolutely."

"I wish I was as positive of my own goodness as you are."

"Take my word for it, then."

She turned away from him to look past the daydreaming guard. "I wish we'd been able to bring a talker with us. I don't know if anybody will pick us up at this range."

"After the talkers the scouts are the ones with the best hearing, right? This one who's been traveling with me, Azure? He and I have become, well, close. Sensitized.

If anyone picks us up it'll be him. We'll call together. And watch the left side of your face. We don't want to show any strain." He nodded in the guard's direction. "He's ignoring us because we don't look like we're doing anything. Let's keep it that way."

"Supposing they do pick us up. What do we want them to do?"

"I haven't thought that far ahead. But you know better than I how good they are at fixing what's broken. It might be interesting to see how they go about taking things apart."

"You're assuming they'll take the risk of helping us."

"I don't doubt it for a minute. I'm a member of their Associative. Friendship doesn't follow form. Ask a thranx."

"I will. If we ever get out of here."

"Ready? On three. One, two..."

The guard continued to gaze out over the sparkling horizon. He was wondering when Frazier would give the word to leave the beautiful but dangerous place. He neither heard nor sensed the explosive cry for help that burst from his bound prisoners.

There was no misunderstanding, no fumbling for the right words. Their cry was picked up and deciphered simultaneously.

"What's wrong?" Azure asked. Evan knew the scout's voice as well as he knew his own. "Are you all right? What's happened?"

"The people who have come here are not our friends. They are the associates of the human who killed Martine's companions and forced her to flee. They have made us their prisoners and plan to take us away with them on their ship. They have plans in mind for you and your world," and he proceeded to detail the likely course exploitation and development would take under the heavy hand of Frazier's superiors.

It was library who finally responded. "You have lived

with us, fought with us, and helped us. You are a member
of the Associative. Your friend is a member by association
with you, and perhaps even more than that. We have not
had time enough to explore the philosophical implications
of all these recent developments but we know who our
friends are. Of course we will help you."

"You're going to have to be very careful. These people
are wearing survival suits. They're not as well equipped
as the one I arrived in, but they're more than sufficient
for dealing with the majority of native animals. That
includes you, my friends."

"But we are not animals." Azure's reply was quietly
confident.

"It may be necessary to hurt some of them in order to
protect ourselves while we are freeing you." That had to
be from library—worried about morality as always—Evan
knew.

Martine had an answer for such concerns. "Do what
you have to do. You say I am a member of your Associative by relation. These people are murderers. They kill
not to defend themselves or to obtain food but for abstracts.
They won't hesitate to kill any of you simply to learn how
you work."

They overheard library addressing the other members
of the Associative. "It is as I thought. These humans are
more advanced in knowledge than we are but their system
of ethics is woefully underdeveloped."

Neither Evan nor Martine spoke up to dispute library's
assertion. If the locals wanted to believe they were morally superior to their human friends, let them. It could
not hurt, and there was always the possibility that library
was right.

"We will come in and free you," Azure told him.

"It's not going to be that easy. I know what you're
capable of, but you've no idea what modern weapons can
do. You're familiar with the barrean's defenses? The kind

that the other physicians installed in Martine? Well, these people all carry devices which are just as powerful."

"We have dealt with the barrean." Azure tried to reassure his friend. "I myself have dodged their attacks on more than one occasion." There were a few barely audible comments from other members of the Associative which might have qualified as electronic snickers. Azure ignored them.

"We will extricate you from your present situation with minimal loss of life," library said with great dignity. "Stay where you are. Give no indication that you are in contact with us or that you know what is happening."

"Naturally. Wait a minute. Don't you want us to tell you what to do, how to proceed?"

A faint suggestion of a mental smile. "Credit us with the intelligence you told your captors we possess. We will come for you before sunset, after we have had the time to bring ourselves to full strength. Until then we need to discuss how we are going to proceed among ourselves."

A last, cheery "Don't worry" came from Azure. Then the only voice in his head was Martine's.

"We'd better try and get some rest. We want to be as alert as possible when your friends come for us."

"I wonder if it's possible to sleep in this position." He struggled until he'd worked his way onto his side. "I doubt it."

But he was wrong.

15

THE CHANGING OF THE GUARD WOKE HIM. Martine was already conscious. Evan blinked sleepily, saw that Prism's intensely bright sun was just beginning to set. Their new guard had familiar features to go with the large needler she wore in her holster.

"Winona, right?"

The woman smiled thinly at him. "Hello again. Give me no trouble and I'll deal you no pain. Shut up and go back to sleep. It'll be easier on all of us." She turned away from him.

A soft voice in his head. "It is beginning."

"What?" In his surprise he spoke aloud. Winona looked back at him and frowned.

"Say again?"

"Nothing," Evan said sheepishly. "Just coming out of a bad dream."

"Better get used to them. I hear they're going to turn you two over to Nodaway."

"They may have restored the station's defensive perimeter," Martine was telling their would-be rescuers. "It's a powerful electric field that runs between pylons, metal posts. You'll have to find some way to avoid it. I'm sure the field is strong enough to wipe your memories if not kill you outright."

"We know about the danger," Azure told them. "We have already bypassed it."

"What?" Evan tried to look over the rim of the wind shield, past their guard. There was no sign that anything was amiss in the camp.

Martine was equally confused. "If the fence is powered up and you came through it you should have set off a flock of alarms."

"We determined not to disturb anything." Library was speaking now. "So we set several of our number to divert the energy flow around us while we walked past."

"That's impossible," Evan said flatly.

"You forget the conduits, my friend. They can carry other things besides water."

Evan tried to envision his friends' approach, several conduits linked together, perhaps forming a neat arch between two charged pylons, diverting the lethal voltage harmlessly through their bodies while the other members of the Associative calmly strolled into the camp beneath this bypass. Since current continued to flow freely between pylons, there would be no interruption. No interruption meant no blaring alarms inside the station compound. It was an elegant solution.

"You still have to watch out for guns," Martine reminded them. "A needler won't disrupt your own personal electrical fields but it will go right through you."

Silence then for what felt like an agonizingly long time. It seemed certain to Evan that the attack had faltered. Had library changed its mind? Had they decided that their human friends were not worth the pain of deaths within the Associative?

Then a pair of warriors clambered over the wind shield and things began to happen very quickly.

One pounced on Winona while the other rushed to free the prisoners. Sharp rotating teeth sliced through the bands that bound Evan at ankle and wrist. He heard a moan from Winona. Thoughts of acid and other local forms of weaponry passed through his mind and he shuddered, not wishing that fate even on an enemy.

As usual, his imagination was worse than the reality. Their guard was lying on the observation deck, her legs curled beneath her, her hands twitching slightly while the other warrior stood nearby. As it worked to free Martine, Evan's rescuer explained.

"No acids. Library forbade it," the warrior told them in its usual clipped, terse phrases. "Been analyzing your old exoskeleton. Gatherers found the necessary ingredients, processors synthesized it. Spray it on your kind of exoskeleton and it kills."

"Kills?" Evan murmured.

"Kills flexibility," the warrior corrected.

Martine bent over the guard, who was still moaning reassuringly. Sure enough, a dark sticky substance now clung to the survival suit at selected points. Where the liquid had hardened, so had the suit, with the result that every joint had been frozen. Their guard could not reach for her gun, could not stand up, could not even run away. Her survival suit had been turned into a straitjacket. And no blood had been spilled.

The warrior reached forward. Winona's moan changed to a whine, but the powerful claws were not reaching for her. They opened the holster and withdrew the needler. The warrior examined it with professional interest. "Doesn't look very dangerous."

"Neither do you."

"Hmph. Own body is better than extraneous supplements." Silicate claws contracted. The metal housing of the needler crumpled like foil.

"What—what are you going to do to me?" Winona blubbered. Her earlier bravado had vanished completely. "What did you do to my suit? Where did these monsters come from?"

"Quiet," Evan ordered her. "And don't call them monsters. They're sensitive." He reached down and shut off her battery pack, eliminating power to her suit communicator. "Don't worry about your suit. You've lived on Samstead too long. The only suit that matters is the one you're wearing next to your bones." He reached down again and unsnapped her hood.

"Please—no," she moaned.

Pitiful, Evan thought to himself. He removed the hood, tossed it over the side of the platform as the sounds of yells and curses began to reach them. All hell was breaking loose below.

He joined Martine at the railing. People were running out of buildings. Some of them were only half-dressed. Every now and then the brief crackle of a needler could be heard.

Initial confusion slowly gave way to a semblance of organization as figures in twos and threes began to gather on the west side of the administration building. Moving in a body and firing as they did so, they began to retreat in the direction of the shuttle.

"Your friends are cutting their visit short," Martine informed her. The guard's eyes went wide.

"No, please, let me go with them! Don't let them leave me here!" She was staring in terror at the warrior who stood over her.

"Why should we let you go?" Martine's reply was cold. "You deceived us and turned us over to Frazier. You'd have shot us without a thought if either of us had tried to escape earlier."

"Please, I was just doing my job."

"Hell, Martine, let her go. Besides, if Frazier and his

people still have any doubts that Prism is home to a Class A population, she should be able to help resolve them."

Martine considered, then turned and bent to grasp their former guard with a sapphire-blue crystalline hand.

"You see that these people, and they *are* people, are highly intelligent. We told Frazier that and he refused to believe us. Remind him." The woman nodded frantically. "This world is off limits to commercial development."

"Sure it is." Her tone was bitter. "Your own company's just going to give up its investment here and walk out, right?"

"That's right," Evan told her, startled at his own words. "We're going to make sure the proper authorities are notified. There's not going to be any unchecked exploitation of Prism. The native sentients are going to be allowed to develop at their own pace and in their own way until they've progressed far enough to qualify themselves for Commonwealth membership." He blinked, gazed dazedly at Martine. "Did I actually say what I think I just said?"

"You sure did," she told him proudly before turning to address the patient warrior standing nearby. "Loosen her suit so she can walk."

"I am afraid there is no way to do that."

"Then cut her out of it."

Its teeth a rotating blur, the warrior obediently stepped forward. The air was filled with a high-pitched whine as it went to work on the guard's survival suit. She cringed, but need not have worried. No physician, the warrior nevertheless displayed a touch delicate enough to cut the suit without touching its occupant. In moments it was split neatly down the center.

Like a snake shedding an old skin, the guard kicked the useless garment aside. Without leaving behind so much as a single thank-you, she was out the window and shinnying down one of the supporting girders.

Leaning over the edge of the wind shield, Evan and Martine watched as their former guard sprinted to catch up to her retreating companions. As they stared, it struck Evan that not all the bursts of light that were spotted around the scene of battle were coming from human weapons. He asked the warrior about it.

"The physicians have been very busy. Conduits can carry many things, and flects can concentrate much energy. The physicians conferred with library. As a result, we have a new type of individual in the Associative, one that is part flect, part conduit, part gatherer, and part warrior—and part something else. Something new." Multiple hands gestured at Martine. "Something akin to what you carry within right upper limb." It moved to the railing and raised itself up enough to peer over the rim. Flat lenses scanned the grounds below. "See, there is one of our new relations at work."

Evan and Martine looked. The warrior was pointing at a shape. It was bright red beneath and silver on top, sliced with grooves of deeper, embedded silver silicate. This new citizen of the Associative resembled a crystalline millipede.

It straightened its tubular body and bent its head. From the back of its neck a thin beam of coherent light emerged to strike at the cluster of retreating humans. The light lasted for several seconds before the head raised. The millipede ducked out of sight as Frazier's panicked troops tried to return the fire.

"I'll be damned." Martine stared wonderingly at this latest product of the physicians' collaborative genius. "A laser with legs."

"So are you, sort of."

"Not quite. I am an intelligence in possession of a weapon, not an intelligence possessed by a weapon."

"Look, there's another one." Evan pointed to where a second millipede was harrying Frazier's staff from the cover of the water purification plant.

There was a great deal of noise and light, but not much death, since it appeared that the humans' survival suits were just able to deflect the attacks. Or were the millipedes capable of generating far more powerful effects but holding back under orders from library? The warriors who'd rescued them confirmed that this was the case.

"Library orders that there be as little killing as possible." The warrior sniffed. Such directives were distressing to its karma.

Frazier's people were stumbling into the shuttle now, their panic and confusion evident even at a distance. "They're being herded aboard." Martine was grinning. "Probably don't even realize what's being done to them."

The shuttle's engines coughed, then roared. The comical collection of half-clad humans must be packed in like fish, Evan knew. They'd be forced to suffer one another's stink all the way up to their base ship.

The rumble of the shuttle's engines intensified, rose to a howl. An unexpected pang of homesickness shot through Evan as the craft roared down the landing strip and nosed sharply upward, heading for the ionosphere. He kept staring long after it had disappeared into the clouds, leaving behind only the echo of its departure. That, and some difficult questions. "You think they'll return to try and retake the station?"

Martine looked dubious. "With what? If they'd brought any heavy weapons with them they'd have used them already. I doubt they have any. They came in expecting to find their man Humula in charge or, at worst, trying to deal with a few stubborn holdouts. An intelligent native lifeform capable of defending itself against modern technology is something out of their worst nightmares. They're going to have to completely reassess their intentions here. Frazier's going to have a hard enough time just getting his superiors to believe him." She chuckled softly.

"Oh, they may be having thoughts about returning home to assemble a better-equipped landing party, but by that time we'll have gotten the word out and there'll be a peaceforcer or two standing watch in orbit."

"I wouldn't lay odds on that just yet," he said suddenly, pointing to the far side of the camp. Smoke was rising into the pristine air of morning.

"Oh my God," Martine whispered when she realized where the smoke was coming from, "the nullspace communicator. I didn't think they'd have time to remember that."

"Neither did I." Evan's expression was grim. "We'd better get over there fast and see if we can salvage anything."

While the station and much of its equipment had been built largely of fireproof material, certain components by their very nature contained flammable ingredients. Unfortunately, that included much of the control-and-drive unit for the deepspace communications beam, an intricate farrago of electronics which had been reduced to slag by the time he and Martine were able to bring the blaze under control. It was small consolation to Evan that they could have done little more had they arrived much earlier. Standard-issue fire-extinguishing equipment cannot smother burning magnesium powder, and that was what Frazier's improvising saboteurs had sprinkled liberally throughout the instrumentation before setting it alight.

Buried in its shaft deep beneath the surface of Prism, the beam generator itself was undamaged, but without the means of activating and directing it, it was completely useless.

Evan tossed his extinguisher aside and dropped tiredly into a chair that had so far escaped the attention of both the fire and Prism's voracious scavengers. "That's it, then. We're stuck."

Martine was staring sadly at the still smoldering control console. "I wasn't thinking. We should have told Azure and the others to secure this building first. I didn't think."

"It might not have mattered." Evan rubbed at his eyes. "It only takes a minute to dump some ignition powder and toss a lighter into the pile."

"I'm no engineer, but if the replacement parts were available, I'd say it might be possible to fix this."

"I'm sure it is," Evan replied sardonically, "except that I'm not that kind of engineer either, there probably aren't enough spare parts to repair the damage, and even if we *did* have the parts and the know-how, we probably wouldn't have the time. Knowing that we're cut off, Frazier and his people will be back here hunting for us as soon as they can acquire some heavy weapons."

Their friends and rescuers gradually trickled into the area, attracted by the twin magnets of lingering smoke and rising despair. Warriors and newly born millipedes took up instinctive defensive positions around the communications building while the physicians moved among them. There were several casualties. Two warriors and one of the new hybrids had been shot up beyond repair.

There was also one possible fatality that instantly roused Evan from his lethargy the moment he heard of it.

"It is to be regretted," the gatherer told him sorrowfully.

"No!" Evan charged outside, was directed to the spot where one of the physicians was working on a motionless, all too familiar shape.

Azure.

Evan fairly shook the ether around him with the force of his mental blast. "He's not dead! Tell me *he's not dead*!"

"He lingers on the thin line between self and the going-away," the physician informed him without looking up from its work. Its delicate hands and tentacles were a blur as they worked over the scout's exploded insides. "Go away now, please, and keep your voice down!"

Evan complied, moderating the intensity of his thoughts but refusing to leave. "Azure. Azure! There's no response. Does that mean that—?"

"It does not. What it does mean," the physician informed him, "is that the system has been so badly damaged that all nonvital functions have been shut down by the body. That includes communication faculties. There is heat damage in the area of the brain, though I cannot yet tell the extent of it. Please the Associative, it has not melted the memory cortex. I will tell you once more only: go away."

Evan took a few uncertain steps backward, tried to analyze this wholly unexpected emotional response. Why was he so upset? What was Azure, after all? Nothing but a primitive lifeform composed of hard, inhuman materials. Hardly better than a talking rock. Sure he had individuality, even personality of a sort, but so did certain fish. Was there anything else?

Only that he was a friend.

A nearby voice startled him, because it was a real voice, not a mental projection. "You must be quite fond of him," Martine murmured.

"If it wasn't for him—it, whatever Azure is—I wouldn't be here now. I'd be in pieces somewhere out in the forest, food for syaruzi and their ilk. I don't think fond is a strong enough term."

"What then?"

Evan couldn't meet her eyes, either of them. "I'm not strong enough to say it." He swallowed hard.

She put her human arm around him. "Try not to worry. You've seen what these physicians are capable of."

"I know, but Azure took a needler burst in the head. I don't know if even the physicians can repair that kind of damage."

She pulled gently. "There isn't a damn thing you or I can do about it. Come back inside and let's put our heads together. Maybe there's something we can do about the transmitter."

"Sure there is. We can piss on it. That'll do as much good as anything else." But he let her lead him away.

"One thing's for certain," Martine was telling him hours later, as darkness enveloped the world, "I'm not going anywhere with those bastards. I'll go back into the forest first and live out the rest of my life there. Try and get the different Associatives to work together. It won't be easy. They limit the population of each Associative because they're convinced they've determined the optimum size for dealing comfortably with their surroundings. In that they're probably right, but this is a new threat, something they've never had to deal with before. It's a threat not just to one or two Associatives but to their collective future. The danger is to all of them and it's going to take a united effort to deal with it. The libraries are pretty sensible. If I can convince them I may be able to win the rest over."

"My friend the integrator," Evan mumbled.

"What?" She eyed him sharply. "What did you say?"

"Nothing. I'm rambling."

"You could at least show some interest." When Evan didn't reply she moved to a nearby desk.

Later, with the station's batteries fully charged, they were able to enjoy the luxury of lights and hot water. They were also able to run the station's information through an intact terminal. Library declared himself fascinated and insisted Martine instruct him in the terminal's operation. As it was simple enough for a child to use, or a nonspecialist, library was soon playing with files and diagrams without her supervision.

"Having fun?"

"Considerable," library told her cheerfully. "Your information is couched in simple terms. We interpret them through the terms we have acquired from Evan and, subsequently, from you."

"That's very clever of you."

"You think so?" A small tentacle waved at the screen. "There is a great deal, of course, which I cannot understand. Charts and visual representations are straightforward, but I do not understand your written codes. Tell me, are there codes which describe this communications system?"

Evan brought himself back to reality. "Everything having to do with the establishment and operation of the station is held in storage. Why?"

"Just a thought. If you could direct us by interpreting these written codes, we might be able to fix what is broken." A brace of cilia indicated the blackened console nearby.

"I don't know," Martine said slowly. "That's an awfully complicated piece of equipment."

"More complicated than you? Or Evan? There is no difference. Only in design. Let us try. I will need the help of other libraries, of many gatherers and processors."

"Here's your chance to start a silicate uprising." Evan grinned sideways at Martine. "Go to it."

Once the crisis was explained to them, members of the many Associatives volunteered to help. By the next day there was no room in the communications building for Evan or Martine, so full was it with busy libraries and processors. They moved to the nearest dormitory and tried to relax. There was little else for them to do anyhow and they could interpret designs and images for the libraries just as easily using the dorm terminal as any other. Besides which the dorm was full of stockpiled supplies which Frazier's personnel had abandoned in their rush to escape. For the first time in weeks, Evan and Martine ate properly.

None of which had the impact on Evan that a small blue shape did on the morning when it came waddling into their temporary abode. There was no mistaking that outline, even taking into account the chunk that was missing from its dorsal side.

"Azure!" He rose from his seat, then halted himself. The mental greeting would have to suffice. Azure's shape made him impossible to embrace. Then Evan frowned slightly. There was something wrong with that quaint waddle. "You're limping."

"Damaged motor control, here." He tapped the top of

his head. "Impossible to repair it properly without risking injury to more sensitive areas. I will live with the disability, though it will limit my effectiveness. A scout who cannot run must perforce limit its activities."

"I'm sorry. It's my fault, for involving you in our problems."

"Nonsense. As we have discussed already, your problems are ours. Besides, it has been decided that it is more important for me to continue to scout you at close range than to return to my former duties. I am also to act as intermediary between you, your people, and the Associatives when necessary. Have you been outside recently?"

"No." Evan glanced over at Martine, who was lying on her cot balancing a portable tridee viewer on her stomach.

"Come. There is something you should see."

They followed him outside. Their pace was restricted because the paths between buildings were full. Evan counted warriors, gatherers, walls, and flects, even slowly moving towers picking their way carefully through the crowd of their lesser relations. He also noticed a pair of huge, massively built creatures holding enormous hands and tentacles out in front of their bodies.

"Those are builders," Azure explained in response to their query. "They've come here from far away. Only Associatives who cannot make use of walls employ builders to raise artificial walls to protect their members." He pointed out something that looked like an ambling exploding star. "That is a distributor, who works in tandem with the talkers of the largest Associatives. And those over there are excavators, who are close cousins of the gatherers and diggers."

The ground trembled underfoot as the silicate horde surged busily back and forth. Evan took Martine's arm.

"I think we'd better have a talk with library. Things are getting out of hand."

"Which library?" Azure asked. "There are dozens at work here."

"*Our* library."

That individual was lying prone on the desk where Martine had introduced him to the station computer many days ago. The two humans had to pick their way carefully through the herd of newly arrived libraries who were busy exchanging information with one another. Nearby, several of the recently glimpsed exploding stars were juggling dozens of private conversations simultaneously, sorting them out of the extraordinary mental babble.

Beyond the library, the rear wall of the admin building had been torn out. Builders and processors and physicians swarmed over something vast and barely visible. What little Evan could see of this oversized mystery gleamed and glistened like moonstone.

He managed to reach library's table. "What's going on?" He nodded toward the hivelike activity which dominated the missing end of the building. "Just because you can't fix the transmitter controls doesn't mean you have to demolish everything else trying."

"You know, it's strange." Library spoke absently and without shifting his attention from the flashing computer terminal.

Evan did his best not to sound exasperated. "*What's* strange?"

"How unnecessarily complex superior technology can be."

The heavily armed woman put down her high-powered monocular and turned away from the shuttlecraft port. "Looks deserted to me. If they're still alive they probably heard us coming down and ducked into the woods."

Frazier leaned over to look past her. "Doesn't matter. We don't have to find them—though I have personal reasons for wanting to. But it isn't critical. All we have to do is burn the place down. Isolating them's the same as

killing them. Oh, and we don't refer to the local flora here
as 'woods.' Forest is more accurate. You'll see why after
we disembark." He straightened, called out to the man
standing near the rear of the cabin. "Everything ready?"

"All set back here, sir."

Frazier spoke into an intercom pickup. "Cannon?"

"Heated and ready, sir."

"All right. Unless something shows itself, keep it aimed
at that tall observation platform in the middle of the camp."
He glanced back to the man standing by the exit. "Open
up."

Twenty armed and armored men and women charged
down the self-extending ramp to take up defensive positions around the ship while the big, turret-mounted laser
on top swung silently toward the center of the research
compound. There was no visible reaction to the hostile
display.

"There's nothing here to worry about, sir. I don't see
what all the fuss is about." The middle-aged woman standing next to Frazier held her rifle cradled loosely beneath
her right arm.

"You weren't here last time or you wouldn't be saying
that." Frazier darkened his suit visor manually, scanned
the grounds as he led the landing party out of the ship
and toward the station.

No one challenged their approach as they crossed the
inoperative fence. They halted and waited for reinforce-
ments to join them. Among this second group was the tall
woman who had been Frazier's second in command during their previous sojourn on Prism.

Her gaze swept over the buildings with interest. "They
did a lot while we were away. A lot of the mess has been
cleaned up. Maybe we *shouldn't* raze this site and start
over elsewhere. Maybe we'll just set up here again. It
would save a lot of time and company money."

"If those two freaks are still around and planning some

kind of ambush, that might be just what they're hoping we'll do."

"Then let's oblige them." The tall woman didn't smile often, and she didn't smile then.

They marched toward the old administration building, turned a corner, and came to an abrupt halt. "What's that?" the woman asked sharply. "I don't remember that being here when we left."

"It wasn't," Frazier snapped. His thumb lightly caressed the trigger of the pistol he was carrying.

To their right, behind the communications building, was a massive, opaque silicate dome three times the size of any of the original station structures. It seemed to change color depending on the angle at which it was being viewed.

"You don't suppose—" Frazier began, but his assistant cut him off.

"Not a chance. I lit the powder in there myself. It would take a shipload of technicians and a supervising communications engineer even to begin to reconstruct the beam controls."

"Then what the blazes is that thing?"

As she had no answers, they changed their course, cautiously approaching the building that fronted on the mysterious dome. The outer double doors were unlocked, just as they'd left them. So was the second inner pair.

Beyond was something they hadn't left there.

"It's been quite a while. We were beginning to think you weren't coming back. Come on in."

"Orgell." Frazier started to raise his pistol.

"Don't do that. We'd rather talk," declared a second male voice.

People emerged from behind storage cabinets and consoles. Not all of them showed weapons, but that didn't mean they weren't carrying any. Of far more concern to Frazier was the confidence they were armed with. And the uniforms they all wore. Most of them were clad in

Commonwealth crimson, but a few wore the aquamarine of the United Church. Standing near the back of the room and smiling that unforgettable half-human, half-Prismatic smile was Martine Ophemert.

The older man who had spoken last stepped in front of him. He had no hair and wore a black-and-red headband of unrecognizable pattern. "I am Rua Tarawera. Captain to you, Mr. Frazier." He extended a brown hand. "Your weapon, please." When Frazier hesitated the officer spoke more firmly. "No unpleasantness, please. Your vessel is already docked to the C.P. *Ryozenzuzex* and its crew disarmed and in custody."

Frazier slumped, handed over the needler. There was no place to run.

"How?" the tall woman next to him asked Evan as she turned in her own pistol. "There was no way for you to get word out. No way at all." She looked past him, past Martine, to the gleaming new communications console. "Those terminals were destroyed down to the floor. I know. I took care of it myself. You couldn't rebuild them, you *couldn't*."

"You're right, we couldn't," Martine admitted readily. "But you forgot about our friends."

"Friends?" Frazier's brows drew together. "What friends? The animals?"

"You saw the dome outside? Yes, of course you did, or you wouldn't have come here first. The 'animals' made that. Our friends. When they're given sufficiently detailed diagrams and a little help, they can duplicate anything. It's a game to them, a puzzle, a challenge. They're also capable of making some interesting improvements to whatever they're working on at the time.

"The instrumentation they put together is unorthodox but it works. The message we were finally able to get off with it wasn't too coherent, but it was effective enough."

"It was kind of an explosive, desperate grunt," Evan told them. "What it lacked in eloquence it made up for in strength. It was picked up and recorded, and someone got curious because it was emanating from what was supposed to be an uninhabited region of space. So some official directed that it be checked out. When I find out who, I'm going to nominate him or her for sainthood in the Church."

Frazier was gaping at him in disbelief. "Then you gave it all away! Now that the government knows about this world your own company won't be able to profit here any more than ours, or anyone else's. This place will be put under regulation. Development will be regulated to death."

"It doesn't matter." Evan smiled. "You see, our company isn't our company anymore."

Martine moved to stand close to him. "We've both tendered our resignations. We're going to stay on here to work with the natives. They have a lot of potential and they're very enthusiastic and anxious to learn. They're not interested in joining our mechanical civilization because they don't have to, but they very much want to learn from it. That new beam amplifier out back—that's half alive. It can't walk and it can't talk, but my, can it amplify! It's sort of a superevolved version of the talker towers each Associative counts among its members—but you wouldn't know about that. It wasn't built; it was hatched. These 'animals' are going to alter Commonwealth technology in ways we haven't begun to imagine."

"Think what you gave up." The tall woman spoke contemptuously as she was led away. "Great fortunes. Power." She shook her head. "Idiots."

"I think not," replied Martine imperturbably. "Which one of us is under arrest?"

When the last of the landing party had been taken into custody, the representative of the United Church on Prism came looking for them. Manheim had been dispatched along with the rescue party to see to the moral development of the natives—should any such development be required. From what he'd observed so far of Azure and library and the rest of Evan and Martine's friends, any extensive Church presence on Prism would be superfluous at best. He was delighted. The Church hated to meddle.

He found them on the observation platform, gazing out across the forest. Prism's sun was beginning to set. The waning light, harbinger of the long night to come, made the forest resemble more than ever an endless ocean of elfin castles, every tower alight, every rampart a sheet of jewels.

"Hello, Manheim," Evan said absently, not taking his eyes from the view. The Churchman didn't blame him. The sparkling panorama was far more pleasant to look upon than his own pudgy visage. He joined them in drinking in the fiery vista.

"I understand you two want to go back out into the forest to try and establish a native city—excuse me, a large Associative—where other natives can come to partake of humanx philosophy and ideas. You won't be able to give them any more advanced technology, you know. Not yet. Against Church edicts."

"There's no need to hurry the technology. They have to realize the time has come for them to abandon their tribal organizations. That's paramount. Introduction of technology can come later. We have no intention of trying to circumvent Church strictures." His tone was firm.

Manheim smiled. "I didn't mean to imply that you did. I've had a chance to review your preliminary reports, you know. I'd like to see this Integrator thing."

"That might be arranged," Martine told him. "From a distance, of course. The Integrator is no respecter of rank. Or sanctity."

"Knowledge like that is why the outpost that's going to be established here will have to rely on you two to get its people safely through the first couple of years. You're the only ones who know this world. I suppose you qualify as the first colonists."

Martine looked down at her right side. "It's more like Prism has colonized us." Evan nodded agreement.

"It's a wonderful thing you've done for these, uh, people. I intend to recommend that you receive full Church support for any projects you wish to initiate."

"That'll be much appreciated," Evan told him sincerely. "Save us from having to deal with the bureaucracy."

Manheim nodded knowingly. "If you'll excuse me, I'd love to stay until sundown, but I have business that needs to be taken care of. The matter of cosigning formal indictments and other distasteful things that are best disposed of as soon as possible. I'll see you later."

"Looking forward to it." They watched as he descended from the platform and crossed the shadowy open ground below toward the administration building.

"What do you think?" Martine whispered. "As far as what's being done about Frazier and his people?"

Evan didn't try to keep the sarcasm from his voice. "I've seen much more of how big companies operate in a crisis than you have, Martine. They'll never make any indictments against his employers stick. Frazier and his underlings will bite their lips and suffer whatever punishment the courts mete out. But you'll never see any Directors undergoing Correction. They'll deny everything, claim that Frazier was operating entirely on his own and without official permission from higher up, and produce the documents to prove it. Charges and countercharges will be filed, the media will have a field day, and within two years it'll be business again as usual. You can't imprison a company. You can irritate it, bleed it, aggravate it, but you can't lock it up."

"That's unfair, and immoral."

"That's business."

It was quiet atop the platform for a long time. The sun was almost down when a third figure joined them. It limped out of the newly repaired lift and complained about the inefficient design. The controls were much too high to be useful.

Evan smiled affectionately down at the newcomer. "Evening, Azure."

"Downtime greetings, my friends. How does it proceed?"

"The disturbed members of our Associative have been restrained and will be repaired." Azure would not be able to grasp the meaning of the term "punishment." "We are looking at one small problem, though."

"What kind of small problem?"

"Our greater Associative has laws that govern how much information, how much of our learning we can share with prim—with new friends. We may not be able to help you progress as fast as library and some of the others would like to."

"Martine told us about such laws." Was that a wink? Just the evening light, Evan decided. "The libraries have been busy with the physicians. Already they have absorbed most of the knowledge that was contained within the dead library here. They will hold it for future study."

Evan's eyebrows lifted. "You didn't say anything about that. No one said anything about it to me—until now."

Azure gave a mental shrug. "We saw no need to burden you with trivia while you were engaged in capturing your disturbed relatives."

"I see. And what are library and the others planning to do with this information they've quietly stolen?"

"You cannot steal information, Evan," Azure said reprovingly. "Library says you can only borrow it. The libraries have one or two projects in mind."

"Better battery systems for your bodies?" Martine asked interestedly. "New variations on the barrean defensive beam?"

"I don't think so. Actually, there is nothing at the moment we want for ourselves. The projects are designed to thank *you*, for what you have done for us."

Both humans expressed their surprise. "Now what could you be doing for us, Azure?"

"Well, I believe one group is trying to design a device that would replace that gruesome soft sac in your torso, as well as the need to constantly fill it with organic compounds, with a system akin to our own, so that you would be able to live as we do, on the clean food of the sun."

"That was suggested to me before," Evan told him, "by the physicians of your own Associative. It's a quaint thought, but even if they succeed I'm not sure I'm ready to substitute solar power for a good steak. What else?"

"They are working on a way for walls to defend themselves from the devices you call needlers. Lastly is a favorite project which is still only in the discussion stage but which has the physicians and processors in particular very excited. It is only in the discussion stage because it would take the combined efforts of hundreds of physicians and thousands of processors to complete.

"They are also afraid that your own people would not understand it, so I must ask you not to mention it to any among your own kind." Azure's somber tone precluded the possibility that the scout was joking with them.

"Well, that does sound serious. What is it? Some kind of superbattery that will enable you to function around the clock? A more refined communications system based on the exploding stars and the talkers?"

"No." Azure sounded at once troubled and excited. "You see, until you came among us, Evan, we had never thought of traveling at night, much less traveling through the night that separates the stars. There was a great deal of information about such matters contained within your machine. So library tells me."

It took a moment for the scout's words to seep through Evan's preconceptions. "You're not telling me," he said laughingly, "that the libraries are thinking of trying to build a starship?"

"No, of course not." Azure was very earnest. "We wouldn't know how to begin *building* a ship to travel between the stars.

"We are going to try to grow one."

ABOUT THE AUTHOR

Born in New York City in 1946, Alan Dean Foster was raised in Los Angeles, California. After receiving a bachelor's degree in political science and a Master of Fine Arts in motion pictures from UCLA in 1968–69, he worked for two years as a public relations copywriter in a small Studio City, California, firm.

His writing career began in 1968 when August Derleth bought a long letter of Foster's and published it as a short story in his biannual *Arkham Collector Magazine*. Sales of short fiction to other magazines followed. His first try at a novel, *The Tar-Aiym Krang*, was published by Ballantine Books in 1972.

Foster has toured extensively through Asia and the isles of the Pacific. Besides traveling, he enjoys classical and rock music, old films, basketball, body surfing, and karate. He has taught screenwriting, literature, and film history at UCLA and Los Angeles City College.

Currently, he resides in Arizona with his wife, JoAnn (who is reputed to have the only extant recipe for Barbarian Cream Pie).